It wasn't easy, but it was...

WORTH IT

by

AMY NIELSEN

A Wild Ink Publishing Publishing Original

wild-ink-publishing.com

Edited by Brittany McMunn, and Laura Wackwitz

Design and Layout by Abigail Wild

ISBN: 978-1-958531-58-7

Danielle, Olivia, Trent, and Barclay, you are each my Number One.

Love,

Mom

"I'm not telling you it's going to be easy. I'm telling you
it's going to be worth it."

Arthur L. Williams, Jr.

PROLOGUE

1980 SUMMER

DAD ONLY MADE GUMBO on good days. Mom only drank on bad ones. So, when Levi and I burst into the kitchen—the scene broke all the rules I knew about my parents.

"How was the fishin'?" Dad picked up a cutting board full of diced peppers, onions, and okra and slid the holy trinity into the stockpot.

"I caught three brims. But Angela made me toss them back." Levi tattled.

"It's not like you were going to eat them." My job was to look after my baby brother and save tiny fish.

Mom wasted no time sharing her disgust at us being lake dirty. "Go scrub up and change clothes for supper." Then to me only. "Make sure your brother properly washes up."

"Yes, ma'am." I muttered through gritted teeth.

After Levi and I properly washed our hands and changed out of our lake clothes, we took our places at the dinner table. My stomach rumbled.

Dad said a quick blessing, and I dove into my favorite dish.

"How do you kids like the gumbo?" Dad crunched a saltine into his bowl.

Levi answered around a mouthful of the seafood stew. "Delicious. Are these the shrimp we caught?"

"Levi, please don't speak with food in your mouth." Manners mattered to my mother.

"Yes, sir. They are. This is what I call 'All the Way Filet' gumbo." Dad held a spoon close to his mouth. A slimy blob spilled over its edge. He spoke directly to it. "These oysters—if they aren't from the muddy bottom of the Gulf of Mexico, they don't go in my gumbo." His neck bulged as the oyster slid down his throat.

I dug out a blue crab claw and snapped it in two. "I want you to make it just like this for my birthday." It's what I asked for every year.

"Got some sassafras branches drying in the garage. Fresh filet powder for that birthday gumbo." After Dad emptied his bowl, he pushed it in front of him and clasped his hands. His eyes met Mom's.

She nodded, then poured another glass of red wine—much larger than the one before.

"Kids, your mom and I have some exciting news."

"Are we getting a pool?" Levi asked.

We'd begged for one since we'd moved in last year after Dad got his promotion. Almost every home in our neighborhood had a sparkling pool behind their sprawling ranch. Except ours.

Dad chuckled. "Not exactly, but how does a beach sound?"

I stopped digging the crab meat out of the tiny claw. "We goin' on vacation?"

"You could kinda look at it that way. We're moving to the vacation capital of the world: Florida."

Levi cheered. "Yeah!"

My brow furrowed. "What? Why?"

Dad unclasped his hands and brushed his fingers through thick, dark hair. "The chemical plant where I work, it's shutting down. When I was gone a few weeks ago—it was to apply for a job down in Florida at Sunshine Citrus. Today I found out I got the job. The citrus industry is exploding down there. This is a great opportunity."

Mom loosened the death grip from the stem of her wine glass and patted my hand. "It's gonna be wonderful. We'll be close to Disney and the most beautiful beaches."

She had a point. All my Mississippi friends would be jealous I was moving to Florida. The ones I'd never see again. "It sounds fun. I'll just miss my friends." I dropped the claw into the bowl, no longer interested in all that work for such little reward.

"Me, too. But we'll both make new ones." Although she punctuated the statement with a smile, her eyes hinted there was more to read between the lines. She downed the rest of her wine. "Be right back. I think Amber's crying."

Levi slurped his last bite, put his bowl in the sink, and headed outside to play.

I glanced around the home that I had thought I'd live in for longer than just a year. In the sunken living room sat the matching floral couch, love seat, and chair Dad had bought brand new when we moved in. My friend Shannon and I liked to make chocolate chip cookies with our moms at the large butcher block island in the center of the kitchen. "Where're we gonna live?"

"I picked out a decent rental in a small town called North Lake. But it's only temporary. Once we get settled, we'll look for a house as big as or maybe even bigger than this one. Maybe even with a pool."

A tear slid down my cheek. I tried to wipe it away before Dad saw it. It wasn't so much that I loved our house, but that I loved that Mom and Dad seemed happier since living in it. We all did. I was worried our happiness would stay here like a ghost. "Can I be excused?"

"Listen, Number One"—Dad only called me that when it was just the two of us—"I wouldn't be moving our family to Florida if I didn't think it was for the best."

The kitchen table sat nestled near an enormous bay window. Right outside it grew the mimosa tree I'd climbed more times than I could remember. Levi's sinewy arms appeared and effortlessly yanked him up a low-hanging, leafy branch heavy with pink flowers.

"Number One, do you trust me?"

Trust him? I trusted him so much that last September, I followed him outside in the middle of the eye of a hurricane—Frederick it was called. Mom hadn't been happy about it. We'd crept around in the pitch dark, surveying the damage, mostly downed trees.

Holding a flashlight for him in the eerie quiet, knowing the howling winds and violent tornados would soon make an ugly return, I hadn't been scared. Not one bit.

I locked eyes with my father. "I trust you." And I did trust him. But how did he know this was for the best? And the best for who?

Because it was in full bloom, the mimosa's canopy hid my little brother in fluffy, pink clouds. "Can I be excused?"

"Sure. We'll talk more about the move later."

I stood to leave.

Dad looked up at me. "Number One, living in Florida... It's something most people only ever dream about."

"Yeah, I'm sure it'll be great." But as I said the words, a foreboding washed over me like the deceitful calm during the eye of that hurricane.

I joined Levi in the mimosa. Straddling my favorite branch and leaning back to brace myself, I floated with my brother in the pink clouds.

I closed my eyes and tried to imagine living in Florida. I saw myself in Mickey ears, splashing in the ocean and building sandcastles.

But the reality would turn out nothing like the dreamy images in my ten-year-old brain. No, this move would play out more like a nightmare.

The North Lake News

August 1987

Staff Writer

Dating back to the Roaring Twenties, central Florida has been a leader in the citrus industry. Boasting small-town living amongst Orange-Blossom scented orchards, North Lake thrived on being home to Sunshine Citrus and supplying not only the state but the entire country with a vast quantity of citrus, from fresh to frozen juice concentrate.

In the last decade, the small town economically benefited from a huge influx of out-of-state newcomers eager to join the booming industry and relocate to North Lake's coveted central Florida moderate climate.

Unfortunately, the residents of North Lake still feel the ripple effects of the devastating freezes from '83 and '85. The unexpected extreme cold temperatures caused widespread damage to citrus trees and resulted in significant crop losses and operational setbacks for Sunshine Citrus.

The resilient residents of North Lake continue to adapt to the ever-changing landscape of the citrus industry of yesteryear. They are harvesting what's left in the dwindling orchards and shifting to new economic opportunities as investors purchase ailing groves to repurpose into housing developments.

While the transition will come with some growing pains, *The North Lake News* is confident that our community can overcome this transition and thrive on the other side.

Change isn't easy. But it's often worth it.

CHAPTER ONE

THE KISS

1987 SUMMER

INNOCENCE IS IRREPLACEABLE CURRENCY, and I was gambling mine away like a secret addiction.

I tucked my newly trimmed Daisy Duke short cutoffs, the ones Dad said never to wear out of the house, and my strawberry-flavored lip gloss into my tattered brown backpack. The same backpack I'd carried to North Lake High for the last two years. The same one I'd start my senior year with. Then I hid my spaghetti-strapped tank under a long-sleeved flannel. Satisfied with my outfit, I ducked into my little sister's very purple bedroom.

Amber sat on the floor next to her child-sized table and filled a chipped teacup with water from a yellow pitcher. Mom had bought the pitcher at a Tupperware party back in Mississippi. Back when she was a Tupperware Party type of mom.

"That's one lucky bunch of tea party guests," I said.

Cookie crumbles and wrinkly grapes sat in front of her plush animals. "Will you play with me?" She gazed at me with large chocolate puppy-dog eyes.

"Sorry, I can't. I'm babysitting Cole tonight. Do you mind if I borrow one of your coloring books and some crayons?"

She jumped up and grabbed my hand. "Okay, but I wanna come with you."

"Sorry. Your bedtime is eight p.m. No later. Plus, you're hosting the most anticipated tea party in all of North Lake. You can't let these VIPs down." I selected a coloring book and a well-used pack of crayons from a plastic bin next to her twin bed and added them to my unallowables. "Levi's here if you need anything."

She stuck out her plump bottom lip and dropped back to the floor. "Fine."

"Thanks. See you in the morning." I stole one more glance at my baby sister playing—alone. My heart and my head told me to cancel with Cole's mother, Addis Simmons, and stay with Amber, but an undefined something else told me to go.

I pushed the door open all the way so Levi could hear her, then darted to the kitchen. My brother sat at the laminate roundtable in the middle of the U-shaped room with a bowl and a box of cereal. Like Amber—alone.

"I'm leaving." I dug out a half-eaten bag of Doritos I'd hidden in the back of a cabinet. Fancy snacks didn't last long in this hungry home.

"So why can't she go? What's one more kid?" He overfilled the bowl with the knock-off corn flakes my father now bought.

"I'll be home too late." It wasn't a lie, just not the whole truth. "I told you. Lay off eating our breakfast for dinner."

"You're not my mother." He shot me an evil eye as he emptied a milk carton.

"Sorry. You're right. Once one of our parents decides to show up, you're off the hook. But stay home."

"I'll watch her. But I'm not promising anything else."

I pecked him on the cheek and ruffled his shoulder-length hair. "Stay home."

He really needed a haircut. With our tight family budget, I'm sure my parents didn't care he'd wanted to grow it out.

Guilt gutted me at leaving my siblings with little to eat and, more importantly, alone. The kind of guilt a mom should have. But she was probably drinking beer with her orange grove friends. Dad was probably still at the dealership. Neither of them my problem.

I hopped on my bike and pedaled to the Simmons' house. The guilt didn't come with me. But something else did—something awakening from deep within the most provocative places inside me. And even though I wasn't sure what it was, I believed Dale Simmons could help me figure it out.

The evening dragged on. Cole reluctantly ate the runny beans and ham his mother had left for him. Then, per instructions not to waste hot water, a concept I knew all too well from my own family's tightening of the belt, I gave him a lukewarm bath and dressed him in too-small pajamas.

I held up the coloring book and Doritos. "Wanna join me?"

"Doritos!" He shouted from the crib-sized mattress he'd long out-grown that sat in the corner of his parents' bedroom.

"One picture, then light's out. You pick." I handed him the coloring book.

He flipped through it. "This one."

A smiling family of bears stood outside a cute cottage—a scene far from both his and my lived realities.

We held cheesy nachos in our left hands and crayons in our right. When we finished the picture, Cole wrote our names at the bottom. "Can you put it on the fridge?"

"For sure. Goodnight." I didn't want to rush him, but the clock ticked.

"Goodnight. I like when you babysit." His little blonde head poked from underneath a dingy blanket.

"Me, too." And I meant it. I enjoyed spending time with kids. But tonight, I hoped to also spend time with someone else.

I grabbed my backpack off the couch and darted to the Simmons' bathroom. A single light bulb sat in the center of the ceiling. I pulled the chain, and the light chased a few cockroaches underneath dust-crusted baseboards. Years ago, that would have grossed me out. Now a few cockroaches didn't faze me.

I shut the stained toilet lid and dropped my backpack onto it. I jimmied off the khakis and stepped into the cutoffs. Then I rinsed the chip crumbs from my mouth and smeared on a thick layer of strawberry gloss. Nope. Trying too hard. I wiped it off with some toilet tissue.

So I wouldn't forget it, I opened the front door and tossed my backpack on the washing machine that sat on the Simmons's front porch. Bonfire smoke infused the summer night air. Had I not been babysitting, Andrew and I would have probably snuck out and been there with the neighborhood rowdies—our new summer ritual. With our good friend

Julie gone all summer, we'd drifted to the dark side. And it had been one helluva ride. But Andrew wasn't my focus tonight.

Back inside, I powered up the rabbit-eared TV that sat atop a larger broken one. A grainy Saturday Night Live rerun I'd seen earlier this year, with some actor pretending to be President Reagan, lit up the home's nicotine-tinged walls. I plopped on the lumpy couch just as a roaring truck engine neared. I jumped, turned the TV off, sank back into the couch, and tugged a frayed quilt up to my nose.

A shiver ran down my spine when the door creaked, and boots clunked the hardwood floor. It's ironic that sometimes when what you want to happen then happens, it scares the shit out of you.

Someone stumbled into the kitchen. The open fridge light confirmed who I thought—hoped—it was. Cole's older brother, Dale, snatched a beer and slammed the door. He stood for a moment and studied the picture I'd attached to the fridge. Then his dark silhouette moved toward the couch.

Toward me.

My chest pounded.

He tried to sit but tumbled forward at my bony legs hidden under the quilt. "Whoa." He steadied himself. "I didn't know you were babysitting tonight." The pale moonlight revealed his crooked smile. "But it's a nice treat you are."

I recoiled into a ball. Fear clashed with desire. I craved them both.

He popped the beer open, took a long swig, and offered it to me.

I shook my head.

"Your call." He polished it off, crushed the can with his boot, then kicked it toward the kitchen.

My voice quivered. "I'm sure your mama will be here soon."

I half wanted Addis to walk in the door right then, and half, maybe slightly more than half, didn't want her to come home at all.

"You sure are a pretty thing. I've always thought that. Now, look at you. Almost grown."

My skin tingled when he brushed my long brown bangs behind my ear. Dale had smiled and winked at me before, but this was the first time he'd ever touched me.

"I can't remember. How old are you now?" He wrapped a finger around the thin strap of my tank top.

Every nerve in my body was aflame. "I'm sixteen, seventeen on Sunday." Even though I'd refused the beer, intoxication consumed me.

Dale's t-shirt hugged his small but toned chest. That, plus his faded baseball cap, shaved years off his age, making him look not much older than when he'd played tight end at North Lake High years ago. "Seventeen, that's practically eighteen in my book. Happy early birthday." He leaned in to kiss me.

Shock forced me to back away, even though this was what I'd been dreaming about ever since I'd started babysitting Cole.

"It's okay. We've known each other long enough. It'll be our secret."

But now in front of him, I didn't know how to feel. "I just—"

Before I could finish my incoherent thought, Dale pressed his lips against mine. A tongue heavy with alcohol and nicotine penetrated my mouth. Deeper and deeper. It slithered down my throat, into my lungs. Oxygen depleted; my body trembled. He pressed harder and crushed my lips into my teeth. A metallic taste mixed with the leftover hint of my strawberry gloss. Unable to interpret pleasure from pain, my head spun. Bodies writhed. Hands explored.

Then he stopped and stood. The bulge in his jeans radiated heat in my face.

He took a flattened pack of Marlboro's out of his back pocket and a lighter out of the front. The flame illuminated his olive skin and then ignited life into the cigarette. Smoke rose to the ceiling like steam. "Goodnight, Miss Angela." He turned, strutted into his room, and kicked the door shut behind him.

My chest rose and my pulse raced. No boys my age ever kissed me like that. A forbidden hunger yearned for something that was probably not good for me, but I wanted it anyway.

CHAPTER TWO

UNDEFINED CRAVINGS

THE NEXT TIME THE door creaked, it was Addis. "Thanks for watching Cole. Can I pay you next week? You know how things are at Sunshine since the freezes."

Even though I wanted the money to buy something new to wear on the first day of school, I let it go. Because I did know how things were at Sunshine. I lived the aftermath every day. "It's fine. Whenever."

A cigarette dangled between long, red-nailed fingers that matched her lips. "Your mama was out with us again. She's so much fun."

"Yep. She sure is a bundle of laughs. See ya later."

I collected my backpack off the washing machine on the Simmons' small front porch. Then unchained my bicycle from the clothesline post and pedaled the ten minutes it took to get to the rectangle where my family lived.

Inside the house, the rental that—seven years ago—my father had said would be temporary, an unexpected voice startled me. "How was the babysitting?"

"Ahh, Dad. You scared me."

He sat in his well-worn recliner, legs crossed, drink in hand, no lights on.

I put my hand to my mouth. My chin and lips stung from Dale's stubble, and the bottom one had started to swell. "Am I in trouble?" Thank God, shadows sheltered me. He couldn't see my forbidden clothes or the marks of my forbidden desire.

He swirled the tumbler. Ice cubes clinked the sides. "No, I'm just waiting for your mother." He took a slow, deliberate sip, not reacting to the strong taste of what I assumed was Scotch. "She's out with the girls—again."

My stiff shoulders dropped. I was off the hook. Mom was on it. Better her than me. "Addis told me."

My father had no idea his daughter had kissed someone who he certainly would not have approved of. I avoided his earlier question and instead asked a generic, "How was your day?"

"Good. Picking up work at the dealership, which will help. You go on. If she's not here in the next few minutes, I'm going to bed, too. Got another early training."

"Okay. Goodnight." I started down the hall.

"Number One?"

"Yeah, Dad."

"Sorry things are a little tough now. I'm working on it."

"It's okay." But it wasn't okay. None of this was okay.

I shut my door, changed into an oversized baseball t-shirt and silk cheer shorts, turned on my box fan, and climbed into bed. Remnants of Dale's kiss pulsed through my veins like liquid fire.

"Angela, psst, Angela." Andrew whispered from outside my open window.

He and I hadn't planned on sneaking out, but I was game. I folded my arms on the windowsill and rested my chin on them. "What's up?"

He pointed on the ground to a passed-out Levi. "This is what's up."

"What the hell?" I jimmied the screen out of my window and climbed out.

"Bonfire tonight in the woods. Last hurrah before school. Found Levi like this at the base of a pine tree and hauled him here."

"Let's get him inside." We picked up Levi and somehow managed to maneuver him through my window. He landed with a thud on my bed. "I'm worried. Ever since he quit the Junior High Weightlifting Team, he's not been the same kid."

Andrew leaned back on our concrete block house. "Maybe when school starts back you can talk him into joining again."

"Yeah, maybe. Thanks again, you're a good friend."

He wrapped his fingers around mine. "So are you." His tender touch contrasted with Dale's aggressive one.

Andrew's family had moved next door to ours the same weekend we'd moved to North Lake. And for the same reason. The lure of a booming citrus industry—only to be shattered by something as simple as the weather. We understood each other.

I went to wrap his hand with my other. But he pulled away.

"I gotta go," he said, then disappeared into the dark.

For the second time in one night, I was left to shake off undefined cravings. Dale and Andrew occupied the same space in my brain, but I had no idea how to label it.

I climbed through my window and popped the screen back in.

Even though he reeked of bonfire smoke, I snuggled next to my little brother.

A vehicle idled outside my open window. I assumed one of Mom's orange grove picking, loser friends dropping her off. Not long after she came inside, angry voices thundered through the house. There was a time in our family when this wasn't how the night ended, a time I'd almost forgotten.

My door creaked open, and a small silhouette appeared. "Sissy, can I sleep with you, too?"

"Of course. Come here." Hot or not, I scooched closer to Levi and made what little room I could for Amber and one of her tea party plushies.

Levi snored on one side of me. Amber whimpered on the other.

"It's okay, Sweetie. Everything's going to be okay." I kissed the top of her head. Then a tear rolled down my cheek because I'd just lied to my baby sister.

Chapter Three

Frail Friendship

By the time Mom woke up, the sun shone through my westward-facing sneak-out portal.

"Hey, Baby Girl. Whatcha doin'?" Her lips stuck together with each word, and dark circles pulled heavy at bloodshot eyes.

"Reading."

"I can see that. What're you reading?"

"My summer reading assignment. Mom, I'm really busy." I only had a few days left to finish *Pride and Prejudice*.

"Sorry. Your birthday's in a few days. Any special requests?"

A car, please. The wish remained silent. She remembered my birthday, shocker.

Pretending to be a good mother was Mom's hangover cure of choice.

"I'll probably hang out with Julie. She should be back today."

"Sure, no problem."

I had yet to make eye contact with her. My gaze remained on the words within Jane Austen's fictional world—one of innocence, functional family, and true love. I turned a page and willed my mother to disappear.

"I'll let you get back to your book." She punctuated the sentence with an inhale as if she had more to say. But she'd never say it. Unspoken words in this family spoke volumes.

The phone rang. "Ange, it's Julie." Levi's deep voice didn't match his youthful appearance.

Mom rubbed her forehead and forced a smile. "Perfect timing."

I dog-eared the last page in chapter fifty-six, then carried a little of Elizabeth Bennet's obstinance into the kitchen with me.

Levi handed me the yellow receiver, attached by a cord to the base on the fruit-papered kitchen wall. I jabbed his chest. "You and I will be talking later."

He shot me a middle finger and then ducked into his bedroom. I assumed to tinker with a broken toaster or hair dryer.

I pulled the phone as far into the hallway as the long-coiled cord allowed. "Hey, I was just about to call you."

"I'm a mind reader—one of my many amazing talents, that and being super, hilariously funny." Julie laughed.

I loved my best friend, but resentment welled at her carefree disposition. "How was the beach?"

"Spectacular, like my perfect tan. You should come over. We can celebrate both your birthday and the last weekend of summer."

I craved a little reminder of what my life used to be. "What's the plan?"

"Some kids are going to be at the dock later tonight. A boom box dance party. It'll be fun. Then we can go to cheer practice tomorrow."

"Oh shoot. I forgot about cheer practice."

"How could you forget about the most important thing of our senior year?" Julie had circled that date on her calendar the day we made the varsity squad last May.

But she didn't know what hijacked my frontal cortex. And the tripled-headed beast left no room for cheerleading. "Yeah, me, too. I can't wait. Hold on. I'll see if Mom or Dad can drive me over later."

I raised my hand to knock on my parents' door. The voices on the other side lured me to press my ear up to it instead.

"Helen, your drinking is becoming a problem. Think about the kids."

"Stop treating me like I am one of the kids. You have no idea how physically demanding that job is. Picking oranges all day knowing half of them have to be tossed from freeze burn. And the worst part, I work there because of you."

"Don't make this about me. There's no way I could've predicted that freeze. And a big part of the move was a fresh start. I didn't want what happened to your mother to happen to you. I thought I was making the best decision for our entire family."

"Well, you were wrong. And don't ever compare me to my mother. Ever."

Rapid footsteps approached their bedroom door.

I darted to my room.

The front door opened and shut, and a car peeled out of the driveway.

Curious and confused, I tiptoed back to my parents' room.

My father sat on the bed, elbows on knees, head resting in hands.

"Is everything okay?" I asked.

His posture straightened. "You hear all of that?"

"Yes, sir."

"Come here, Number One."

I sank onto the bed next to him.

"Your mother's struggling. It's tough for all of us. But she's a good person." He patted my knee. "Don't you worry. This is our issue. We'll work it out."

I wanted to be a normal teenager, celebrate another year around the globe, hang out with my best friend. Not be my dad's therapist.

"It's Friday night. What're you doing home anyway?"

Dad never forgot. "I was going to ask you or Mom to drop me off at Julie's. Sunday's my birthday."

"Oh. I'm so, so, sorry. Of course. I'll take you. And I'll make you some birthday gumbo when you get back, 'All the Way,' just how you like it."

"That sounds great. I can't wait." Then I remembered Julie was still on the phone.

I dashed to the kitchen and picked up the dangling receiver. The Bangles blared from the other end. "Jules! Jules!" I yelled into it.

The music's volume lowered. "Don't mind me. I've just been brushing up on my walking like an Egyptian. What took so long?"

"Nothing. I'll be over soon." Time for me to brush up on pretending like my life didn't suck.

It took less than fifteen minutes to get to Julie's house, but her neighborhood belonged on another planet. Gorgeous homes surrounded several lakes, and fancy cars parked on cobblestone driveways. I had lived in a community like this once, but I doubted I'd ever live in a sprawling ranch on five acres again.

Julie's parents sat in matching leather recliners in front of their enormous wood-framed console TV, arms stretched toward the other, hands held. They'd watched TV like that for as long as I could remember.

Mrs. Davis stood. "Angela, dear. Look how much you've grown in a few short weeks."

Julie's mom smelled like fresh Jasmine. My mother used to smell like Giorgio perfume, now she smelled like cigarette smoke and stale beer. Mrs. Davis's hug made me hate my life.

Mr. Davis offered his typical wink and nod.

Julie sprang down the winding staircase in a cute pink romper. Juxtaposed against her newly bronze complexion, her stylish blonde hair looked even lighter.

"Ange, I missed you so much." She took my hand. "Come on. Tell me everything I've missed all summer."

She talked nonstop. First, about her internship at the hospital and how she couldn't wait to go to nursing school. Then about her beach vacation. The fishing, the laying out with her two older twin sisters by the resort pool, the surf lessons she nailed day one, the cute lifeguard—white noise.

"Ange, have you heard a word I've said?"

A few loose bricks from my wall tumbled down. "I'm sorry. My parents. Their arguing. Mom's drinking." Burdening my best friend with my problems wasn't my style, but internally imploding wasn't either.

She attempted empathy. "I can't imagine what that's like, but please know you can always tell me anything. That's what best friends are for." She changed the subject to something she could relate to. "Now, let's get ready for the dock party. Dancing is a miracle mood lifter."

We rummaged through her closet and teased our hair. I went through the motions. But as the Aqua Net stiffened Julie's plump curls, resentment stiffened my hollowing heart. She had it all: concrete college plans, a solid moral compass, and a supportive family. She had everything I didn't. A distance simmered between us, and I wondered how long before someone turned up the heat.

CHAPTER FOUR

BIRTHDAY BLUES

JULIE TORE OPEN THE curtains. Sunlight poured into her room. "Wake up, sleepyhead. Mom made chocolate chip pancakes. Then after church, we're taking you to lunch for your birthday." She wore a floral dress with an oversized bow tied to her side ponytail. She looked twelve.

The last thing I wanted to do was sit in a pew next to her while she prayed to a God I doubted existed. "Nah, I gotta get home. Spend my birthday with the family." First Friday's disaster dock party. Then Saturday's cheerless cheer practice and family night Uno. I was ready to get back to where I didn't have to pretend to be someone I wasn't.

"Your loss. Those hot guys we met Friday night from Mayflower Prep are coming."

I changed out of one of Julie's matchy pajama sets into the same Bermuda shorts and over-sized t-shirt I'd worn all weekend. "Correction, those guys you met."

"You didn't even try." She fluffed her Pepto Bismol pink comforter. Julie took her favorite color to the extreme.

I threw my stringy brown hair in a scrunchy. "Sorry, flirting with guys out of my league and dancing with hoity-toity private school girls isn't my thing." Jumping into the lake and sacrificing myself to the alligators was what I'd really wanted to do.

"Stop underestimating yourself. You're prettier and smarter than all those girls combined. Everyone knows it but you."

She was wrong. I used to be.

"Time for breakfast," called Mrs. Davis.

After the sickeningly sweet pancakes, I crawled into the Davis's van and squeezed between Julie and her sister, Wendy. Karen sat in the back with one of her friends. Ruffles, perfume, and laughter suffocated me. I'd been so eager to leave my house and come here, but now I couldn't wait to be home. My misery didn't like company.

Mr. Davis opened the door for me to exit. The family cheered, "Happy Birthday," as I climbed out.

"Bye, Ange! Senior year tomorrow. Have a great rest of your birthday." The van backed out and disappeared around the corner, taking the blue sky with it.

What I didn't see or hear when I opened the front door told a depressing story. A pot of gumbo didn't sit simmering on the stove. A family wasn't bustling around the kitchen prepping for one of its members to turn a year older. My house was empty and silent.

I searched every room. In the kitchen, a barely legible note sat on the table.

Angela and Levi,
Picking your mom up from one of her friend's houses. Amber is with me.
Dad
Happy Birthday to me.
The front door opened. Levi beelined to his room.

I followed him. "Where've you been? You smell like weed."

He pulled off worn sneakers and flopped on the bed, not bothering to push the piles of clothes on it off. "Leave me alone. I'm tired."

"You're stoned. What's going on with you?"

He pulled a thinning sheet over his face. "Leave."

"Fine." I slammed his door shut. This family was a freaking pressure cooker, and all of us were about to explode. I needed to release some steam.

I picked up the phone and dialed Andrew's number. A number I'd known by heart for as long as I'd known my own. "Hey, it's me. Whatcha doing?"

"I was gonna call you later. Happy Birthday. Been getting a head start. Reading through each syllabus. Senior year tomorrow."

Even Andrew had his life together better than I did. "Wanna hang out later? You know, after everyone's asleep? I never got my last summer sneak-out hurrah like you did."

"Ange, I can't. I really gotta buckle down now. First in the family to hopefully go to college."

"For sure. I was just asking in case you wanted to. I've got so much to do before tomorrow. Priorities." As I had drifted away from Julie, I'd wanted to drift toward Andrew. Apparently, the feelings weren't mutual.

"I'll see you at the bus stop bright and early. Jules said she'd meet us at the usual spot."

"When did you talk to her?" I'd never known them to have a private conversation. They were each my best friends, not each other's. At least that's how it used to be.

"Oh, we talked on the phone after she got home from church. I wanted to catch up. Find out what she'd been up to—no big deal. See you in the morning. Gotta go."

His abrupt hang-up sent my mind whirling about what else he or she hadn't told me.

CHAPTER FIVE

SPLITSVILLE

THE SUN HAD LONG dipped behind the scraggly North Lake palms by the time Dad's company car, a dark brown Chevy Cavalier, crunched the gravel driveway and woke me from a restless nap on our dated floral couch. We didn't own the matching love seat anymore. Not enough room in this pitched as temporary, now permanent, rental.

Amber entered first, sniffling, puffy-eyed and clutching an adult sneaker and a woman's purse.

"Come here, Sweetie." I reached out.

She dropped Mom's things on the coffee table, collapsed next to me, and buried her tiny head into my chest.

Dad hauled our inebriated mother inside and dragged her into the bedroom. I loathed seeing her drunk. Even more, I loathed Amber seeing her drunk. But I really loathed what I now had to do.

"I'll be right back."

I pulled off the one shoe Mom had managed to keep on. It took Dad and me both to maneuver the clothing off her one-hundred pounds of lifeless flesh. After we threaded her limp limbs into pajamas, we covered her near-comatose body with their faded comforter. A pathetic routine I was all too familiar with.

For dinner, Dad made Hamburger Helper for the three of us. The other two members of the Carter family failed to make an appearance. Halfway through the somber meal, Dad smacked himself on the forehead. "The gumbo. Your birthday. I'm so sorry."

Amber piped in. "Sissy, it's your birthday? I'm gonna go make you a card right now."

"Guys, no. It's fine. I don't feel like celebrating. And Amber, you have to go to bed soon. It's your first day of second grade tomorrow."

Dad apologized again. "I'm so sorry. I'll make it up to you."

He was overwhelmed and I knew it.

The rest of the evening, I helped Amber pick out her first day of school outfit and she helped me pick out mine. I'd deal with Levi in the morning. I assumed Dad would deal with Mom.

"Call now for your chance to win tickets to this week's CWF, Championship Wrestling from Florida match." I hit snooze. But instead of catching a few more z's, I thought about when Julie and I had snuck close enough to the ring to get Barry Windham's sweat on us. We didn't shower for days. *Could I be that girl again?*

After a second snooze, I turned off my clock radio, threw on a pair of jeans, and the t-shirt Amber picked out the night before. Mom had bought me the pale-blue V-neck at a surf shop in Daytona last summer. That was the last time we'd gone anywhere as a family.

I brushed on a bit of blush, tossed my hair in my signature scrunchie, and made my bed. Then I headed to the kitchen for some quick breakfast before meeting Andrew at the bus stop.

Despite my less-than-perfect life, the first day of senior year felt like a fresh start. Maybe I'd buckle down like Andrew. Maybe I could salvage the parts of my life I hadn't yet ruined.

My father hunched at the kitchen table in the same crumpled clothes as yesterday, receiver to his ear.

I stopped short of entering.

"Yeah, Mike. I appreciate it. That's all I need is one bedroom for now. It's just me." Dad turned around and noticed me standing in the hallway. "Thanks. We can work out the details when I get there. Gotta go."

He hung up the phone and shuffled back to the table in front of a "Best Dad" coffee mug.

"What was that all about?" My gut instinct told me I didn't want to know.

He closed his eyes and inhaled the mid-August humidity. "I need you to handle Levi and Amber this morning." A flat monotone accompanied his demand.

"Why? Where're you going?"

At his feet sat an overstuffed duffle bag. His stoic demeanor lost its grip. His body trembled. Sobs erupted.

I'd never seen my father cry. It terrified me.

He wiped his unusually unkept stubbled face with the tail of his button-down. "I can't take this any longer. I can't focus at work. I'm trying to learn a new career, and this, Helen's—your mother's—drinking is constantly on my mind. I've asked her to go to marriage counseling and AA. She refuses."

I didn't want to know how this ended. My heart hoped one thing, but my brain connected the dots to something else—something I couldn't fathom. Something terrible.

He stood, pinched between his eyes, and blankly stared out the small kitchen window where Amber's rusting swing set sat. "I have to get out of here. I'm renting a room from a buddy at work."

Suddenly there was no air in the room. "No. You can't leave. What about us? What about Mom?"

"This must seem sudden. And I'm sorry. But me staying isn't helping, so maybe me leaving will."

He faced me. "Sometimes in life, you must make difficult decisions. I hope one day you understand this one." Then he placed his hands on my shoulders, piling the weight of the world on my small frame. "Do you trust me?"

Back in Mississippi, he asked me the same question before we walked outside during the eye of Hurricane Frederick. But a Cat 4 storm paled in comparison to the catastrophic threat my family was under.

"I want to trust you," I said.

"That's good enough for now." He picked up the duffle bag and opened the front door. "Once I'm on my feet and can afford a bigger place, you, Levi, and Amber will be welcome to join me. But until then, I have a big ask."

"What is it?"

"Take care of your brother and sister. They're gonna need you."

In other words, do what I'd already been doing. "Take care of the kids. Got it." The kids, I was still a kid.

Then my father walked out the front door.

And I thought I could have a fresh start senior year. *Joke's on me.* Karma had one twisted sense of humor.

Chapter Six

Fresh Start to Failure

Amber whimpered as she pulled last year's Holly Hobbie backpack on her shoulders, and we readied to walk to the bus stop.

"Honey, it's fine. Dad and Mom have some things to work through. It's normal family stuff." *Thanks, Dad, what a lovely way for your kids to start a new school year.*

"But he didn't even say goodbye." Her buttered toast sat uneaten on the coffee table.

"It's not like he moved to the moon. We'll see him soon. He's just gotta get settled." Having to defend my father's selfish move to Amber infuriated me.

I popped my head into Levi's room to see if he'd followed my orders. But he was still in bed, just like his mother.

"I told you ten minutes ago to get up and get dressed. You're gonna miss the bus."

He rolled over. "I'm not going" He tossed one of his flat pillows at me. "Get out."

"Whatever. I'll walk over to the Junior High and get your schedule. But you're going to school tomorrow."

Andrew greeted us at the bus stop. "Good morning. Well, look at you Miss Amber. Second grade this year, right?"

Instead of the flushed cheeks and girlish giggles Andrew usually drew from her, Amber offered a flat, "Yeah." Then she squeezed my hand.

"Everything okay? Where's Levi?"

I bore my eyes into him and shook my head to shut him up. "Everything's great. He just wasn't feeling well." I faked a smile.

The school bus rolled to a stop and the three of us climbed aboard. Amber and I slid into a bench seat together. Neither of our dispositions matched the rest of the animated students eager to greet old friends and make new ones. Andrew sat with some of his last year's friends across from us.

When the bus stopped at the elementary school, I told Amber, "You're gonna have a great day today. Mrs. Hunter is the best second-grade teacher. Julie and I are picking you up after school and you're coming to cheer practice with us."

Her sad eyes sparkled a little. "Okay. Bye. Love you, Sissy."

"Love you, too." I peeled her thin arms from around my neck. "Go."

She wiped a watery eye and slipped into the line of kids exiting at the elementary school.

Andrew slid into the seat next to me as the bus pulled out. "Something's going on. Tell me."

I appreciated that he cared. But I didn't want to talk about it. "It's not a big deal. Dad moved out. I'm sure he'll be back."

"Ange, I'm sorry. What about your mom?"

"She's currently in a self-medicated coma."

"What!"

"She's still sleeping off last night's drunk fest. Like Levi. The Carter family at its finest."

"That sucks."

"Yep."

The bus pulled into the shared parking lot of North Lake Junior High and North Lake High. The seventh through ninth graders went left, the direction Levi would have gone, and Andrew and I followed the tenth through twelfth graders to the right.

Julie waved from the gum tree. The old oak was a North Lake High staple. Daily students dotted it with gum faster than janitors could remove it.

Andrew sped up and when he reached her, they fell into a warm embrace.

My eyes burned.

When I got closer, Julie said, "I already checked the homeroom sheet. You have Mrs. Minich. Me and Andrew have Mr. Robinson."

My eyes went from burning to flame-throwing. "That's convenient for you both."

She crinkled her manicured brows. "What's that supposed to mean?"

"Nothing. And good morning to you, too." My two best friends seemed more interested in each other than me.

"Why are you so grumpy? It's the first day of our senior year." Julie high-fived Andrew. "I still cannot believe it."

They drifted into a flirtatious conversation that didn't include me.

I walked away before I said something I'd regret.

Andrew shouted, "See you at lunch."

I waved without turning around.

Maybe I should've stayed home like Levi. School wasn't the escape from my shitty life I'd hoped it would be. It was just an extension.

Mrs. Minich's emerald dress accentuated her fiery red hair. "Good morning, Angela. Glad to have you in homeroom this year. Here's your schedule."

"Thanks." I liked Mrs. Minich okay enough. She'd run the Glee Club I was in sophomore year. Back when I had something to feel glee about. I plopped down at a desk in the back row. Erika Sterling sat next to me. Lovely. She and her valley girl wannabes with their popped-up collars compared schedules. Erika was on the cheer team like I was. Only for her, hunky guys in letterman jackets lingered close.

I scanned my schedule. Everything looked good except Algebra II. Math and I weren't friends.

The bell rang and students scattered.

Julie sat in the middle of a row of desks in Mr. Conway's room. She waved me over.

"So glad we have second period together," she said. Then wasted no time sharing that she and Andrew had been talking about me behind my back. "Sorry about your dad, Ange. I'm your best friend. Why didn't you tell me?"

"Because I don't want to talk about it."

Fortunately, Mr. Conway shushed the class and handed out the syllabus. A lecture ensued and senior year formally began.

Third-period biology was annoying. Mrs. Van talked more about her pregnancy than the normal first-day-of-school stuff. That was gross. I didn't want to think about one of my teachers "doing it."

After school, I met Julie in the senior parking lot. Over the summer she'd inherited her twin sisters' blue Ford Escort when they bought a Jeep together.

"How was your day?" Her tone was bright. "Oh my gosh, did you see Mrs. Van? She looks funny with that baby belly. And can you believe Erika and John are finally official?"

"Fine. It was fine. Let's just go."

We pulled into the parent pick-up area to gather Amber, who now didn't have a parent to pick her up. I yanked myself out of my funk for her sake.

"Hi!" I smiled. "How was Mrs. Hunter's class?"

"Great. My best friend from last year, Christie Hulsey is in my class. Are we going to cheer practice?"

"Yes, we are." Julie chimed in.

At practice, Amber stood next to me. She beamed when Coach Kim said to her, "You keep this up and maybe you can cheer a real game with us this year."

Amber's moves were better than mine. I used to love chanting the corny lyrics paired with sharp moves and exaggerated facial expressions. Now my arms flailed, and my face struggled to form the thinnest of grins.

"Angela, we're at cheer practice," Erika said. "Not sad practice. Liven up." She flashed a bright smile.

I clenched my fists and only for Amber's benefit plastered a fake grin across my taught face.

Julie and Amber chatted on the drive home. When we got there, she told Amber to go in because she wanted to talk to me.

"I know things are tough on you right now. But you gotta pull yourself together. Kids' parents split up all the time."

Her words slapped me. "You seriously have no idea what I'm dealing with. You're so outta touch with reality. You and Andrew both. I hope you two enjoy your senior year. Together. I gotta go."

I slammed the door to her car and stormed inside to see what other shit life was about to throw at me.

Chapter Seven

Three Garbage Bags

The last month my role as the family matriarch had drained me on all fronts. Mom was useless and Dad gave every waking moment of his time to Clark's Cars. Filling both of their shoes meant I had little time to wear my own.

"What do you guys want for dinner?" A few boxes of mac and cheese and some cans of soup dotted the sparse cabinet that served as our pantry.

"I'm leaving. Don't worry about me." Levi put a worn denim jacket over his white t-shirt. His facial hair had grown into a patchy beard.

I snatched a blue and yellow box and slammed the cabinet door. "Where're you going?"

"None of your business." He grabbed a half empty two-liter bottle of soda off the laminate counter and took a big swig right out of the bottle.

I ignored it. I couldn't risk getting him angry, not when I needed information. "Please, just tell me where you're going and what time you'll be back. Nothing more."

He wiped a hand across his mouth and put the bottle back on the counter sans lid. "Sorry, not happening."

I snatched the lid off the counter and twisted it back on the plastic bottle now less than half full. "I walked over to the Junior High last week and talked to your old weight-lifting coach. He's gonna talk to you."

He jabbed a finger in my chest. "Stay in your lane."

I swatted his hand away. "You used to love weightlifting."

"There are a lot of things about this family that used to be. I gotta go." He paused at the door. And with a calmer demeanor said, "Ange, I know you're just trying to help. And I appreciate it. I'll try not to be too late."

"Thank you. I love you."

"Yeah, me, too." Then he left.

I didn't know what was going through my brother's head, but I did understand how hard it was to give a damn about anything with your family falling apart.

I pulled a tarnished pot from a bottom cabinet. "It looks like mac and cheese again?"

"Yeah, my favorite." Amber grabbed my hand. "Why is Levi always sad?"

"I don't know. Hey, I have an idea; we could be his personal cheerleaders. Maybe Coach Kim could help us make up a special Levi cheer."

She started cheering, "Give me and L, give me an E,"

Then I joined in, "Give me a V, and an I. What's that spell, LEVI!"

I picked her up and swung her around the room. Amber was the only reason I hadn't quit the squad. But a month in, I didn't know how much longer I could keep up the act. It was just one more place I had to pretend to be a normal teenager.

The phone rang. I pinched the receiver between my shoulder and ear and started making the mac and cheese.

"Hey, Number One," Dad said. "I have some good news. We got a trade-in that I think is perfect for you, an older model but low mileage. You're doing a lot to help with Levi and Amber. I'd like to buy it for you as a late birthday present. The boss is going to work out a payment plan."

His offer caught me off guard. "Seriously?"

"You bet. I'll pick you up tomorrow after school and bring you to the dealership, and we can take care of the paperwork." He cleared his throat. "How's your mom?"

I thought about last weekend when I had woken up to find her passed out on the kitchen floor in a puddle of vomit. He needed to know the truth. "Not great. The drinking is worse. My grades are suffering because I'm dealing with Levi, who doesn't want me to deal with him, and Amber, who needs a parent to raise her, not a sister."

"Honey, I'm doing everything I can to expedite getting a bigger place. Help me through the next few months, and hopefully, we're all together again under one roof."

Since divorce papers arrived last week, by "all together again," he didn't mean Mom. "Sure, I'll do whatever I can."

Although I appreciated the car, it came with a catch. He'd expect more from me. Drive the kids here; drive the kids there. By proxy, that enabled Mom to continue to skirt her responsibilities. It was a perfect arrangement for everyone—except me.

After dinner, I turned on cartoons for Amber. "I have a math test to study for. I need you to watch TV for a while. When I'm done, you can take a bubble bath."

"Okay. When's Mommy coming home?"

"Soon. She probably had to work late." It was my go-to for *I have no idea if she's drinking on a wooden pallet in the orange grove or if the Sunshine Citrus pickers stopped off at Uncle Tuck's.* Mom had always been a casual drinker, but now it was as much a part of her daily routine as eating and sleeping, probably more.

After about an hour of studying, laughter from a rowdy crowd and blaring music emerged and shook my bedroom walls. Mom was home.

I slammed my book shut and barged out of my room. Amber was not going to bear witness to whatever the hell was going on out there.

Some guy I didn't recognize hunched over several white lines on our coffee table. Bodies gyrated as if in a dance club.

Amber sat on the floor clenching a doll, gaze focused on colorful grainy images on our rabbit-eared TV.

I turned off the boom box and yelled to the room. "Are you kidding me? Really? Amber, come with me. Everyone better be gone by the time we come back in."

The guy covered the white dust with his hand and mouthed, "Sorry."

Mom lay passed out on the couch next to him.

This was my father's fault.

I grabbed my little sister's hand and led her out the back door. I sat her on her rusty metal swing set and pushed her until my pounding chest slowed.

"Amber, tell me what was happening inside."

"I couldn't hear the cartoons because of the loud music."

I exhaled. "Mommy and her friends are so silly." I wanted Amber to have the kind of childhood I had, the one before my parents' de-evolution.

When the last of the cars left the driveway, I told Amber, "Okay, time for that bubble bath."

Inside, I sent Amber to collect some toys and her pajamas. I turned on the water and poured in a couple capfuls of Mr. Bubbles. I wished I could take a warm bubble bath—wash away the pain, the hurt, the disgust of what my parents were doing to us.

"I got all five of my Little Ponies and my Strawberry Shortcake pj's." At seven years old, Amber had already lost so much, and she had no idea. To her, our dysfunctional life was normal.

"When I come back, I'm going to check that each of these Little Ponies is nice and clean, even behind the ears." I hoped that would buy me some time. Because I didn't care if she was drunk or not, I was confronting my mother.

I sat down on the couch next to her. I used to think she was the most beautiful woman, petite with short, trendy dark blonde hair. I had looked up to her, wanted to be her. Now, I didn't want to be anywhere near her.

She moved a little, opened sleepy eyes, and asked, "Hey, Baby Girl. Where is everybody?"

"I made them leave. Do you know what one of your loser friends was doing while Amber was in the room?"

She didn't answer.

"Let's just say he was about to inhale something white and powdery." I let that sink in a few beats. "Mom, what're you doing?"

Tears welled in pale green eyes. She covered them with her hand. "Things are really hard on me right now. I'm doing the best I can to deal with everything."

"Things are hard on you. What about me? And what do you mean by 'deal with everything?' You're dealing with nothing. I'm the only one doing anything to try and hold this family together."

She continued to cry.

"You're not the mom I used to know. The mom I knew baked cookies with her kids, not neglected them. She had fun bowling with her friends, not using drugs with them." A fiery rage ripped through my body and words I'd held back far too long erupted all over my mother covering her in a layer of shame.

She could hardly speak through the sobs. "I'm so sorry. I just don't know what to do."

"Well, I have an idea. Instead of being a shitty mother—don't. You can start there." I pushed a button.

She shot up. "It is what it is. No matter what you think of me, I'm still your mother. And while you live under my roof, you need to show some respect."

"Respect. What's to respect? And trust me, if I had anywhere else to go, I'd be gone." Heavily armed with the one weapon that would hurt her the most, I went for the jugular. "You turned out just like your mother."

She fell back onto the couch, curled into a fetal position, and wailed.

I didn't care. I stomped to my room and slammed the door. I picked up the math book off my bed and threw it at the wall. The framed photo of the cheer squad fell, and the glass shattered. I hoped my words had broken something in my mother that needed to break like she was breaking us.

The pendulum of her life had swung so far from where it started; I didn't think it would ever turn back. If things didn't change, it would detach and level everything and everyone in its path.

The following day, after school, Dad picked me up to do the paperwork for the car. I assumed Mom was picking up Amber and Levi. I withheld telling Dad about the night before. I wasn't trying to protect Mom. I just didn't want more chaos in our family. We had enough already.

I sat across from him in his cubicle at the dealership. After I'd signed the last paper, he slid the keys across his desk. I closed my fingers around them. Finally. "Thanks so much for the car."

Then he took out his wallet and handed me some cash. "Here's a little extra money for gas, but now that you're a car owner, time to find a job."

Perfect. Now he expected me to go to school, take care of his other children, and work. "You bet. I'll start looking right away."

The rusty Ford Fairmont was far from my dream car, but any form of transportation came with perks. I wouldn't have to ride the bus or depend on Julie anymore, and I could come and go as I pleased. Well, depending on the kids.

On the drive back home, confronting my mother again flashed across my radar. But I decided I'd table it. The night before, I'd delivered my message loud and clear.

When I got home, Mom's car wasn't in the driveway. Not surprising. What was surprising were the three small white garbage bags on the front porch. I opened one—my clothes. I opened the others—also my clothes. Suddenly, it hit me.

My mother had kicked me out.

Betrayal, outrage, and rejection churned in my stomach like a storm. She had really done it. What had I done that was so terrible? I was the only one taking care of her kids. She needed me. Worse, what would happen to Amber and Levi?

I tossed the bags in the backseat of my car and took off. My heart shredded into a thousand pieces as my home disappeared in the rearview mirror.

CHAPTER EIGHT

CLAYPIT HILL CLIMB

JULIE HANDED ME HER phone. It was one of those cool new clear ones where you could see all the fluorescent wires on the inside. But nothing was cool about who she wanted me to call.

"Call him now. He's your father. He needs to know where you are."

"Fine. But I don't need you giving me a play-by-play."

"No problem. I'll be in the bathroom getting ready for the game."

I dreaded making the phone call I'd avoided.

"It's a beautiful day. Thank you for calling Clark's Cars. Your Number One Dealer. How can I help you?"

The woman's sugary voice triggered a nerve. "Can I please speak with Richard Carter?"

"Of course, Darling. I'll put you through to his office."

His office? That was new.

"Hello, Richard speaking." Even though anger lingered, his warm voice filled me with a familial sense of safety—a constrictive safety.

"You have an office?" What else had he not told me?

"Hey, Number One. Yep, your old man got a small promotion to Sales Manager. Hopefully, I can afford a place big enough for all of us soon. Work's been so busy, I haven't had a chance to call or see you kids. Can you bring Levi and Amber by this weekend?"

"Maybe." I wanted to say, *how about you come pick your children up in your company vehicle rather than asking your teenage daughter to bring them to you?* But I didn't.

"I called to tell you I'm temporarily staying at Julie's. Mom and I got into an argument."

He let out an exaggerated sigh. "I admit this isn't fair to you. But I did ask you to give me a little time. I need some help here. Part of the reason for getting you the car was to help with Levi and Amber."

His attempt at guilt-tripping me wasn't going to work. I wasn't his employee. "I can't do this right now. I understand your difficult position but think about mine. Mom and I fight all the time. Why are you allowed to leave but I'm not?" I didn't tell him the truth. That I hadn't left willingly. That Mom kicked me out. I needed to regain agency. I needed him to know I was in charge of me now. And as much as I worried about my siblings, he was their parent—not me.

He took a few seconds to process. "I'm sorry. I'll handle their transportation. Take your time."

"I gotta go. Julie and I are cheering tonight." Although nothing about me felt cheery.

"Number One, I love you. Things will get better. I promise."

"Bye, Dad." His words implied love, but his actions implied self-preservation.

The football game was a blur. Julie, Erika, and the rest of the squad nailed the exaggerated smiles and sharp moves. I flung my limbs around like someone who'd just jumped off a bridge plummeting to their death.

After the game, Coach Kim chased after me, her thick, blonde ponytail swung behind her. "Can I talk with you for a minute?"

Julie read the room, or rather she read the football field sidelines, "I'll meet you in the locker room." Then she pom-pommed away with the rest of the cheer squad.

Coach Kim had never pulled me aside. But it's not like I could say no. "Sure. Sorry I was a little off tonight. It won't happen again."

"No, you're fine. That's not it." She held her clipboard of cheer titles to her chest. "It's… you've missed several practices. And your grades are slipping. Is anything going on?"

Coach Kim was only a few years older than me. She'd probably understand. "My parents split. I've had more responsibility with my siblings."

I held back about Mom kicking me out. A teacher might report something like that to the police. As much as I hated both of my parents, I didn't want them in trouble or my siblings in foster care.

"Sorry to hear that. The guidance counselor, Mr. Givens, he runs a Teens of Divorce group before school. Maybe that would help. Maybe you and your brother could both go. Talking to some other kids going through the same thing might help."

That was her way of offering help? Send me to some lame teen support group. *No way.* "Thanks. I'll check it out."

"To stay on the squad, you must pull your grades up and not miss any more practices. Got it?"

"Got it." Everyone kept wanting more from me, but I wasn't a renewable resource. Eventually, I needed something—or someone—to fill my emotional tank because I was running on fumes.

As I walked toward the locker room, someone behind me called my name. I turned. Dale Simmons stood in tight jeans and cowboy boots. Absent a baseball cap, his thick wavy hair brushed passed his shoulders.

My heart fluttered. "Hey. What's up?" With all that had been going on in my life, I'd forgotten about Dale. But seeing him filled me with an overwhelming yearn.

"That's a sweet cheer uniform." He peered through the orange and white garment onto my bare skin. His gaze drew goosebumps. "Whatcha doing after the game?"

I cocked my head to one side and twirled my hair. "No plans. What're you doing?" A smile, a real smile, formed on my lips. Lips he'd kissed.

"Roger and me are headed to the clay pit for a little hill climbing and any other trouble we can get ourselves into. Wanna join?"

Julie wouldn't be thrilled with the idea. But we were going. "Sure, can my friend, Julie, come, too?"

"The more, the merrier," he grinned.

"Give us about a half-hour, then pick us up at the entrance to Four Lakes. That neighborhood on the edge of town between here and Mayflower."

"You got it. See you in a few." He winked and pointed a finger gun at me before disappearing into the crowd.

Dale Simmons and hill-climbing at the clay pit sounded thrilling and dangerous. I needed them both.

I sprinted to the locker room.

Julie was sifting through her bag. "Where've you been? We gotta go. My house again?"

"Yeah, I mean, I don't have anywhere else to go until I figure some things out. You still haven't said anything to your parents, right?" I opened my locker and grabbed my bag.

Coach Kim clapped her hands. "Hurry up, Ladies. We don't have all night."

Julie whispered. "No, because they haven't asked. To be honest, if they do, I won't lie. If they knew, maybe they could help you."

I slipped my jeans on under my cheer uniform. "No way. Please don't tell them. Let me handle this." Like Coach Kim, Mr. and Mrs. Davis must've had their suspicions. But this was my problem, one I preferred not to share.

"I have a surprise. Remember that little boy I used to babysit? Well, his older brother Dale and his cousin Roger invited us to the clay pit tonight to go hill climbing." Despite my enthusiasm, I expected Julie to oppose.

"Those older guys. Gross. No way. Plus, even if I wanted to, which I don't, my parents would never allow me."

"You don't have to go. But I'm going."

"I can think of a thousand things less disgusting than the clay pit." Her eyes widened and a sheepish grin grew. "I have an idea, let's call Andrew and see if he wants to go to a late movie?"

A confusing pain stabbed me when she mentioned his name. I was the one that had introduced them when he moved in next door to me. I was the bridge between them. But now she'd built her own bridge. "How about you and Andrew go to a movie together? I'm going with Dale."

She gritted her teeth. "Fine, I'll go. I don't want you to be alone. But it's a terrible idea. I've heard what goes on out there."

What goes on out there was exactly why I wanted to go. "Jules, live a little."

"Don't forget it was me who said this was a terrible idea." She yanked her jeans out of her bag and stomped into a stall to change.

When we got back, she told her parents we were taking a walk around the lake. They bought it. No doubt it was the first lie she'd ever told. I did feel a little bad about that, but guilt wouldn't numb my pain. What I hoped to find at the claypit might.

"If you can't tell, I'm less than happy," Julie said as we headed down the street to meet Dale and Roger.

"If I can't tell? Don't worry. You wear your emotions on your face as vivid as a Care Bear does on their stomach."

"Good analogy, but not funny."

"And I appreciate you coming. I'm just ready to experience something different, something fun."

"I'd hardly call going to a clay pit where a bunch of drunk hicks drive trucks up hills fun. Sounds more like a death sentence to me."

A jacked-up truck's rumbling exhaust ended our short conversation. The lumens from roll bar lights blinded us. We stepped back from the road and held hands. My palm sweated in hers. Maybe Julie was right. But it was too late to back down.

The massive machine slowed. Hank Williams, Jr. sang "Country Boys Can Survive."

Roger leaned out of the window. "Well, looky here. We got us a couple of cuties all alone in the middle of the night on this empty road. What do you say we show these two little ones a good time tonight?"

The aroma of cigarette and cannabis smoke drifted out of the cabin.

"Sounds like a great idea to me, Cuz." Dale hopped down and opened the door to the extended cab.

Julie hoisted herself up first.

I climbed in after.

Julie and I buckled up and huddled together in the tiny dark back seat. Dale handed us each a beer. I popped mine and chugged in hopes of calming my nerves.

Julie held hers, unopened, and rolled her eyes.

Roger roared the engine to life, cranked the music, and the guys hooted and hollered the whole way to the dirt road that led to the clay pit.

The pickup tore through the foliage of the one-way entrance with no regard for the possibility of an oncoming vehicle. The guys belted out the song's lyrics, oblivious to any potential danger.

I double-checked my seatbelt.

At the clearing, my eyes widened at not only how high the clay pit's sides were but how many trucks were climbing at the same time. I tossed my empty beer can on the floor and reached out to hold Julie's hand.

She squeezed it tight.

"Let's go, ladies." Roger accelerated toward the hill and up the only space left big enough for his truck.

Julie and I screamed as Roger gassed up the steep incline. Headlights illuminated the dark sky. At the top, he let off the gas, and the truck rolled down the bank into the clay pit. Weightless bodies thrust around the truck's cabin. Hair swirled in all directions. The adrenaline was more intoxicating than the beer.

"I'm done. Let me out." Julie shouted, and she hit the back of Roger's seat.

Roger laughed but pulled out of the clay pit and parked near a small group. She jumped down, slammed the door, and bee-lined toward a roaring fire. Roger trailed close behind. If he expected anything from her, he could forget it.

Dale leaned over the seat and asked, "Wanna go somewhere a little more private?"

I bit my lower lip. "Sure."

He slid over to the driver's seat, and I climbed up front. He lightly tapped the gas and steered us away from the rowdy crowd. When the light from the fire vanished, Dale slowed to a stop, turned off the ignition, and popped in a cassette of slow country music.

"Let's go lie in the back and look at the stars." He grabbed a blanket from behind his seat. The sky was black as coal that night. Looking at the stars was code for something else. Something else I was ready and willing to do.

My heart pounded. But this wasn't as much about a crush on Dale Simmons as it was about me.

I initiated a kiss. It started off gentle, then accelerated to intense hunger. Tongues penetrated deep down throats. Bodies pressed into each other. It was time. I unbuckled his jeans.

He stopped kissing me. "Are you sure?"

"Yes. One hundred percent."

In the bed of Dale's truck on a thin blanket, dark nothingness consumed me. I disassociated from my body and floated, far away from my patronizing best friend, drunk mother, demanding father, and needy siblings. I was above them all, making my own decisions. Doing what I wanted when I wanted. No longer a victim of my circumstances. Goodbye, little girl—you are a woman now.

CHAPTER NINE

TWO DAYS TO TWO WEEKS

BECAUSE I NEEDED TO conserve gas, on Monday morning I rode to school with Julie. As I chewed a piece of tasteless gum, she sang along to "I Melt With You" by Modern English. Like the song's lyrics, Julie's future was open wide. Mine was tasteless gum.

Fortunately, she hadn't interrogated me about Dale—yet. Until she did.

She popped the Valley Girl soundtrack out of the Escort's tape player. "I know you don't want to tell me what happened with Dale."

I'd rather listen to her sing about her future than answer any questions about mine. "Then why are you bringing it up?" I laid my head against the window and shut my eyes.

She waited as long as she could stand it. "Like it or not, you're my best friend. And it's not even about Dale. You need to talk to an adult about what's going on with you. You need advice I can't give."

"I don't need anyone's advice. I'll figure it out." I pulled the hood of my sweatshirt over my head, hoping she'd get the hint I wasn't interested in continuing this conversation.

But she didn't. "That's it. I don't see you trying to figure anything out. I don't want to be mean, but you can't just stay in this state of... What's that word? Purgatory. You have to do something."

Even though I missed my family, especially Amber, the last week and a half had been the break I needed from all the responsibility. But apparently, break time was over.

"Right now, purgatory is my comfort zone. I'll let you know when I decide if heaven or hell is my next stop." I grabbed a pair of sunglasses from her dash to hide my watering eyes. She didn't know how good she had it. But I did. And I was starting to hate her for it.

She shook her head in frustration. Because it was all she had to offer, she gifted me her silence the rest of the drive.

Andrew was waiting for us at the gum tree. "Hey, what's up?" He greeted us both, but his gaze fixated on Julie—all dolled up in a new sleek pink and white striped jumpsuit.

"Good morning, Andrew. I'm over here." I gave him an exaggerated wave.

He offered me a half-assed, "Hey, Ange." Then the two of them disappeared into a chuckling chit-chat of teenage shit that didn't matter—homework, prom, school lunches. Their voices morphed into a garbly echo as we all stood next to a stupid oak tree dotted with chewed gum.

I took the wad out of my mouth. "Pardon the interruption." Then I thrust my hand between them and smashed the gum into the tree's rough bark. "Enjoy the rest of your day."

I gripped the straps of my backpack and took off for homeroom. I'd rather watch Erika flirt with her quarterback boyfriend than have my two best friends ignore me.

The rest of the week was equally awful. To dodge Julie and Andrew, I didn't sit next to them in class and stayed in the library during lunch.

The only good news of the week was a job posting on the library bulletin board for a teaching assistant at the elementary school's after care program. I both needed the money and liked kids. So maybe it would work.

Back at Julie's place, to avoid her parents, I kept to myself.

But by weeks' end, Mrs. Davis, pretending to collect laundry, cornered me alone in Julie's room. "Angela Dear, can I have a word?"

I sat up in Julie's bed, my stomach in knots. "Yes, ma'am." I had no other option than to agree. Julie's parents had always been kind to me, and they weren't the type to pry. But I'd been at their house for almost two weeks. This was bound to happen.

She grabbed my hand. It had been a long time since a mother had touched me. I wanted to jerk away—protect myself from becoming soft.

"I've watched you grow up right alongside Julie. You've been coming in and out of this house since you were ten years old. I've seen you get awards at school for good grades and watched you cheer at more football games than I can count."

I know she didn't mean it but reminding me who I used to be made me feel worse about who I was now. But I couldn't be her again. That carefree girl from Mississippi now knew what it meant to be poor. To be homeless. To be unwanted.

"You're like another sister to Julie. And we love having you here. But at some point, I'm going to need to step in and talk to your parents."

I jerked my hand away. "No, ma'am. Please don't do that. I'll work things out with them soon. I promise."

A concerned look settled onto her face. "Well, is there anything you'd like to talk about? I'm a good listener."

Mrs. Davis may have seen me come and go in and out of this house for years, but she didn't really know me. Or my family. She couldn't possibly understand what my life was like behind-the-scenes. But I had to give her something.

"It's nothing really. My mother and I are just arguing. You know, normal teen mother-daughter stuff." Poor choice of words. Mrs. Davis and her teen daughters rarely argued. "That and my dad moved out. It's just been an adjustment. That's all."

"I'm so sorry. This must be a challenging time for your family. We're happy for you to stay as long as you need to—you know, while you adjust."

I exhaled a little relief, but there had been an ever-so-slight tone of disbelief under her voice. "Thank you, Mrs. Davis. I really appreciate your understanding."

"Of course, Dear." She grabbed the empty laundry basket and left.

I sank back in the bed. I had to figure something out. I could call Dad. Maybe he could get a bigger place now. I could call Mom and apologize. Maybe I could help her. But why weren't they calling me? I was the kid here.

Julie bounced in; hair wrapped in pink sponge rollers. "Get up and get ready. We're going to meet Andrew at the mall tonight. I'm not letting you sleep your life away."

"I don't want to go to the mall. You go. I'm tired."

Before she had the chance to launch into a tirade about me wasting my life, the phone rang. Julie answered and her nostrils flared. "Just what you've been waiting for—it's Dale." She rolled her eyes, then dropped the phone on the bed and retreated into her bathroom.

I pressed the ice-cold receiver to my warming face and muttered a shaky "hello."

"Hey, it's me. Whatcha been up to?"

My heart raced as I searched for a reply. "Just been hanging out." Even though Julie wasn't in the room, I expected she was listening.

"Daddy's grillin' some ribs, and Mama said you could crash here this weekend. If you want."

Staying with Dale wasn't at the top of my list. I'd already gotten from him what I thought I wanted. But I was done with the stifling Davis household. "Sure."

Julie bolted out of the bathroom, half the rollers still in. "Well?"

I nonchalantly replied, "Dale asked me to stay the weekend with him." Then I collected my clothes from around her room.

"And you agreed? Listen, a one-night stand with him is one thing, which I assume is what happened at the claypit. But staying the weekend with him is a whole new level of an initial terrible idea." She yanked a t-shirt from me. "Plus, we already have plans."

"I'm staying at his parent's house for a couple of days. That's it. And I really don't want to be third wheel with you and Andrew." I yanked the t-shirt back.

She threw her hands in the air. "What's that supposed to mean?"

"Nothing. I'm just tired of everyone telling me what to do."

Her voice softened. "Dale's trouble and you know it."

I shoved my clothes back into my garbage-bag luggage. "Well, for now, maybe that's exactly what I'm looking for. Because if you haven't figured it out, I got nothing else."

She handed me some of my clothes off the floor. "Ange, I miss my best friend. I want to help you and so does my family. But you have to let us. The situation with your parents sucks and it's totally not your fault. But you have a choice. And if that choice involves Dale Simmons, it's a path I won't follow you down—no matter how much I love you."

"Thanks. You just helped making my decision a little easier." I threw the bags over my shoulder and headed toward her door. As much as I hated to think of losing my best friend, I had to be somewhere I could breathe. The perfection here was suffocating.

"Wait—be careful."

I turned around.

Julie stood in her meticulously decorated bedroom with its ensuite bath, half her blonde hair fell in large curls, the other half in pink rollers.

Have fun at the mall tonight. I've got a date with the devil. "Why? You're careful enough for the both of us."

Then I walked out, tossed my clothes into the backseat of my car, and again drove away from somewhere I didn't belong.

When I got to Dale's, I parked in the backyard. Mom didn't usually drive this way, but I needed to fly under the radar and regroup. I also needed to convince Addis not to say anything to my mother if they crossed paths. I left my bags in the back seat in case I changed my mind. But it's not like I had anywhere else to go.

When I got out of my car, a couple of mangy hunting dogs barked at me from cages. I shivered, feeling like I was about to walk into a cage myself.

A barefoot Cole ran toy dump trucks through a sandbox made of two-by-fours. Too long bangs covered his eyes. "Are you here to babysit me?" he hollered.

I wanted to take him inside and bathe him. "Not this time. But I'm here to stay the weekend with your family."

"Yay! Can we color and watch cartoons?"

"I don't have the crayons and coloring book with me this time. But we can for sure watch some cartoons together."

Dale's dad sat on a bucket smoking a cigarette and drinking a beer next to the fifty-five-gallon drum he'd haphazardly converted into a meat smoker. His job as a trucker for Sunshine used to keep him on the road. But as the citrus dwindled, so did his deliveries.

"Hey, John. The ribs smell delicious."

He tilted his head my way. "Two more hours. Dale's inside."

I knocked. Addis answered. "Come on in. How's your mama? I haven't seen her since I got laid off from Sunshine. I heard she and your daddy split up. They weren't right together anyhow. He was too controlling."

Addis was the town gossip. If I didn't shut this down, my parents would know where I was before night's end.

"About my parents, they don't know I'm here. I'd like to keep it that way. I need a little space."

"Of course. Dale told me all about it."

Aha, now I knew she wouldn't tell—Dale. She'd lie, cheat, and steal for him. For now, my secret was safe.

About that time, he strutted into the living room—shirtless, denim cut-offs hung slightly below the waistband of his underwear. "There's my girl. Come on back here and get settled."

Each time I'd seen Dale before had been through the lens of desire. But since I'd satiated that hunger, the reality of who he really was came sharply into focus—a full-grown man with the trace of wrinkles pulling at his eyes, stained teeth from years of smoking, and a slur to his speech as if he was never fully sober.

My heart dropped. I sheepishly followed him into his tiny bedroom. Push-pinned towels blackened the windows. A shabby blanket covered the low bed. The only artwork was a single deer head and a stocked gun rack.

Dale shut and locked the door and shoved me to the bed; his mouth and hands were everywhere.

I pushed him off. "Hey, I just got here."

"And I've been thinking about this ever since the clay pit. You must've too, or you wouldn't have come."

Why did I come? Maybe because no one who cared about me would want me here. It was a twisted rationale, but it was the only one I had.

Other than eating ribs on John's tailgate, Dale and I stayed in his room most of the weekend. I never watched cartoons with Cole. He probably forgot I was there anyway. Dale only left to get us food or booze, then he'd climb back into bed. Since neither of us showered, by Sunday a mix of sweat, stale beer, and half-rotten food smell filled the room. It was the worst two days of my life. And then two days turned into two weeks.

CHAPTER TEN

LIMITED OPTIONS

"TURN OFF THE DAMN alarm. I don't have to get up for another hour," Dale complained.

"Sorry, I've got that job interview this morning before school." My head throbbed—courtesy of another well-earned hangover.

"Job interview?"

"The one at the elementary school. I told you about it like ten times this weekend." But he was already snoring again.

Someone knocked on the bedroom door. "Dale, I made you some breakfast. Open up."

I jostled him. "Wake up. Your mama's at the door." I wasn't about to answer it. Since staying at the Simmons' place, my limited interactions were run-ins at the bathroom. I did my best to stay hidden in Dale's bedroom.

"Just open it," he said then rolled over.

I grabbed a Mason Jar off the side table and took a gulp of warm water infused with a disgusting hint of sulfur. Every house in this town enjoyed the taste of rotten eggs with their well water. Then I unlocked and opened the door.

Beady eyes looked me up and down.

I felt exposed in a tank top and cheer shorts.

Addis held a plate—one plate—filled with runny eggs and lumpy grits swimming in butter. The breakfast's aroma mirrored the odor of the water. I tried not to inhale.

"Hi, Addis. Thanks for letting me crash here the last couple of weeks. With everything going on, I really needed the downtime." Through the thin walls of her home, I was sure the noises from her oldest son's bedroom told a different story. I should've never left Julie's. This was a mistake.

"Dale needs to get up and eat. Too busy having—downtime—I guess. And he's gotta work today." She shot past me and sat on the bed next to him. "Dale, Sweetie. Mama made you some breakfast. I'll put it on the floor. When you get up make sure you eat every bite, ya hear."

"Yes, Mama," he moaned.

She grabbed some of his dirty clothes off the floor, glared at me one more time, then bolted out the door.

Well, good morning to you, too, Addis.

Dale crawled out of bed and pulled on his underwear. Then he used a piece of burnt toast to slop up the runny egg.

I dug some clothes out of a garbage bag for school. Pretty soon I'd have to ask Addis if I could use her washing machine. I'm sure she'd love that.

Dale came up behind me, wrapped his arms around my waist, and whispered, "Let's have another sick day and crawl back into bed." His breath reeked. I couldn't believe I'd ever been attracted to him.

"I don't think your mother wants me here." Her icy demeanor made that clear. But Addis didn't need to be concerned with me trying to steal her baby boy from her. All I wanted to do was get away from him.

"Don't worry about Mama. I'll talk to her. She'll come around. Mama knows I get what I want." He kissed my cheek.

My skin crawled. I didn't want to stay, but I was too dirty to go back to Julie's, and it wasn't a filth you could wash off.

"I gotta get ready." I grabbed my clothes and makeup bag and tiptoed to the bathroom praying I wouldn't run into Addis.

I didn't recognize the reflection in the mirror. My cheeks were sunken from recent weight loss. My eyes were bloodshot from too much booze coupled with lack of sleep.

But it wasn't just my appearance. Makeup could mask the dark circles under my eyes but not the darkness growing inside me. I smeared on concealer and blush, then brushed my tangled hair. I needed that job. As my cash dwindled, so did my limited options.

CHAPTER ELEVEN

JUDGMENT FREE ZONE

I KNOCKED ON THE door to the room where the aftercare program was held. A plump older woman with curly gray hair and glasses answered. She looked like the type of woman who baked pies and put together jigsaw puzzles of landscape scenes, like the grandmother I wished I had.

"Hi, Angela. I'm Mrs. Elliott, the aftercare program director. Come on in and have a seat. Tell me a little about yourself."

I crossed my fingers in preparation for the half-truths I'd mastered over telling outright lies. "Well, I'm seventeen and a senior this year. I want to go to college, but I don't know what I want to study yet." College. Even saying the word sliced off a little piece of my soul.

She scribbled some notes on the back of my application. "Great, so why do you want to work here?"

"Well, I need a job." I shouldn't have sounded so desperate. "My little sister, Amber, she's seven, and I've always had fun with her. I like to help her learn new things. I also like babysitting. When I read the posting about this job at the high school, I thought I'd give it a try."

She took off her reading glasses and let them dangle from a chain around her neck. "Both sound good. I want to hire someone motivated to work and having experience with children is a big plus."

By the end of the interview, miraculously, Mrs. Elliott offered me a job as a teaching assistant in the homework room, working with elementary-aged kids.

She also said Amber could come with me. I hadn't seen her much since Mom had kicked me out.

"Mrs. Elliott, thank you very much for this opportunity." Something tiny sparked inside me—hope.

Lines appeared at the corners of her round eyes and mouth. "I've got a good feeling about you. I think you'll be a great role model here for our students."

Mrs. Elliott's confidence in me made me want to step up, at least temporarily, from the newest lowest version of myself. She was the type of person I didn't want to disappoint.

The morning dragged on for what seemed like forever. I was bursting to tell someone about my new job. So instead of hiding behind a study carrel in the library, and even though it had been awkward between us, I joined Andrew and Julie in the cafeteria.

The second I stepped onto the sticky floor I nearly gagged. No matter what was on the hot-lunch menu the odor was always the same, and not in a good way.

The fluorescent lights illuminated obnoxious teenagers packed into tiny booths. It was too late to turn around and bolt to the library. Julie had already spotted me and was waving me over.

I slid into the booth next to her and across from Andrew.

"Did you get kicked out of the library because it's that time of year for the Sophomore Sex-Ed talk, or did you come here willingly?" She popped the lid back on her Tupperware bowl. Every day her mom packed her the same damn salad.

"I can leave." Suddenly I had no interest in telling them anything.

"She was joking," Andrew said. "Right?" He glared at Julie.

"Of course, I was joking. But this 'Avoid Julie and Andrew' tactic, I mean why? What're you trying to hide?"

"First off, you were the one who told me if I left and went to Dale's our friendship was basically over." My stomach growled. I didn't understand how I could be both nauseous and starving at the same time.

"You know that's not what I meant."

Hunger pains scraped my insides. "Are you gonna finish that salad?"

Julie popped the lid back off and slid the bowl in my direction. I scarfed what little was left. "Thanks."

"You're welcome. Maybe you should try the novel concept of eating during lunch. Back to the reason you've been avoiding us?" Julie cocked her head.

Andrew opened and closed his milk carton.

I shrugged. "I guess because I just didn't have anything good to share." It was time to shift the conversation. Get them off my back. "But I do now if either of you care to know."

"Of course, we do." Andrew piped in.

"I got a job. Working at the aftercare program at the elementary school. I'm kinda excited about it." It was the first time in weeks I had good news to share, and I liked how it felt.

"That's really awesome," Andrew said.

Julie's eyes lit up. "It's perfect. You should go to college to be a teacher." An annoying enthusiasm oozed out of her every pore. "You've always been so good with Amber. I'll ask my guidance counselor at North Lake Community College about their education degree when I meet with her next week."

"I don't need you asking your guidance counselor anything on my behalf. Besides, it's just a job. I only took it for the money." My excitement waned and envy welled. Julie and Andrew had college plans and parents to hold their hands through them. My parents didn't even know where I slept each night.

"Sorry, I'm only trying to help." Julie changed the subject to even more annoying topics. "You've told us about the job, we also want to know how things are with your parents and with—Dale?" Her voice slowed, and her nostrils flared when she said his name.

I didn't want to talk about my parents or Dale. but I couldn't totally avoid the question. "My parents. Dad's working all the time. Mom and I still haven't spoken."

"And—Dale? Like are you living there?" She did that nostril flare thing again. Like she could smell his stench on me.

Andrew fidgeted in his chair like he would rather be anywhere but here. He took a bite of square pizza and looked out the window. He and I had once been the twosome on the other side of Julie. But he'd crossed over her bridge. I was totally alone.

"Fine. Everything's fine."

She pushed. "Ever since you've been staying there, you've missed a lot of school, cheer practice, and both games. Coach said she's going to talk to you—again."

I clenched my fists under the table. "Julie, stop it. I don't want a lecture from you. And don't talk about me behind my back. I'm probably quitting cheer anyway because of the job."

"What? Why? You love to cheer. Being senior cheerleaders was all we used to talk about. Who are you, and what have you done with the real Angela?"

I imagined my fist in contact with her smooth jaw. "I don't have to listen to this." I yanked my backpack out of the booth and bolted up. "Maybe I'll quit school like my brother apparently has. Some of us grow up a little faster than others."

Julie stared at Andrew like she needed backup.

He dropped his pizza crust onto his lunch tray. "Ange, no. So close to graduation. It doesn't make sense."

Great, now she'd also turned Andrew against me. "What I choose to do with my life doesn't need to make sense to you. So back off."

Like Julie, he pressed. "Ange, we're worried about you. Julie and me, we want you to really think about what you're doing."

"What I'm doing? I'm not doing anything any different than you, Andrew. You drink and go out and have fun, or at least you used to. We used to. You never lectured me when we were partying together. And Julie, stop acting like you're above me because you don't. Both of you, stop with the judgment." It was too late to turn back. I made my choice.

"I gotta get to class." With Dale, there was no judgment. Maybe it was time for me to let go of how miserable I was there and embrace the Simmons' lifestyle as my own. Because currently, it was my only option.

CHAPTER TWELVE

MISS JONES

THE CLICKETY CLACK OF thirty students trying to finish the same typing drill as me didn't deter me from finishing first. I had to get to the office before dismissal. I raised my hand. "Mrs. Lovejoy."

She scuttled over on her twenty-four-inch legs—half that height from her stilettos.

"I'm done with the vowels drill. Can I go to the office and make a call?"

She scanned my document. "You did miss one *e* for an *i*. But other than that, good job. Yes, you're dismissed."

"Thanks." I pulled the document out of the typewriter and shoved it into my backpack then darted to the office.

Thankfully, the office was quiet and the phone available. I dialed the number to the dealership and the receptionist had my dad on in a flash. "Dad, I have some good news. I got a job working at the aftercare program at Amber's school, and she gets to go with me."

"That's great, Hon. Listen, I don't have much time—Gotta sales meeting in a couple of minutes. Can we talk later, and you can fill me in on the details? That'll definitely help as far as Amber's concerned, for sure."

His biggest take-away from our short chat was now he didn't have to deal with Amber in the afternoons.

A line of students needing to use the phone had gathered. I hung up without saying goodbye and offered the phone to the girl behind me.

"Thanks," she said her grin full of metal braces.

What if I needed braces? Who would take me to the orthodontist? Who would pay for them? I darted out of the office—desperate to get away from normal teenagers I could no longer relate to.

I put the conversations with Dad, Julie, and Andrew on the back burner and drove to the elementary school. I couldn't get there fast enough. My first stop was Amber's classroom.

"Sissy." Her face lit up when she saw me. "What're you doing here?"

I bent down. "I have a surprise. I got a job here at the aftercare program and every day you'll get to go with me."

"Yeah. Some of the kids in my class go." She wrapped her arms around my neck. My heart warmed. Hers was the only real love I had in my life.

We walked into the building of the aftercare program, and I introduced Amber to Mrs. Elliott.

"Nice to meet you, Amber. Follow me, Ladies." She led us to a large room. Giggling children filled chairs at several tables. Bookshelves overflowing with school supplies lined the walls. A tall, thin woman stood at the front.

"Miss Jones, this is your new assistant, Angela, and her little sister, Amber. Miss Jones teaches fifth grade here at the elementary school and works with me in the afternoons."

"Hi, I've seen you around here, Amber. It's a pleasure to have you both." Miss Jones looked to be in her late twenties. Her black pencil skirt and pale blue button-down blouse fit her like a glove. She'd feathered her dark blonde hair perfectly on each side. Even Farrah Fawcett would be jealous.

The night before, as I lay intoxicated in Dale's bed, she probably drank herbal tea out of a fancy teacup while she graded papers. I didn't belong in the same room with someone as unblemished as her.

"Thank you. We're glad to be here," fumbled out of my mouth.

Pale pink lips offered me the kindest smile. "And I'm more than thrilled to have you."

Miss Jones and I went student to student. I listened with awe as she effortlessly spoke with each one about that day's homework and upcoming tests, every word rich with encouragement and sincerity.

"Angela, Miss Lauren here has a spelling test on Friday. Here's her list of words. Can you give her a practice test and see if she's prepared?"

My hand shook a little as I took the list from her. "Of course. Yes, ma'am."

Through a quivering voice, I did my best to emulate Miss Jones as I spoke to Lauren. Julie's comment about me becoming a teacher lingered in the background.

"Hi, Sweetie. You're going to do great. And if there are any words you have difficulty with, I'll spend as much time with you as you need until you know them."

The little girl smiled up at me. "You're pretty and nice. Just like Miss Jones."

In that moment, my senses turned acute. The waxy smell of well-used crayons, the sound of chalk scraping the chalkboard, the warmth of a child's kind words; those sensations buried themselves in my soul, took root, and sprouted.

The rest of the afternoon, I walked around the room and helped other students with their homework. I helped one learn the colors of the rainbow. He'd never heard of Roy G. Biv. I also made sure Amber finished all her math problems. Every now and then I'd glance up and notice Miss Jones smiling at me. I didn't want the day to end.

"Wonderful job today. Mrs. Elliott sure knew what she was doing when she hired you. If you want, maybe we can work it out with the high school, and you can come observe in my classroom. If you think that would be something you'd be interested in."

My heart warmed. "Yes, thank you. I'd love that. I really enjoyed today, even more than I expected."

"I can tell. You're a natural. I'll contact the guidance counselor at the high school and see when we can set that up. See you girls tomorrow."

Amber grabbed my hand. "Sissy, I really like Miss Jones. I'm glad you got this job."

"I am, too, Amber. I am, too." I couldn't stop smiling.

Walking out of the building, I wasn't the same person who walked in. I knew what I wanted—more than anything else in the world. I wanted to be just like Miss Jones. In one day, I'd gone from considering quitting school to now knowing what I wanted to do with the rest of my life. I wanted to become a teacher.

CHAPTER THIRTEEN

HOUSEWARMING HANGOVER

ON THE DRIVE BACK to Dale's, my head slowly drifted out of the clouds where dreams of becoming a teacher were possible and back into the brimstone and hellfire of my real life where they weren't.

When I pulled up to the Simmons' house, I forced myself out. Addis was hanging a load of sepia-colored laundry on the clothesline. Apparently, she'd never heard of separating by color. The sight was a reminder that I still needed to ask her to use the washing machine.

John was sitting on that damn bucket smoking, probably on his second pack of Marlboros already. I didn't see Cole anywhere.

Dale shot up as soon as I walked in. "Hey, I've been waitin' on you to get home. I've got great news. My Aunt Joan's gonna rent me her trailer for cheap."

"Huh?" My thoughts scattered.

With wild eyes and an ecstatic grin plastered across tobacco-stained teeth, he clarified. "We're getting our own place."

In what sick and twisted world did Dale think me moving into a trailer with him should even be an option? Did he forget I was a freakin' teenager and he was a grown man?

"Wow, that's just great." What I really wanted to say was, *Great for you. It's about time you moved out of your parents' house, but I think I'll pass.*

On the other hand, as bad as living alone with him in a trailer sounded, maybe it would buy me some time to either patch things up with Mom or come clean to Dad. And at least I'd have a place to study to pull up my grades, in the event I really wanted to pursue this teaching idea. In the interim, this could work.

"When do we move?" I regretted the words as soon as I said them.

"Whenever we want. All we gotta do is bring our clothes. She left most everything when she moved in with her boyfriend. I thought we'd go check it out this afternoon and probably move on Friday. Roger and some of the guys wanna come over on Saturday and throw us a housewarming party."

Great. We haven't even moved in, and Dale was already planning parties.

The trailer park, Sunshine Estates, sat next to the Sunshine Citrus orange plant. But it hardly deserved the word estate in its name. About forty trailers were parked on tiny overgrown lots. Trash, pets, and kids littered crumbling asphalt streets. I'd pedaled past by on my bike a few times but never expected to live here. I hoped it wouldn't be for long.

The trailer I was lucky enough to move into sat at the end of Orange Blossom Street on the left. But after climbing the rickety steps to the backdoor that led to the kitchen, I felt anything but lucky.

Several half-dried gel air fresheners sat on faded green laminate countertops. They failed to mask the stench of years of oily cooking. Peeling patterned linoleum covered the leaning floors. A couple of the walnut wooden cabinets were missing doors, exposing beat-up cookware. A picnic-type table sat opposite the cabinets.

Dale passed by me and entered the wall-to-wall wood-paneled living room. I followed him. The pale afternoon light barely made it through the filthy windows, but enough to illuminate a dark brown sofa draped with an Afghan, some black vinyl chairs patched with duct tape, and a scuffed coffee table.

Dale had described it as furnished. Yeah, with someone's roadside giveaways. Since the condition of the interiors wasn't far off from his parents' decor, I guess he didn't notice.

He stood in the center of the living room on the burnt orange shag carpet, arms spread wide. "Well, what do you think?" He beamed as if he'd inherited the Taj Mahal. Not that he'd even know what the Taj Mahal was.

"It has potential." The potential to be the most disgusting place I've ever seen.

"Let's check out the bedroom." He grabbed my hand and dragged me down the hall. On the left, we passed the only bathroom and an empty bedroom. The bedroom on the right housed a rusted brass four poster bed covered with a sickeningly floral comforter. Dale wasted no time shoving me onto it.

"Baby, this is our place. We can do whatever we want. Whenever we want. Let's celebrate." He kissed my neck and started undressing me.

That first time, that was me choosing to live on my terms, but since, it was me accepting his. And living with him in this trailer was nothing to celebrate. But for now, I had a role to play. Until I could figure out how to get what I wanted, Dale would get what he did.

I raised my hand to get Mrs. Minich's attention. She meticulously folded her newspaper before coming to me.

"Can I leave a few minutes early? I'm not feeling well."

"Did you fill out your agenda for the week?"

I pointed to the pages as I held my hand over my mouth. Any second, she'd be calling the janitor to come sprinkle that gross-smelling pink stuff over the vomit I was about to expel all over her classroom floor.

"Looks good. You can go."

I grabbed my backpack and sprinted to the bathroom. Once everything in my stomach was in the toilet, I flushed. Then rinsed my mouth with water from the faucet and wet my face. I hoped this passed by the time I had to go to work. I didn't want to show up with remnants of my weekend house party hangover.

I couldn't imagine Miss Jones ever hungover. There were some things I had to do with Dale to keep the peace. But not this one. I was done. No more partying. If I wanted to be like Miss Jones, I needed to start acting like it.

In second period, Julie whispered, "I heard about the move—and the party. News travels fast in a small town."

"I'm sorry I didn't tell you or invite you over. It was just Dale's friends. Plus, I knew you wouldn't come anyway." Another wave of nausea hit me. "I'm still hungover. I'm going to lay off the partying for a while." I hoped she'd latched on to that last part, give me some credit.

She whispered while taking down her notes. "A hangover shouldn't last two days. Maybe you're pregnant." She narrowed her eyes and raised her voice. "Yeah, you should probably stop the partying."

"Excuse me?" I couldn't believe she had the nerve to suggest what she did. "Yeah, no. I'm sure I'm not—that."

Shock shot through me because she was right about one thing; a hangover shouldn't last two days. I wracked my brain, trying to remember when I had my last period. I knew for sure I hadn't had one since that first time with Dale at the claypit.

Most of the time, we used protection. Except the few times when he, or we, were too drunk to think about it. I had planned to get on the pill soon. But soon hadn't happened yet. This couldn't happen to me. Could it? *Oh shit. Oh shit. Oh shit.*

I would just stop thinking about it because what Julie had suggested was ludicrous. But telling yourself to stop thinking about something means that's all you think about. Thanks a lot, Julie, for the pink elephant you tossed my way.

While my mind spun at her damning insinuation, she'd effortlessly gone back into her normal world of just taking down notes in social studies. Like she hadn't just given oxygen to a manifestation that could ruin my life—even worse than its current state of ruin-ness.

CHAPTER FOURTEEN

A THIN BLUE LINE

EVEN THOUGH I WAS excited for my second day working with Miss Jones, it was difficult to concentrate. As I walked around looking over students' shoulders in the homework room, my mind reeled at the unfathomable possibility of what Julie suggested.

Last year, there was a pregnant girl on campus. Rumor was while she visited family out of state, she got knocked up by some rando she met at a party. As her belly got bigger, we saw less of her at school. Eventually, she stopped coming. I'd forgotten about her until now. I didn't even remember her name.

I wondered if that's what happened to pregnant teenagers—they slowly faded away and everyone forgot they existed. Like that picture of Marty and his siblings in *Back to the Future*. If Julie was right, and I was pregnant, would she and Andrew forget I ever existed? Would my parents? What would happen to me when I disappeared?

"Miss Angela," a student called my name. "Can you help me with this writing prompt?"

"Sorry, sure." I read the prompt aloud to Lauren, the same third grader I'd worked with before. "What do you want to be when you grow up and why?"

She looked up at me and smiled. "I want to be just like you, Miss Angela."

Her sweet words spiraled me into imposter syndrome. When Mrs. Elliott hired me, she said I'd be a good role model for the students. That couldn't be farther from the truth. I swallowed my guilt.

"Honey, I think what the prompt means is what do you want to be when you grow up. Like a nurse or a teacher." Those last words out of my mouth stung. Julie would be a nurse. Despite how much I wanted it, I'd probably never be a teacher.

The rest of the afternoon dragged on. I did my best to hide my growing anxiety. It wasn't working. Julie's accusation occupied all of my available headspace.

At the end of the day, Miss Jones asked, "Is everything okay? You seem a little quieter today than yesterday." She placed her delicate hand on my shoulder.

I wanted to scream at her. *No, things are not okay. My father abandoned us. My alcoholic mother kicked me out. My younger brother and little sister are fending for themselves. I'm living with an older guy in a run-down trailer park, and my best friend thinks he got me pregnant.* But of course, I didn't. Instead, I replied, "I'm just a little tired today. That's all."

She laughed. "I totally understand. Working with children is rewarding, but it's equally tiring. Get some rest tonight."

Rest. I needed a hell of a lot more than rest to fix the problems in my life.

As I was dropping Amber off at the address formerly known as my home, Levi shuffled up the driveway.

"Bye, Amber. See you tomorrow," I said, then called to my brother. "Hey, Come here."

A pale, gaunt face took a drag from a cigarette. Then a bony hand dropped it to the ground and a worn sneaker crushed it. "Long time no see, Ange."

A skeletal version of my brother stood outside my rolled-down window.

"Same. How are you? I haven't seen you at the Junior High much." Not like I had any room to judge.

He shrugged his slouched shoulders. "What's the point? Since you left, I had to step up. Man of the house now."

Guilt gutted me. My absence had forced Levi to fill my empty shoes.

"That's not your job. Don't quit school. There's an electrician or an engineer in you dying to get out."

"The only thing I'm dying to get out of is this town. Good to see you. Don't be a stranger." He turned toward the house.

My heart wanted to follow him inside. Reclaim my role in the family. Take care of the siblings I loved so much. Even though I didn't think about Levi as much as I did Amber, seeing him made me want to be the big sister I should've been all along. But after what my mother did to me, I couldn't—no I wouldn't—face her. Not once had she tried to contact me since kicking me out. No messages through Amber. Nothing.

"Take care, Levi. Love, you." It killed me leaving them.

I couldn't go back to the trailer yet, so as a distraction, I decided to visit Julie at work at Spin City Laundry. Her parents were up to that parenting thing again—making her get a job she didn't need to learn responsibility she already had. Plus, we argued so much lately and I didn't like it. It wasn't her fault. She was only worried for me. And if our roles were reversed, I would've been worried about her, too.

Seconds after I arrived, I realized it was a mistake. Because Julie wasted no time bringing up the last topic I wanted to talk about.

"Ange, you must take a pregnancy test."

I glanced around at the customers in the laundromat. "Shh. I came here to see you because we haven't hung out much lately, and to ask if I could wash my clothes here, not to discuss that again."

She moved a load of laundry from a washing machine into a dryer, then grabbed my arm and dragged me into a corner of the room.

"You need to know. Because if you are, there are some things you need to start doing, and more importantly, some things you need to stop. Trust me; I pretty much know everything about pregnancy because I did a report on it last year."

I jerked my arm away. "A report hardly makes you an expert."

"I'll pay for the test. You have nothing to lose. Either you are, or you aren't. Taking a test won't make you pregnant." She wasn't going to let this irrational fixation go.

"Fine, if it'll make you stop talking about it."

She pulled a ten-dollar bill out of her pocket. "Here. Go to the grocery store next door and buy one of those new pee-on-a-stick tests. My aunt used one."

"You're so annoying." I snatched the bill and stormed out of the laundromat.

This was about as stupid as the time she insisted we sleep inside a kitchen cabinet to spy on her sisters. We got home from the skating rink and emptied the large island of cookware and filled it with pillows, blankets, and our tiny bodies. The next morning, we did overhear some juicy details of their Saturday night dates, until our giggling spoiled our cover.

My pursed lips softened briefly into a smile at the innocence of the whole thing, then quickly thinned again.

Nothing about this was innocent or funny. I pushed open the grocery store door. Frigid air slapped my cheek. Like it wanted me to snap out of the life with Dale and back to the one when Julie and I had more in common than not. But that life didn't exist for me anymore, and if Julie was right, and my nausea wasn't from a hangover, then mine was about to get worse.

I had no idea where to even look for this test, and I wasn't going to ask anyone. I walked up and down every aisle, including the produce—as if I'd find pregnancy tests somewhere amongst zucchinis and papayas. Finally, I found them next to the feminine products. What a horrible place to put them. *Oh, late on your period? Here's a visual reminder of what you won't be using for at least nine months.* I wished I was here buying tampons instead. I'd even be willing to wear a pad to have my period right now.

At least ten different obnoxious pink and purple boxes plastered with labels such as "99% Accurate," "6 Days Sooner," and "Results in Under Three Minutes" covered the shelves. I grabbed a two-pack labeled "Earliest, Most Reliable Results" and concealed it under my armpit. Then I took the walk of shame to the check-out and scanned the lines. I didn't want a teenage cashier; they might know me. I didn't want an older cashier; they might know my parents. I chose one who appeared to be in her early twenties. Safe enough.

She grabbed the box, entered the price into her register, and glanced at me.

"It's for a friend." I lied.

She stopped chewing her gum—she knew. "I have a son. He turned six last week." She blew a large bubble then popped it. "I'm only twenty-three."

I quickly did the math. She would have been about my age when she had her son.

"Tell your *friend*; it's going to be okay. Becoming a mother was the best thing that ever happened to me. It changed my life for the better."

She smiled, handed me the bag, and I got out of there as fast as I could. Knowing she had a baby when she was my age made it seem a little too possible.

Back in the laundromat, Julie and I huddled together in the restroom. "Okay, three minutes. Here, hold my hand," she said.

I refused to watch the stick I'd just peed on. Instead, I read the poster on the wall reminding employees to wash their hands after using the restroom. When I was little, my mother said to sing Happy Birthday twice to reach the recommended twenty seconds. I focused on singing Happy Birthday in my head, rather than think about why I was really in this bathroom. I squeezed Julie's hand, and closed my eyes, *Happy Birthday*...birth...a baby...my stomach rolled. No way, not me.

Her voice broke my scattered thoughts. "Ange, there's a thin blue line."

A thin blue line. What did that mean? I didn't want to know. *Jules, please don't.* But she continued to confirm my worst fear.

"According to the directions, that's a positive. You're pregnant."

I pushed her out of the way and vomited into the toilet. Each heave sent me deeper and deeper into denial. *No way. Not me. Not this. Not with Dale.* Julie held my hair back until I was done, then handed me a wet paper towel.

"Are you okay?"

I wiped my face. "No, I'm not okay. Maybe it's not right. I'm going to do the other one."

"I'll be right outside the door." She stepped out of the bathroom and left me alone with thoughts that had escalated from scattered to panic.

My hands trembled as I peed what little urine I could muster on stick number two. This time I didn't invite Julie in. I waited and watched, horrified as the seconds ticked by, and another thin blue line formed before my eyes. Twice confirmed, I was pregnant. I felt the color drain from my face.

I opened the bathroom door and struggled to hold up stick number two. "You have to promise you won't tell anyone." Until I could process what this meant, I couldn't let this get out.

She didn't hesitate. "You know you can trust me."

Lately, my life was one big secret. But this one, this secret, even if Julie pledged to keep it to her grave, my time to hold her to it was limited.

"What're you going to do?" she asked.

I shrugged. Overwhelm and dread consumed me. "I have no idea. I suppose at some point, I'll have to figure it out."

She flung her arms around my neck and squeezed. "No, *we* will figure it out."

She could have said *I told you so*. She'd given me ample warnings not to be with Dale. She'd encouraged me to talk to an adult for help. I took none of her advice and now I was paying the ultimate price. I didn't deserve a friend as good as her, but I was glad I had one.

"Thanks. I really have to go. Dale will be wondering where I am."

She pulled away from me and smiled. "See you tomorrow. You better be at school, or I'm coming to get you."

"I'll be there." I held back tears, terrified of what tomorrow and the next day and the next would look like. But at least now, I finally knew I'd have my best friend by my side. For the first time in a long time, I wasn't alone.

True to form, when I got back to the trailer, I found a passed-out Dale sprawled across the couch. An empty aluminum frozen dinner tray balanced on his stomach. Remnants from the party littered the place. It was hard to tell which beer cans he'd consumed with his Salisbury steak, mashed potatoes, and corn, and which I'd helped empty over the weekend.

I tossed my backpack on the kitchen table and then threw a slice of bologna between two pieces of white bread. I'm sure it wasn't for me, but Addis had spent what little she could afford to help us with our first round of groceries. For that, I was thankful.

I pulled out my biology textbook and tried to focus on the assigned reading. But I couldn't focus on anything else but that thin blue line. Those results had to be wrong. How could something that cost ten whole dollars give accurate enough results to basically ruin my life? My plan was to use living here as a launching pad to bigger and better things. But now I realized that plan might backfire.

At the laundromat, with Julie, I had felt genuinely cared for. But back inside this filthy trailer in Dale's presence—coupled with the repulsive thought that his child was growing inside me—was a stark reminder that the life I wanted didn't want me.

CHAPTER FIFTEEN

FIRETRUCK TABLE

I WAS STARTING TO dread sitting next to Julie during second period.

"You need to call a doctor. I asked my aunt. That was the first thing she did when she found out she was pregnant."

It had been several days since I'd peed on the stick. And she'd brought it up every single day since. Julie seemed to forget she had a life outside of mine. Or maybe she was just doing a good job of hiding it from me.

"You told your aunt?" I whispered through pursed lips.

"Of course not. I promised you. I asked, like in general when a girl gets pregnant, what's the first thing to do." She smacked herself on the forehead. "Crap. I bet she thinks I'm pregnant. I guess that was a dumb move on my part. Whatever. Anyway, the point is, you need to call a doctor."

"Even if I wanted to, I can't afford it. Plus, that test could be wrong. It's from a grocery store. And other than puking a couple of times, I don't feel any different. It's not like I'm craving pickles and ice cream. If that's even a thing."

"Well, go get a second opinion—from a doctor." She shot me a sarcastic grin.

Mr. Conrad shushed us, and we kept quiet the rest of the period.

I flipped the pages in my American history textbook. The words blurred into one inky blob. A second opinion—Julie made a great point. That's exactly what I was going to do. I didn't trust the reliability of a ten-dollar grocery store pee-on-a-stick test, no matter how large the font read "Reliable."

The rest of the day, my confidence grew. When the last bell rang, I dashed to the office and made it first in line to use the school phone before the masses ensued. I called Mrs. Elliott and told her I had a doctor's appointment. I didn't, but hopefully, my lie would be true by day's end. My next call I couldn't make from the school office.

Mounted outside a nearby convenience store, the locals called The Caddy, was the closest pay phone. After school, some teens met there to sip frozen soda, and others met on weekends to convince of-age customers to buy them beer and cigarettes. I didn't belong to either group.

I picked up the heavy tethered phone book, turned to the Yellow Pages, found Physicians, Pediatricians—then bingo, Dr. Carson. I dropped a quarter in the slot and dialed the number.

"Hello, Dr. Carson's office. Can you hold, please?"

Without allowing me to answer, elevator music filled my ear, followed by thoughts filling my head. I crossed my fingers and repeated, *I'm not pregnant, I'm not pregnant* until the woman's voice returned.

"Sorry, how can I help you?"

I squeezed my eyes shut and forced the words out. "Hi, when I was a kid, well, I'm only seventeen, so technically still a kid. Dr. Carson was, um, is, my pediatrician."

Feet shuffled behind me. A few frozen soda sippers were waiting their turn to use the phone. I turned my back to them and whispered, "I was wondering, do you guys do tests to be sure someone isn't, um, I mean, I missed my period."

"Do you need a pregnancy test?" The way she asked so bluntly made it seem like an everyday question. But pregnant at seventeen was anything but every day. I hoped the kids behind me couldn't hear her through the receiver.

"I guess. I mean, I don't think I am, obviously, but just to be sure." I cupped my hands around my mouth. "I did the pee on a stick test, which showed a blue line. My friend said to get a second opinion."

"Yes. Honey, you come on up here this afternoon. We can do that."

"One more question, how much will it cost?" With gas prices climbing up to seventy cents per gallon, I barely had enough money left before my next paycheck just to drive to and from school and work.

"There's no charge for those visits."

I breathed a sigh of relief. "Thank you so much." Finally. Once I got the answer I was looking for, maybe I'd call my dad and tell him everything. I didn't know if the guy he lived with would agree but sleeping on a couch sounded more appealing with each day that went by.

"All yours," I announced as I hung up the pay phone and faced the annoyed pimple-faced teens who were probably ordering pizza, not scheduling pregnancy tests.

At Dr. Carson's office, I approached the receptionist and whispered, "Hi, I called about a half-hour ago and asked someone here if you could give me a test because I missed my monthly you-know-what."

"Of course. Have a seat. Someone will be right with you."

Moms and dads filled the waiting room, mostly moms, and children of all ages. A bookshelf overflowed with picture books and toys. Snotty toddlers fought over them. I sat in the only empty chair next to a woman nursing a newborn. Gross.

Mom used to bring me here each year for my cheerleading physical. When I left Dale's trailer, I'd ask Coach if she'd let me back on the squad. I missed cheering.

A few minutes later, a nurse motioned me to come back with her. She led me to a small room with a firetruck-inspired examination table.

"Hi. I'm one of Dr. Carson's nurses, Lynn. You've been here before, right?"

Needles pricked my skin from the inside. "Are you going to call my parents?"

"No, Sweetie. This test is confidential and complimentary, meaning you don't have to provide any personal information or pay a fee. Take this cup into the bathroom and fill it to this line with urine. Leave it on the table and go back to the waiting room. When I have the results, I'll call you back here again. Do you have any questions?"

"No, ma'am." I wanted this over as quickly as possible. Then I'd try to salvage what I could of my former life, which didn't include having a baby with Dale Simmons.

I took the cup into the bathroom and followed her instructions. Worry consumed me less this time because I knew the results would be negative. That ten-dollar test had to be wrong.

A few minutes later, the door opened, and Nurse Lynn waved me back again and led me into the same room. "Have a seat," she solemnly said as she pointed to the firetruck table.

I hopped up, crinkling the paper cover in the process. *Okay, let's get this over with.*

Nurse Lynn sat on a stool next to the table and asked, "When was your last period?"

Why was she asking me this? Just give me the results so I can leave. I gave her my best guess.

"Your test results were positive. And by the date you provided, you're likely anywhere from six to eight weeks pregnant."

The walls of the small examination room closed in. "Excuse me. Are you sure?"

Panic swept through my body until it reached my belly. The belly she confirmed where a baby was growing.

"Yes. False positives are very rare, and this is an early detection test. I don't know your situation." She grabbed something out of a drawer and handed it to me. "Here's a pamphlet for the Health Department. If you don't have insurance, they'll take you as a patient free of charge. Because you're so young, I'd like you to contact them as soon as possible."

Out the examination room window, a sullen-eyed woman with a round belly carried a toddler and held a preschooler's hand. *Was that an image of my future life?* One kid after the other, each draining my body of all remnants of my former self. That bubbly cashier at the grocery store probably had no idea she'd also be a sullen-eyed woman after a couple more of the *best things that ever happened to me* happened to her.

"Honey, do you have any questions?"

Questions? I didn't even know where to begin. I started with something external as opposed to internal. "How long before I start, you know, showing?"

"That varies. You're young and pretty tiny. At around three to four months, you may notice your clothes getting tighter, and you might have a small baby bump, or it could be a little longer."

My dry mouth managed a sticky, "Thank you."

She stood and opened the door. "Good luck. Don't forget to call the Health Department. And when you get close to delivery, give us a call. Dr. Carson would be an excellent pediatrician choice for your baby."

"Of course." I couldn't wrap my head around needing a pediatrician for someone other than my siblings or me.

In my car, tears erupted. I screamed and pounded the steering wheel. I wouldn't be getting back on the cheer squad. I wouldn't be going to college. And for the final nail in my coffin, I wouldn't be leaving Dale's place. That was the worst realization of them all.

I shoved the Health Department pamphlet under the seat. I didn't want Dale to find it and ask questions or force me to make any decisions until I had some answers. And right now, I didn't even know what questions to ask and to whom.

CHAPTER SIXTEEN

SCARLET LETTER

DALE LOADED A SMALL cooler with some beer from the near-empty fridge. The only edible item was the leftover Hamburger Helper I planned to eat for dinner.

"I'm going over to Roger's. Don't feel like drinking by myself again tonight."

I was at the kitchen table, doing what I did every night—struggling to focus on homework. "Sorry, you know, school and—stuff." Dale still didn't know what *stuff* meant. And since I hadn't been partying due to *stuff*, he was gone more, allowing me small chunks of much-needed respite. Even though I'd never been the type of person who wanted to be alone, isolation, even in this run-down trailer, was now the only way I felt safe.

"Later." He swung the strap of the soft-sided cooler over his shoulder and left.

I shut my textbook and gave up on the depressing character study of Offred from *The Handmaid's Tale*. Being controlled by men felt too close to home. Dale didn't even fully understand how he'd trapped me, but I did. And I feared when he knew, he'd wield that power over me until I had none of my own left.

The rest of the evening, I folded laundry. Julie let me come to Spin City each week and wash for free. While I worked, I watched a grainy *Beauty and the Beast*. Dale had wrapped aluminum foil around the rabbit-ear antenna, but it didn't really help. I guess he got an A for effort.

Once upon a time, the fairytale-inspired series had been my favorite show. I spent many nights lying in bed imagining being in love like Vincent and Catherine. But the only thing I had in common with either of them was Vincent and I both lived in filth—him in a sewer, me in this trailer. And unlike his sewer, this trailer was not the setting of a fairy tale, and nothing about my story hinted at a happy ending.

As I reached to switch off the TV, a news anchor announced, "It's eleven o'clock p.m. Do you know where your children are?"

I froze. The nightly public service announcement was supposed to remind parents who needed reminding to check on their kids and make sure they were home and safely tucked into bed. My parents must not watch TV past eleven o'clock anymore. Otherwise, how could they not wonder where I was?

The PSA also made me think about Levi. Now that I worked for Mrs. Elliott, I saw Amber Monday through Friday. But I rarely saw my younger brother. And the last time I had, he hadn't look good. I needed to make more of an effort to stay in contact. I couldn't bear one more person in my family headed down a path of destruction. Unlike me, an almost grown-up, he was still so young. Maybe there was time for me to try to save him.

The back door opened. Dale stumbled in. My respite was short-lived.

I yawned and stretched. "Hey, I'm going to sleep. I'm really tired." *Please, please. Just let me go to sleep.*

Within seconds his hot, humid breath prickled my neck as if he was breathing the cockroaches that scuttled on our trailer's floor onto me. "No, no, no. My girl isn't tired."

I pushed him away and turned off the TV. "Yes, I am. I'm going to sleep."

He pressed a plastic bag into my chest. "I got you a present."

"Huh?" I reached inside and pulled out a skimpy, scarlet red, cheap-looking piece of lingerie. An unexpected chuckle surprised me. "You've got to be kidding." Then the chuckle escalated to a maniacal laughter. The absurdity of this moment, Dale gifting me lingerie—he was crazier than I thought. And I was crazy for not seeing it from the beginning.

"No, I'm not. Me and Roger went to that club over by the edge of town. Them girls dance real nice. I knew my sexy girl could do it better. The gas station next door had that. I had to get it for you." His crooked smile made me think he actually thought I would appreciate this.

My laughter ceased and my body burst into flames. Dale and Roger had gone to a strip club, and he got so worked up he wanted me to give him a private dance. No way in hell I was parading around in front of him in that thing. "Well, thank you for the—gift—but I'm gonna pass. I got school tomorrow, and as I said twice already, I'm really tired." I shoved the bag back to him.

But instead of taking it, he pushed me onto the TV. The aluminum foil crinkled at my weight. He pushed harder. The antennae wires pierced my skin and something warm and wet bubbled underneath my night-gown.

Sour saliva sprayed my face. "Put it on. It'll be fun. I don't ask for much. One of the reasons I got us this place is to do what we want."

"Stop. You're hurting me." The edge of the TV pressed into the small of my back, which felt like it was about to break.

He put a hand up to my neck and squeezed. Not too hard, just enough to let me know I didn't have an option. "Put it on. Let me see how good you look."

"Okay, okay," I begged through jagged breaths.

He let go of my throat, pulled me up, and lightly tapped one cheek as I coughed. "You'll see. It'll be fun." He smacked me on the rear and laughed. Then he dropped to the couch, lit a cigarette, and ripped off his t-shirt. Sweat beads formed.

I dragged my feet to the bathroom and shut the door. I fell onto the sticky floor next to the toilet and into it my stomach expelled what little food I'd eaten. Then I collapsed and curled into a fetal position, just like the one inside me.

My body convulsed, and violent tears erupted. *Why? Why? Why?* What had I done besides just be born to deserve this? And unless I could find a way out, this entire disgusting cycle would repeat when my child was born.

Maybe I could squeeze out through the tiny bathroom window. Dale was so wasted maybe he'd pass out. Maybe he'd forget about the lingerie. I could throw it in a garbage can behind someone's trailer because that's what it was—a piece of trash. I was a piece of trash—trailer trash. I belonged in a garbage can.

A rapid knock at the door was followed by, "Hurry up. It's getting late."

"Okay, okay. I'm coming." I pushed my limp body off the floor, then slid the blood-stained nightgown off my shoulders and let it fall into the puddle of tears on the bathroom floor. Mom had given me the flower-covered gown with a matching robe for Christmas a few years back. But the robe didn't make it into the garbage bags she'd so lovingly packed when she kicked me out. Even my own mother likened me to trash.

I wiped the blood off the stinging cut on my back as best I could manage. It took three bandages to cover the long scrape from the TV antennae.

Then I grabbed the loose elastic sides of the pale green underwear with the word Monday printed across the front, pulled them down, and stepped out of them. I should have been wearing my Tuesday underwear. Not these stupid Monday ones. I used to obsess over the most mundane of life's details. But the days of the week didn't even matter anymore. Nothing mattered.

Standing naked in the tiny bathroom, I should've been cold. It was late fall, and Dale still hadn't paid to have the propane tank filled. But instead, fueled by fear and rage, dread and disgust, my body was aflame. This must be what hell felt like. And I was the devil's bride.

I stepped into the scarlet red, lacy garment and slid it passed the small bump where a fetus grew inside a hollow womb—the devil's child. Then slipped the thin straps over my shoulders. My boobs nowhere near filled the cups intended for full women's breasts. I looked like a little girl playing Slut-Whore Dress-Up. *Slut. Whore. Pregnant. Pathetic.* I was all of them. I was North Lake's real-life Scarlet Letter.

I splashed cold water on my face to try and stop it from burning. But it wasn't cold enough. I wanted to plunge my entire flaming body into a basin filled with ice-cold water. To lower my body temperature to where I couldn't think. To where I couldn't breathe. Until this—all of this—stopped— dead—cold.

The gas station lingerie gift-wrapped me to Dale. My womb gift-wrapped a baby to me that would anchor me to him. It didn't matter what he did to me anymore. For all I cared, he could break me one bone at a time until there was nothing left to break. Then toss me into a garbage can where I—a piece of trailer trash—belonged.

I opened the bathroom door and walked toward the living room bathed in a pale, smoky light—sultry music drifted from a boom box. I stopped, took a deep breath of the cannabis and nicotine-laced air, then willed prey to sacrifice to predator.

CHAPTER SEVENTEEN

SMOKE BREAK

THE ALARM JOLTED ME awake. I'd changed it from music to just an annoying buzzer days ago. Since my most recent *encounter* with Dale, I wasn't in the mood for music anymore. I wasn't in the mood for anything anymore. I threw on a pair of my looser-fitting jeans and one of his oversized sweatshirts.

He'd fallen asleep on the couch, and I didn't bother to wake him as I left for school. Roger could have that unpleasant job.

School and I had an on-again, off-again relationship—mostly off. Nausea consumed me in the morning, hunger by midday, and exhaustion all afternoon. But third-period Biology was the worst part, even worse than watching Julie and Andrew live their best lives.

Flaunting a trendy snug maternity dress, Mrs. Van stood at the chalkboard drawing a diagram about digestion. She dropped the chalk and bent over to pick it up. "Oh, sorry, class. The baby kicked. It gets me every time." She laughed as she rubbed her seven-month obnoxiously pregnant belly. I hated her.

By lunchtime, I was about to chew my arm off. Several tables were scattered around the cafeteria entrance surrounded by the North Lake High senior class. Andrew and Julie were huddled around one, talking to a salesman-looking guy. When I saw what was on the table, I lost my appetite.

Julie flashed a bright smile at Andrew as she wiggled a finger jeweled with a sparkly ring—a class ring. "What do you think?" she asked him, drawing out each word in a flirtatious tone.

He nudged her as I approached. "Hey, Ange. How's it going?" He said loud enough to get Julie's attention.

"Fine. I'm fine." I responded without attempting to make eye contact with him.

Julie yanked off the ring and dropped it on the table. "Oh, hi. We, um, are just looking at class rings."

"Whatever. I just came to tell you I won't be eating lunch in the cafeteria anymore." It was the only thing I could think of to give me a reason to about-face and run. I'd been hiding in the library with the other school outcasts most days anyway.

"Why?" Andrew asked as if it was the most shocking statement he'd ever heard a person say.

"The smell of the place makes me want to puke." That wasn't a lie. But it was more than that. I couldn't stand being around laughing teenagers making plans. Not one of them in the entire smelly cafeteria had any idea what I went home to.

"Well, okay. I mean, I understand. But we always save you a seat, so if you change your mind..."

"Not necessary. Let someone else join you at the cool kids' table." She was probably relieved. She and Andrew could freely talk about whatever stupid shit they wanted to. I darted away before they had a chance to debate.

But I didn't go to the library. I went to the bathroom. The one by the bleachers that was always empty so I could cry and scream in private. I threw my backpack on the cold tile floor, then collapsed next to it. Something had to change. This, whatever *this* was, was unsustainable. *This* was eating me alive one bite at a time.

After the last bell, I headed to work, the only place that I didn't want to hide. But soon, Mrs. Elliott and Miss Jones would discover I was a fraud. A *Slut-Whore-Scarlet-Letter-Pregnant-Pathetic* fraud. And when they did, I expected they would turn on me like the rest of the world had.

———

"I spoke with the guidance counselor, and he said you're welcome to check out of school early one day to visit my classroom."

Miss Jones and I were stacking the chairs at the end of the day so the janitors could mop.

I'd been waiting for this, and I had a response prepared. "I appreciate the offer, but I've decided teaching isn't for me. I don't want to waste your time." What a stupid idea. I had to face that I'd never go to college, much less become a teacher. And the sooner I did, the quicker I could let go of the regret.

Her bright smile faded. "Oh. Well, if you change your mind, the offer still stands." She quietly stacked a few more chairs. "I hope I'm not overstepping here."

Which meant she was about to overstep.

"I'm not privy to much about your personal life, and you aren't obligated to share. But you're a smart girl, and you're fantastic with children. If you want to be a teacher, there isn't anything stopping you."

She had no idea an obstacle larger than Mt. Everest—although currently, it was the size of, I don't know, maybe a microscopic parasite of some kind—stood in my way. "Thanks, but I've changed my mind. I'm not going the college route. It's not for everyone." I turned to my sister. "Amber, hurry up, let's go. Sorry, I've got to get her home."

I dreaded the day when she and Mrs. Elliott found out the real reason why I'd changed my mind. I should quit now. But I needed the money—badly. Still, there was no use in visiting an elementary classroom to learn about a career I'd never have. I'd gotten myself pregnant at seventeen. College was off the table, with-child and sullen-eyed was on.

"Sissy, why don't you talk to me as much as you used to?" Amber asked on the drive home.

Even my little sister had picked up that something was off with me—*off*, to put it mildly. "I'm so sorry. I've just got a lot of stuff on my mind with school and work."

When I got to Mom's, I put the car in park in front of the home I wished I could run into. But instead, I offered my baby sister a part of me I knew she needed. "I've been meaning to ask you if you want to check out that new park in Mayflower. I heard some kids at aftercare talking about it. It sounds fun."

"Really? Wilbur Park? Sarah Jane said she went there, and it's awesome. It's got all these bridges and tunnels. When can we go?"

"We'll go soon. I promise." Taking Amber to the park—a normal afternoon—I craved it. Because nothing else in my life was normal.

"Bye, Sissy." Amber hopped out of the car and ran inside.

Mom and Levi were carrying in a couple of bags of groceries. I hadn't seen her in weeks. She smiled and waved at me. I choked back tears and pretended I didn't notice. I'd never shed one more over her again. *How in the hell was I supposed to know how to be a mother in just a few months when Helen Carter was my lived experience?*

The sudden urge to go to the bathroom yanked my attention, and I backed out quickly. I drove back to the trailer with the window down, hoping the cool wind would distract me from how badly I had to pee.

I burst through the door and sprinted to the toilet. The small bathroom window I had wanted to climb out of a few nights ago framed a neighbor's trailer. Mold streaked down the vinyl sides, and duct tape covered broken windows. Toys littered the overgrown backyard. Children lived in that filth, and I was about to bring one into mine. I got up and tried, without success, to button my jeans. It was over—time to let the proverbial cat, or baby, out of the bag.

The back door slammed. Dale was home. When I told him about the pregnancy, the door on my life would also slam shut.

I approached him on his couch island. Had he not been wearing his dirty work boots; I would have thought he'd been there all day. "Can I talk to you?"

"Yeah. When's dinner? I'm starved. We framed up two houses today with no lunch break. That idiot boss of mine. His overbooked schedule ain't my problem. What is it?"

I dropped onto the coffee table directly across from him and stared down at the shag carpet. A baby would crawl on it in a few months. I should clean it.

"Well, do you have something to say or not. I'm hungry." He crushed a cigarette into a full ashtray.

I kicked off my shoes and twirled the nylon fibers with my toes. It was too rough for baby skin.

"Can you spit it out? I hope you don't need money. Shit's tight this month."

He'd have a heck of a lot more of it if he cut back the cancer sticks, beer, and other recreational daggers. "Sorry. No, I don't."

Telling him meant soon everyone would know. My parents, Julie's parents, Mrs. Elliott, Miss Jones, Amber, Levi, every nameless face at school, everyone in this goddamn town would know what Angela Carter and Dale Simmons had done.

"If you aren't going to tell me, then move your skinny ass so I can see the TV."

Oh, you mean the TV you nearly broke my back on. That TV? The one with the half-ass repaired antennae.

I dug my fingernails into my palms. *Tell him. There's nothing left he can do to you that he hasn't already done.* "I've felt kind of sick the last couple of weeks, mostly in the mornings. And I realized I was late for my monthly, you know—visitor. I took a test. It was positive." I hoped he'd put two and two together. I didn't want to say it out loud.

"A test, what kind of test?" He had to be playing dumb.

I spelled it out a little more clearly. "The one where you pee on a stick and a blue line means positive. Mine showed a blue line."

Dale wasn't known for his intellect, but he solved this simple equation. "Are you trying to tell me you got pregnant?" He sat up and backed away from me like I had a contagious disease.

I didn't get pregnant alone. It takes two. But I just nodded. Accepting responsibility would probably help this go a little better for me.

"We may be together, but we ain't married." His sharp words pelted me. "I can barely feed us and pay all these bills, much less add another mouth. How long have you known?" He twisted his neck from side to side, veins bulged, and bones cracked.

I quickly lied. "I just found out yesterday. It suddenly hit me that I was late. I guess I didn't realize with everything going on, the move, school, work."

"Well, how far along are you? Can't you, you know, do something about it? Heck, I'll even offer to pay half. That is if it's mine." He stuffed a hand into the waistband of his jeans and jutted his chin.

I knew what he meant by *do something about it,* and it wasn't an option. And the audacity of him to say, *if it's mine.* He was the only one. "I can't. For one, in Florida, a minor, which I still am, needs parental consent. My parents don't even know. Plus, I think I'm too far along."

A minor could move in with an older man, and he could impregnate her, but that was as far as her decisions about her body went in the good ole state of Florida. I didn't have a choice. I was going to be a mother at seventeen. "And as far as your other comment, of course, it's yours. I've never been with anyone else, and you know that."

"Whatever. Fine. It's done. I'll call Mama later and see what we oughta do. She's wanted grandbabies for a long time." He sat back, lit a cigarette, and stared at the TV. At that moment, I wished I could have a smoke break.

Addis would have plenty to say about it. But if the *we* he referred to included her, not happening. She wasn't part of this equation. I didn't even want Dale to be a part of it. But I had no choice there.

The news would travel fast in North Lake, like the speed of light fast. And I didn't care who heard it from their mother's sister's husband's cousin's girlfriend, except for one—my father. I needed to be the one to tell him.

CHAPTER EIGHTEEN

NUMBER ONE

I parked my car in the dealership customer parking lot and met my father in the outdoor showroom.

"Hey, Number One." He walked toward me with open arms.

I melted into his chest. Then pulled away at the light scent of his fresh shower so he wouldn't smell Dale's cigarette smoke on me. As much as it was good to see him, the reason for my visit made me more nauseous than my condition.

"What do I owe for this lovely Saturday morning surprise?"

"I just wanted to stop by and check out your new office and chat." I swallowed, willing the nausea to subside until this conversation was over.

"Well, follow me." He ushered me through an indoor showroom filled with shiny cars and led me into a private office in the back. Posters of new Chevrolets lined the walls. The air hinted at new car leather and stale coffee. He pulled one of two smooth chairs out for me across from his large desk.

My father sold brand new expensive cars from his luxe office, while his pregnant teenage daughter lived in a trailer park with an older man. And, to make matters worse—he had no idea.

"How are you?" I'd small talk transition into the real reason soon enough.

"Good. I've been working about sixty-plus hours a week, but sales have picked up, and I got this promotion." He waved his hands, showcasing his new office.

At least one member of the Carter's had succeeded in self-improvement since the collapse of our family. "The office is nice. You should be proud." Never mind the rest of us have gone to hell in a handbasket.

"You know, it's perfect you showed up today. I was going to try and track you down later, which lately has been difficult to do." He pointed at me with a ballpoint pen.

I half-doubted his comment. It had been difficult for him to track me down because he hadn't tried. A concerned parent making a couple of phone calls could've done the trick. "Yeah, I've been about as busy as you, I guess."

"Well, my hard work is paying off. This week I moved into my own place. It's only a two-bedroom, but we can try and squeeze in a set of bunks in one and the couch is available anytime you all might want to stay over."

Are you kidding me? His offer was about four months too late. Life hated me. Time to give my father a reason to. "Thanks. I appreciate it. But that's kinda why I'm here. There's something I need to tell you."

Although the grudge of being abandoned by him lingered, his respect still meant the world to me. And I was about to reveal something that would change how he thought about me forever.

Since he was a straight shooter, I didn't drag this conversation out longer than necessary. I opened my mouth, and let the ugly truth claw its way out, shredding my soul in the process.

"I'm pregnant."

An uncomfortable silence filled the room. I couldn't bear my father's disappointment. But more than anything, I wanted him to stand up, embrace me, and tell me everything would be okay. Tell me that he'd help me figure out what to do.

He shifted in his office chair and adjusted his tie. His features flattened, and he shook his head.

"Are you mad?" My words came out meek and small.

He closed his eyes and took a deep inhale before opening them. "No, I'm not mad. Any other details you'd like to share?" He held the ballpoint pen as if he was about to take notes.

Now I had to divulge just how low I'd plunged because *pregnant by whom* was the worst part. "Addis Simmons who I used to babysit for—Dale is her oldest son. After things got bad with Mom, his family let me stay with them. Then he and I moved in together in that trailer park by Sunshine Citrus. And now I'm—we're—having a baby."

Dad recrossed his legs. "And why am I just hearing about this now?" he asked in an unexpectedly calm voice.

"I'm sorry. You've been working so much, and I wanted to tell you in person. But he's a hard-working guy with a close-knit family." The words tasted like the vomit that had plagued me the last few weeks. I didn't want to lie to my father. I wanted him, everyone, to know the truth. To save me. But I also didn't want anyone to know I needed saving, to know how weak I was. How pathetic.

He placed the pen in a mug on his desk, leaned forward, and clasped his hands together in front of him. His features softened, and a half smile emerged. "Do you know the reason I call you Number One?"

"Because I was your firstborn?"

"That's part of it, but there's more."

My curiosity piqued.

"When your mom found out she was pregnant with you, I was only nineteen, and she was eighteen, not much older than you. I played in a rock band, and we lived in a tiny trailer, similar to those over at Sunshine."

"Yeah, you've told me all this." My father was a storyteller. And even though the beginning of this one sounded familiar; my gut told me I was about to hear something new.

"Your grandmother, she put your mom through hell. One night, we were visiting. She was drinking, ran out of booze, and wanted us to buy her more. I said no. Your mom was afraid your grandmother would go herself after we left. But I said her mother would probably pass out before we were out of the driveway." He stopped talking, closed his eyes, and tilted his head back.

Then I was the one shifting uncomfortably in my chair, fearing how this might end. "Are you okay?"

"Sorry. After we left, your grandmother was walking in the direction of the liquor store, and there was an accident. The driver didn't see her until it was too late. We don't know what really happened. But to me, it was my fault. Then I was the one with the drinking problem. Your mom almost left me several times, and she wouldn't have been wrong."

"Oh my gosh. I had no idea. I can't imagine how you, how Mom, felt."

"It was rough. But, a few months later, you were born." He smiled as he choked back tears. "You became my Number One. My number one reason—for everything. And when Levi and Amber came along, you all were Number One. You just happened to be the first. Even the move to Florida was for you guys. In hindsight, maybe it was a mistake. But at the moment, I thought it was the best decision for us as a family. I'm telling you this because you're about to have your own Number One. It's a big responsibility. But I believe in you."

I expected disappointment. Not encouragement. I'd never appreciated him more. "Thanks. For telling me all this."

He opened the drawer on his desk. "We got some new keychains in. This one's for you." He slid a blue rubber keychain shaped like a number one over to me. It read *Clark's Cars: Your Number One Dealer.* "That's your reminder."

I bit my bottom lip. A tear slid down my cheek as I held the keychain.

What he said, I got it. Even though sometimes good intentions fall short, he was still trying to be a good father.

He handed me a tissue.

I wiped the tear away. "Can you do me a favor?"

He nodded. "Anything."

"Can you tell Mom for me? We haven't spoken in weeks. And I think, after what you've told me, I think she needs to hear this from you."

The cyclical nature of our interwoven stories wasn't lost on either of us.

"Of course. I also think I should be the one to tell Levi and Amber, with your permission of course and your presence. Your situation could be confusing for them."

He was right. Talking to your kids about teen pregnancy should come from a parent. Deep down, I wished he'd taken the time to have that conversation with me. But in retrospect, how would he have known he needed to? And he was dealing with so much himself. I was done being angry at him. I needed him. "I think that's the right thing to do."

"Good. We'll tell them together. And soon, we'll sit down again and discuss your plans through this. You're not alone."

"I appreciate that—more than you can possibly know. I can't wait to see the new apartment. Maybe I'll come by tomorrow afternoon, and we could tell them then?"

"We can probably make that work. Amber will be over. Not sure about Levi. He's kinda attached to your mother lately. But I'll do my best."

"Okay." Time to ask for one more favor. "Levi and Amber, please just get them out of there as soon as possible."

He shook his head. "Don't think for one minute I'm not fully aware and involved in what's going on. You only need to worry about yourself and that baby."

He got up and wrapped his arms around me. This time I didn't pull away. I was his little girl again. For the first time in a long time, something familiar filled me from within—unconditional love.

"I love you, Dad."

He kissed the top of my head. "Love you, too, Number One."

When I got back to the trailer, I sat in my car for a few minutes before going in. Through the kitchen window, I could see Dale doing something. But I couldn't make out what.

From out here, he didn't look so bad. The hazy film on the windows filtered his stained teeth and acne scars. He looked like how I remembered him from when I was younger when he had played football and done normal teenage things.

But life hadn't been kind to him, just like it hadn't been to me. He grew up in poverty with parents who weren't pushing him to be a better version of themselves. Partially because they didn't know how. It was a cycle that so many families fell into. I didn't want us to continue it. We were having a child together. Maybe, somehow, I—we—could break that cycle. Maybe it could end with us.

I walked inside and the mystery of what Dale had been doing was solved. On the table sat a disassembled shotgun. "Hey," I said.

"Hey. Huntin' season starts tomorrow. Roger and me are headed out, early. Just givin' ole Winnie the Winchester here a proper cleaning. You know, for good luck."

Various tools and substances littered the table along with gun parts. Although I didn't understand the whole sport of hunting, I respected the passion. At least for this one thing, he had that. "Good luck tomorrow. Hope it goes well. Long day. I'm gonna grab a snack and go to bed."

"Yeah, no problem. I'm gonna finish up then I'm headed to bed, too. Don't wait up, though," he said as he pushed a brush of some kind down a smooth barrel. "Oh, I told mama. 'Bout the baby. She's real happy. You know—for us."

Him telling his mom this soon, maybe that was a good sign. "I told my dad, too. He's also. You know, happy for us."

He gave me half a smile and then said, "Well, goodnight."

"Goodnight," I replied.

I couldn't sleep. A thousand thoughts tore my attention in all directions. But the one that took front and center was my life was about to change—drastically, and maybe it was for the better. As Dad said, I was about to have my own Number One.

Chapter Nineteen

Complicated Family Dynamics

Although Dale struggled to get up on weekdays for work, he was up and gone by four o'clock a.m. to hunt Sunday morning, no problem.

I tossed and turned from the time he left until daylight. Dad hadn't told me how he would break the news to my siblings that I was pregnant. I assumed he had a well-scripted plan designed to paint a picture that appeared a little more wholesome than its reality. Exactly what I'd tried to do when I told him.

When I got up, I poured what was left of a box of generic corn-flakes into a plastic bowl. Then grabbed the milk jug from the fridge. Fortunately, the smell hit me before I poured. The label showed seven days passed the expiration. Dry cereal was probably best for my morning sickness anyway. Then I took the drive of shame to my father's new apartment.

I knocked, and Dad greeted me.

"Number One." He came outside and shut the door. "I wanted to give you a heads-up that I've given a lot of thought to how I will present this to Levi and Amber. I don't want you to be hurt or upset. Just know they're still kids, and this is a sensitive subject I need to handle with care. You trust me?"

His off-the-record comment gave me pause because it was as if he'd forgotten I was also still a kid, but I had no choice but to trust him. "Yes, sir. I do."

He kissed the top of my head. "Good. Come on in."

I felt he was more concerned about my sibling's reception of my news than how it affected me. But he was their dad, too. My pregnancy couldn't be undone, but their innocence could still be saved.

He led me through a small living room to a round table in the middle of the kitchen. The furniture looked used, but comfortable and homey. Levi and Amber were each finishing a plate of fluffy pancakes swimming in sweet-smelling syrup.

"You hungry?" he asked.

My stomach turned somersaults, but I couldn't discern if it was hunger or nausea. "No, thanks. I just ate." I didn't want to risk throwing up, feeling like I was going to was bad enough.

"What's this all about anyway?" Levi asked as he put his plate in the sink.

Syrup dripped from Amber's chin. "Did we do something wrong?"

"No, no." Dad reassured. "No one's in trouble. I just wanted to get everyone together to share some news about your sister."

Six eyes bore into me. Eyes that were supposed to look at me with love. I didn't dare speak. Dad had made it clear he wanted to be in the driver's seat for this conversation.

He brushed a hand through his thick, dark hair and then clasped both hands in front of him on the table. He'd done this same thing before telling us we were moving to Florida.

I could still picture that gorgeous Mississippi home. But it felt more like a dream than a reality.

Dad cleared his throat.

A lump formed in mine.

Then he addressed the room. "Our family has been through a lot these past few months. And I know it's been hard on everyone. Especially your sister. After she left your mom's house"—

My mouth dropped open. I didn't put my own clothes in garbage bags. But he didn't know the whole story.

—"she moved in with a family, the Simmons family, that she used to babysit for. She needed a little space to... breathe, and I can relate to that."

Space to breathe. What a joke. The way he'd made me feel supported when I told him a day ago, he'd now jerked that rug from underneath me.

"During her time there, their oldest son, Dale, and your sister started having feelings for each other. He's been there as a shoulder for her as our family has gone through this—transition. And even though I don't necessarily agree with it, because of your sister's age"—he cleared his throat again.

Here it comes. You can wipe any guilt or responsibility off your shoulders, Dad. Just pile it on mine. I'm used to it.

"She and Dale have moved out on their own and have decided to have a baby together. Your mother and I had her when we were not much older than she is."

I stared at my father in utter disbelief. Dale and I did not decide to have a baby together. He was lying to my siblings. Being pregnant wasn't my choice. Neither was getting kicked out and having no other place to go. This was forced on me by his and mom's bad decisions.

"Sissy, you're having a baby?" Amber's face went from confusion to elation. "When? Do you know if it's a boy or a girl?"

Dad nodded at me. Finally, permission granted for me to speak on my behalf. "I think sometime in April. I don't know if it's a boy or girl yet. But you'll be one of the first to know."

My brother shook his head and tossed his bangs out of his eyes. "Dale Simmons, really?"

"Levi," Dad interjected. "Only positive comments allowed. Our job is to fully support and encourage your sister."

But I hardly felt supported or encouraged.

"Sorry. Congratulations then, I guess. Dad, can you take me back home? I've got—things to do."

"I'll take you home," I suggested.

"Can I come, too?" asked Amber.

Dad answered for me. "No, let them have some time alone."

As much as I was annoyed with him, I did appreciate that. "I'll drop him off and come right back and then take you to the park."

"Fine. Okay." She then skipped off and disappeared into a room.

In my car, Levi fumbled with the radio until he found a rock station and blared ACDC so loud the speakers turned into a staticky rendition of "Hells Bells."

"Hey, you're gonna blow the speakers. I volunteered to take you home so we could talk. Not to listen to this noise pollution."

He put his foot on the dash, then lit a cigarette and rolled down the window. I didn't bother protesting.

"What then? What do you want to talk about?"

"You seem mad at me. What did I do to you?"

His bony hand flicked cigarette ash out the window. He'd lost even more weight since the last time I'd seen him. He then took another long inhale before speaking. "I just don't get it. Moving out, getting knocked up by Dale Simmons. None of this is you."

I didn't want to unravel my father's fictional tale of Dale and I welcoming a love child, but I wasn't going to uphold the whole lie. "First off, just so you know, I didn't plan to get pregnant. It just happened. I assume Dad's little tale back there was more for Amber's benefit. And moving in with him wasn't really my choice either. In case you don't remember, Mom kicked me out."

He huffed. "It's not like you wanted to be there. You hate Mom. Admit it."

"I don't hate her. I hate her lifestyle."

Staring out the window he said, "If her lifestyle is so bad, why are you working so hard to emulate it?"

"Maybe you're right, and maybe you're wrong. But it's not too late for you." What he said sank in, but I wasn't the only one. "Can I ask you a question?"

"Depends on what it is. But go ahead. Shoot." He flicked the cigarette out the window.

"Why did you quit the wrestling team?"

Levi wiped his eyes. "It's complicated."

I pulled into the driveway, parked, and turned the radio down. "I'm a good listener." My brother wasn't one to share his feelings, so I wasn't sure what to expect.

He met my gaze. "When Mom stopped coming. She'd never missed a match those first two years. But then, well you know the rest."

I knew exactly what he meant. She'd always come to watch me cheer also. But when dad got laid off from Sunshine and she had to go work picking citrus, that was the beginning of the end for the Carter family.

"Levi, I'm so sorry. But just because she failed doesn't mean you have to. You're young. It's not too late for you."

He got out of the car. "Yeah, it is," then slammed the door and went inside. As I put the gear shift in reverse, a curtain moved. Mom was on the other side. She smiled and waved.

She had no idea how much the boy who just went inside loved her. And she one-hundred percent did not deserve it. But instead of ignoring her, I waved back—for Levi.

CHAPTER TWENTY

WORD ON THE STREET

BY THE TIME I got to school on Monday, girls I didn't think had even known my name a week ago bombarded me with thousands of questions.

"Do you want a boy or a girl?"

"Have you thought about names?"

"Does this mean you and Dale will get married?"

Over and over, I replied. "I haven't thought about it." Or "I don't know." And that was the truth. Girl, boy, I guess it would be one or the other. And I had to come up with a name? I'd never even named a pet. And marriage—to Dale Simmons. No way. Not ever. But since we were having a child together, we'd always be connected. I hated to even think about it.

Aside from the questions from the girls nosy enough to ask, most kids turned away when they saw me, then cupped their hands to whisper in another teen's ear. But I knew what they were saying, "Angela Carter is a slut. Whore. Pregnant. Pathetic."

Whispers continued as I walked down the hall to switch one textbook for another. I found Julie and Andrew huddled together at her locker. I avoided them as much as this small, stifling campus allowed, which meant I had to see them together more than I wanted to.

"What do you want to do this weekend?" Andrew was asking Julie as I approached.

Her eyes widened when she saw me, and she kicked him in the shin.

"Ouch, what was that all about?" He winced in pain.

"Hey, Ange. I was just telling Andrew that my family finalized our summer plans for that RV road trip." Julie was a terrible liar.

"I hear that new movie *Dirty Dancing* is the perfect choice for date night. You guys should probably go see it." Even though I wanted to be, I really didn't have any reason to be mad at them. They were just doing the things I would've been before I turned into knocked-up trailer trash.

Andrew spoke first. "Ange, I'm sorry about what's going on with you. But I know, if anyone can make this work, it's you."

"Make this work? What does that even mean?"

"What he means is you're one of the smartest people we know. And this situation isn't ideal. Not in the least. But we've talked, and you can do this. Whatever being a teen mom entails, you've got us by your side." Julie tried so hard to keep supporting me. But at some point, I expected our lives would splinter.

"Sorry. I know you guys mean well."

A student messenger tapped me on the shoulder and summoned me to the guidance office. Even though I worried about what he might want, I waved Julie and Andrew off, relieved the conversation was over.

Mr. Givens was waiting for me in his office. "Hi, Angela. Come on in. Here, take a seat." Although neat, his office was bursting with books and memorabilia of his entire probably thirty-plus career in education.

My cheeks warmed as I sat in the worn chair. "Am I in trouble for something?"

"No, no. Not at all. I brought you in for a couple of reasons. For one, Miss Jones called and said you no longer want to visit her classroom. I just wanted to tell you in person that I have no problem with a visit. I encourage all students here at North Lake High to pursue their dreams. If yours is being a teacher, seeing what that's like in action is a good place to start."

Now, I knew why I was here, and it wasn't about me visiting or not visiting Miss Jones' classroom. "I'm sorry, I just changed my mind. It happens, you know."

"I understand." He shook his head as a transition from the fake topic to the real one. "I also asked to speak with you because I've heard some things around the campus, and I wanted to talk directly to you. Do you know the things people have been saying?" Mr. Givens brushed a hand through his long, gray beard. Raised bushy eyebrows waited for my response.

I hung my head in shame. This man knew what I'd done in the back of a pick-up truck at the claypit, in Dale's parents' house behind nothing but a thin wall, and on both the tattered couch and lumpy mattress of the trailer in which we lived. Maybe not the details, but he knew what a girl must have done to end up pregnant.

As much as I hated myself for crying in front of him, I couldn't stop it. The questions from those nosy girls, the whispers in the hallway, my best friends falling in love, knowing I'd never go to college, never be a teacher, it was all too much. I might as well strip down naked in the courtyard and let them all stone me to death, just put me out of my misery because my life was basically over anyway.

He slid over a box of tissues. After a few minutes, I wiped my eyes and met his gaze. "I'm about three or four months along. I think anyway."

"Do you know what you're going to do?"

"No. I mean, I haven't thought much about it. I guess I haven't really gotten that far."

"I'm concerned. Your grades have been inconsistent all year. But in looking over your records from before, you've been an honor student until this year. Don't let this impact your grades again, and most importantly"—he pointed a thick finger at me—"don't quit school. Promise me that."

Just so he'd let me leave, I agreed. "Yes, sir. I promise."

He stood and beckoned me with his hand toward the door. I followed his lead. "I'm not done talking with you about this. I'm going to do some digging, I'll get with you in a week or two, and we'll make a plan. We'll get you across that finish line with a diploma in your hand. And if you need anything, anything at all, come see me. If I don't have the answer, I'll find it. Deal?"

Although I replied, "deal," it was uncertain, unreal, and out of reach. As a little girl, I'd always envisioned walking across a stage in a long robe with a cap on—a balding old man would hand me a diploma. I'd celebrate and hang with friends all summer. Then in fall, I'd pack my bags and head off to a college campus somewhere to live in a dorm and join a sorority. Pregnant at seventeen was not part of the vision.

I didn't want to disappoint Mr. Givens, my dad, or Julie, but what did it matter? At some point, I'd be forced to quit school because when my pregnancy ended, something else would begin. And that something else I couldn't just shove into my backpack with my textbooks when I went to school. That something else would require all of what little of me was left. That something else would cement me to Dale Simmons

like a concrete block hell-bent on plunging my corpse to the bottom of
the ocean.

CHAPTER TWENTY-ONE

CONSEQUENCES

INSTEAD OF DRIVING, I left my car at the high school and walked the two blocks to the elementary school. After half of North Lake High's interrogation and being the rumor mill's target by the other half, the crisp fall air and sunshine gave my brain a much-needed reset.

Some of Levi's old weight-lifting friends were playing basketball at the community court. A year ago, he would've been out there with them. Now he was forced to pick up the jagged pieces of our broken family—more specifically as mom's caretaker.

At least I was able to help with Amber. Her innocence was a refreshing reminder that even though I'd lost mine, maybe I could help her hold on to hers.

When I got to Amber's classroom, she asked the question I expected to hear a lot over the next few months. "Hi, Sissy. So, how long again until you have the baby?"

Since I still hadn't gone to the new doctor like I'd been told to, I didn't know for sure. "I think in about four or five months."

"Yeah, that's after my birthday. I'll be eight when I become an aunt."

She grabbed my hand and asked me another question, the one I didn't want to answer. "When can I come see where you live and meet your boyfriend?" She giggled.

It mortified me to think of her, or anyone, stepping foot in that trailer or meeting Dale. But eventually, everyone would bear witness to the filth in which I lived and the individual who put me in it. "Soon. I'll have you over soon. I want to get it nice and clean before anyone comes."

When we walked into the building, Mrs. Elliott approached us. "Hi, girls. Angela, I need to talk to you. Amber, can you go help Miss Jones?"

"Sure." As Amber skipped away, the air in the room thickened.

Most conversations that start with *I need to talk to you* are followed by something you don't want to hear. What I dreaded most, Mrs. Elliott and Miss Jones peeking behind the curtain, had arrived.

"Please sit." She motioned toward a children's table.

I dropped into a small wooden chair—fitting because that's how I felt, small. Inch by inch, life was crushing me. Soon I'd be the size of an ant, and Dale could finish me off with one swift blow of his boot.

"I don't like to ask the staff personal questions. But I must ask you this one, and I need you to be honest with me. Are you pregnant?" Eyes heavy with kindness and concern waited for an answer I didn't want to give.

But I had to tell her the truth. I dropped my head as tears threatened me for the second time in one day. I was one giant disappointment to everyone.

"Yes, ma'am, I am." As soon as I said the words, fear forced me to look at her and beg because I knew what was coming next. "It won't interfere with my job, though. I promise. I still want to keep working here. I need to keep working here."

She reached for my stiff, clammy hand and held it between her soft, warm ones. "First off, are you okay? Do you know what you're going to do?"

There was that question again. Everyone stop asking me that. I'm the kid here. But I just shrugged.

"You're wonderful with children, and no doubt you'll be a great mother. But the students here look up to you as a role model. Watching your pregnancy progress may be confusing since they know you are only a teenager. And I'd have parents who'd probably not approve. I've been dreading all day having to tell you this. I really like you. But I can't keep you employed here at this time. I'm very sorry."

I pulled my hand from hers and covered my eyes. I couldn't hold back the tears any longer. *I hate me. I hate me. I hate me.*

Mrs. Elliott stood and hugged me until my body stopped convulsing. "Honey, you are a bright, lovely young lady. I've had suspicions you were going through some challenges the last few months. Yet you still walked in here with a smile on your face. It won't be easy, but I believe in you. Miss Jones believes in you. When you started here, you told us both you wanted to be a teacher. Don't give up on that dream. It can still come true."

No, it can't. I was just fired from a job I loved, and I completely understood why. "Amber. I need to get her."

"Miss Jones and I already talked about it. Amber can continue to come free of charge. We will pick her up from her classroom each afternoon, and you can pick her up at six o'clock. I hope that helps."

Although being on the receiving end of her charitable act of kindness made me feel even worse about my life, I thanked her.

"This moment doesn't define you. You can work hard and rise above it. Remember, it may not be easy, but it'll be worth it."

I couldn't bear to be in her presence any longer. "Can I please go?" The day had almost beaten me to a pulp.

"Of course. Take care. If you need anything, please, let me know." She gave me one more hug before disappearing through the back door. The door I should have walked through with her.

Instead, I burst out of the front door and ran to my car. I'd just lost the last thing in the world I had left that was just for me. I wanted to crawl into a dark hole and disappear. But I didn't even have a hole to crawl into. I could drive until I ran out of gas. Then sleep in my car wherever it stopped.

Anything sounded better than depending on Dale for everything. I couldn't go back to the trailer yet and listen to whatever condescending things he might say about me getting fired and complaining about money.

Instead, I cranked the car and headed to see the only person who gave me more than she took. Even though things had shifted between us, she was still my best friend, the best friend I didn't deserve to have.

CHAPTER TWENTY-TWO

FOLDING FITTED SHEETS

THE FRESH AROMA OF clean laundry made me feel dirty. I wanted to stuff myself in one of the washing machines until the stench of the trailer disappeared. But since that wasn't an option, at least my thoughts could disappear while mindlessly helping Julie fold laundry.

But I should've known better because Julie wasn't the type of friend to let you sit back and ignore your problems. She was the kind who held your hand while she forced you to face them.

"Okay, so how much money do you need per week, bare minimum, to survive?"

"I mean, Dale pays most of the bills at the trailer, so all I need is money for gas, car insurance, and to eat. Maybe like twenty-five dollars a week."

"Done. You come here in the afternoons, help me fold laundry, and I'll pay you."

I was already Mrs. Elliott's charity of choice. I couldn't also be Julie's. "No, way. I cannot let you do that."

"You can, and you will. It's not like I'm actually paying you. I get paid by how much laundry I get done, not hourly. Plus, I don't need the money. My parents only make me work, so as my dad says, 'I understand the value of a hard-earned dollar.' Blah, blah."

As humiliating as it was, I had no choice but to accept her offer. "Okay and thanks."

"No problem, I'd ask them to hire you outright. But you know, because of your situation, the owner, I mean, he's more Catholic than my parents. No offense."

Her comment lodged next to a thousand other bullet holes. The same message came at me like a firing squad from all directions. Being a pregnant teen made me unworthy.

Then she loaded another round of ammunition and fired. "Now we've solved one problem. Up next, how's it going making that doctor appointment?"

I was worse than less than. "I can't afford a doctor, and you're not paying for that. I don't want to ask Dale for the money, either. It's not like he has any extra."

"He's the father. It's his job. You need to see a doctor and make sure everything is okay with you and the baby."

Suddenly I remembered the pamphlet I'd shoved under my seat for the Health Department. I let go of my end of the fitted sheet we were failing to fold. "I'll be right back."

I reached under the seat. It was still there. I scanned it. It talked about the importance of prenatal care for a healthy pregnancy and listed addresses and phone numbers for multiple offices. One location was close to the trailer park. Again, Julie was right. It was time to find out what the heck was about to happen to me.

I went back in and showed her the pamphlet.

"Good. Call them right now." She pointed to the phone on the desk. She didn't give me a flipping break. But at least, unlike everyone else, she was helping me figure out what to do, not just asking me what I was going to do.

Since we were the only ones in the laundromat, I slouched to the desk, picked up the phone, and dialed the number.

"Hi. My name is Angela Carter. I need to make an appointment because I'm pregnant." Even though she obviously already knew, saying this out loud, in front of Julie was belittling.

"No, ma'am. I don't have insurance."

Julie handed me a pen and pointed to the laundromat's desktop calendar.

"Yes, I can do next week. Yes, afternoon is best." I scribbled the appointment down. "Thank you."

I hung up the phone. "Okay, done. The appointment is next Wednesday, right after school. So can you lay off me a little?"

"Nope. Sorry."

I couldn't do any of this without her. I should stop feeling jealous of her and Andrew and try to be happy for them. I needed her in my life. "Ugh, you drive me crazy sometimes, you know."

"Yep, I know. And don't plan on it ever stopping. I love you too much." She tossed an air kiss in my direction. I pretended to catch it and threw her one back.

The last thing I wanted to do was face Miss Jones, but it was time to pick up Amber.

"I gotta run. Thanks again. See you tomorrow. Good luck finishing up with that fitted sheet."

She smiled and wadded it into a big ball.

Dad had this joke, *If you don't do well in school, you may end up folding fitted sheets for a living.* It turns out it was more like a prophecy. For Julie, it was temporary. She'd already enrolled in college for next fall. For me, folding fitted sheets could become a permanent career.

I waited until most of the kids were gone before entering Miss Jones's room.

"Hey, I was hoping to see you this afternoon." Her voice was soft and tender. Too kind for what I deserved.

Standing next to her made me long for a do-over of the last several months. To be un-pregnant. "I'm so sorry. I didn't mean to let you down."

"You have nothing to be sorry for. The only thing you need to worry about is taking care of yourself and having a healthy baby. I also wanted to let you know that I spoke with your guidance counselor again. I told him to let me know anytime you're ready for that classroom visit. Having a baby doesn't mean you can't also have a career. It only means you might have to work a little harder to make it happen."

A little harder? Really, just a little?

Encouragement wasn't action. It was inaction. It was like telling someone you would pray for them but not doing anything tangible to help. It was a cop-out. Every adult only gave me cop-outs. Every single one of them failed me.

"That's not an option for me anymore. Thanks for allowing Amber to continue. It's overly generous of you and Mrs. Elliott."

Miss Jones couldn't see past her privilege. I'd never be anything like her, and now, I almost didn't want to be. Her kind of privilege reeked worse than trailer trash stench.

Folding fitted sheets, so be it.

Chapter Twenty-Three

All Fired Up

Addis' car was in the driveway. I tiptoed up the rickety steps and twisted the knob to the backdoor.

Dale lay sprawled in his usual spot on the couch partaking of his usual after-work beer and smoke-fest.

Addis stood next to an old brown playpen dotted with animated animals. "All four of your cousins' kids used this and she was about to throw it out and I rescued it just in time."

Their heads jerked in my direction when my backpack landed with a thud on the kitchen table.

"Oh, hey. I was just showing Dale this playpen I picked up for my grandbaby." She smiled like she'd just delivered a twenty-four-carat gold bassinet.

That thing Addis expected me to put my child in, looked like it belonged in a dump. Which meant it complemented the rest of the trailer's decor. "Thank you, Addis. Very kind."

"My baby boy's gonna be a daddy. I'm going to get one for my place, too. For babysitting." She squealed and bounced up and down.

I knew she didn't care much for me. But she'd do anything for Dale. Maybe helping me could be for him. I'd take it.

"Bye, Dale. Don't forget to come by next week for dinner. I'd invite you too, but I know you work late at the elementary school. I'll have Dale bring you home a plate. You know, for the baby."

I gritted my teeth. "That would be great, Addis. For the baby." Her mentioning the elementary school slapped me with the reality that I needed to tell Dale.

After she left, I plopped down next to him on the couch. We both stared at the playpen.

"This is real, huh?" he asked.

"Yep." I answered.

"Mama's gonna drive us crazy," he said.

"Yep." I answered. We shared a laugh. It didn't last long before it turned into an awkward silence.

I had to tell him about the job. I didn't want him finding out some other way. And since he was in a decent mood, I took advantage of it.

"My job your mom was talking about, at the school, they had a talk with me today."

"About what?" he asked.

I pointed to the playpen. "That. The baby."

"What about the baby?"

Comical moment between Dale and me—officially over. "They're concerned parents will complain and the students will be confused about a pregnant teen working there." I hated telling him this. I hated that it was true. I wasn't good enough to work at the school anymore. Just like my mother kicked me out, Mrs. Elliott had, too.

He grabbed the sides of his head. "Please, don't tell me you got yourself fired."

"I didn't get myself fired. Pregnancy got me fired and you got me pregnant." I'd pushed it. I knew it as soon as the words came out. I scooted away from him to get out of arm's length.

He smashed the beer onto the beat-up coffee table and the liquid splashed everywhere. "Don't for one damn minute blame me. I didn't do anything to you. You should've been on birth control. That's not on me." His volume rose with each word. "I'm trying here. Trying to support us. Trying my damnedest."

Two things kept Dale's lid on. One was not having to give me money. Two was me giving him more of what he'd already taken. But one day, I feared that lid would explode. I just didn't want it to be today. "It's fine. Calm down. Please. I got another job. Working with Julie at the laundromat." I held my breath hoping he wouldn't ask how much money I'd be making, because it was less than half.

Thankfully he didn't. "Get this damn thing outta here. It's blocking the TV," he said as he kicked the playpen.

I didn't say anything else. I got up and dragged the thing down the hall to the empty room where my child would begin a shitty life.

Chapter Twenty-Four

Heartbeat

Although the health department reeked of antiseptic, it wore the wear of thousands of underprivileged patients like me. Worn plastic seated chairs lined the waiting room walls. Sun-bleached posters featured pregnant torsos at various stages, along with birth control options—an odd juxtaposition.

When a nurse called me back, Julie waited until I was changed into my paper garment before joining me in the treatment room. "This place seems pretty nice," she said as she surveyed our surroundings and attempted encouragement.

A knock at the door startled us both. "Come in." I managed.

"Hello. I'm Dr. Patton. It's a pleasure to meet you—both." He walked in carrying a couple of folders, which I assumed contained the stack of papers I'd filled out in the lobby. Papers in which I divulged my deepest, darkest secrets. This man, this stranger in a white coat, now knew them all. He hadn't laid a hand on me, yet I already felt violated.

I crossed my arms in front of my chest. Despite the freezing temp in the room, the paper gown stuck to my perspiring skin. "Hi. It's a pleasure to meet you as well." But nothing about this was pleasant.

Since I had no insurance, I couldn't afford to go to a private obstetrician. The Health Department and this Dr. Patton was as good as it would get.

Julie introduced herself. "Hello, Dr. Patton. I'm Julie, the annoying best friend."

Dr. Patton smiled as if this whole experience was normal. "Good to meet you, Julie, the annoying best friend."

He glanced at a page inside one of the folders. "It looks like you're about four months along. How are you feeling so far?"

Weird—an adult asking how I felt. "Okay, I guess. I mean, in the beginning, not great, but better now."

"Totally common. The first three months are the first trimester. During that time, your body is adjusting to pregnancy hormones, which can cause symptoms such as nausea and fatigue. Now you're in the second trimester. Those hormones have leveled, and you should feel pretty good for the next couple of months." He handed me one of the folders he was carrying.

"Since this is your first pregnancy, I put this together with some pamphlets and other information you might find useful. I also included the phone number of the clinic here, my direct extension, and my home phone. If you have any questions at any time, feel free to call."

"Thank you." He handed me the folder and I passed it to Julie.

Dr. Patton continued. "My job is to get you and this baby to the end of your pregnancy with you both as healthy as possible. It's a partnership between the three of us. I'm going to do my job. And yours is to listen to what I tell you and take my advice. Well, most of it anyway." He chuckled. "Your baby's job is to grow and stay put until it's safe for him or her to come into the world. Got it?"

"Got it." Despite sitting on a table in a cold examination room wearing nothing but a paper gown, for the first time in a long time, I felt safe. I trusted Dr. Patton, and he didn't know how rare that was for me.

"The first thing we're going to do is listen to your baby's heartbeat—with this little guy." He held up a small electronic-looking box with a wand attached by a long-coiled cord. "It's called a Fetal Doppler. It's perfectly safe for both you and the baby and won't hurt at all. I'll move it around on your belly until we find your baby's heartbeat. How does that sound?"

Julie clapped her hands.

Was I supposed to be excited? I didn't know how to feel anymore. I laid back and clenched my jaw in preparation for whatever was about to happen to me.

He moved the wand around on my belly. Nothing but static came from the speaker. He moved it around a few more seconds.

Then—thump, thump, thump.

"Aah, there we go. Your little one is very busy in there. Listen to this."

Thump, thump, thump.

As the rapid heartbeat filled the room, mine stopped. An unexpected tear slid down my cheek.

"That's the coolest sound ever," said Julie.

Words to describe the sound of that heartbeat didn't exist for me like they did for Julie.

Thump, thump, thump.

Each beat of that heart pushed out my fear, my doubt, my shame. A feeling I couldn't label flooded in. It was as if that tiny heartbeat created a brand-new emotion that never existed until now. I could've listened to that sound forever.

"One-hundred and forty beats per minute. Perfect. Your baby sounds great," Dr. Patton said as he scribbled some notes into a folder.

Julie held my hand through the rest of the exam as Dr. Patton explained everything he was doing and why. It wasn't as bad as I thought it would be, mostly because all I could think about was that tiny beating heart inside me. After the exam, he left for a few minutes for me to get dressed.

"You did awesome. And he seems like a great doctor. And we heard your baby's heartbeat. I'm so pumped." Julie pressed a fist into an open palm and grinned from ear to ear.

"Thanks, it means a lot, you being here." And it did. I couldn't imagine having shared this moment with anyone else. She was with me the first time I heard the most beautiful sound in the world. But even in this state of elation, a sadness lingered. I wondered how my mother felt the first time she heard my heartbeat. And if it was anything like how I felt, how could she have done to me what she did?

Julie turned around and I changed back into my clothes. "I'll be here as often as I can. You aren't alone."

I didn't have many people to lean on, but I was damn lucky to have her.

Dr. Patton knocked before re-entering. "That's a good friend right there."

"Trust me, I know." Julie and I smiled at each other. And I knew, without a doubt, she and I would be best friends for the rest of our lives. She was as much a part of my baby's beginning as I was. As I crossed the threshold from child to mother, my best friend held my hand through it.

"Because of your age, I want to see you every two weeks. When you reach somewhere around six months, you'll come in for a sonogram. We'll use a different type of wand on your belly, and through sound waves, we'll be able to see an image of your baby on a video screen. And sometimes, we can tell if it's a boy or a girl. If you want to know. When you get closer to full-term, at about thirty-six weeks, you'll come in every week."

Then he handed me a huge bottle of large pills. "These are prenatal vitamins. I want you to take one every day. And drink plenty of water. All right, see you in two weeks. Remember, call if you have any questions."

Finally, after all this time, I had an adult in my corner, giving me some direction. A roadmap was beginning to form. "Dr. Patton, thank you."

"The pleasure's all mine. You two ladies have a nice rest of your day."

On the ride home, Julie talked nonstop. "I can't wait to see if it's a boy or girl. I hope they can tell. What do you want? I think you're having a girl. I'm going to be an aunt. This is so crazy."

Although I engaged Julie in conversation, I was only half paying attention. An unfamiliar calm embraced me. The noise that came non-stop let up a little, at least for today. Pregnancy was no longer something happening to me. It was something happening for me. Pregnancy was giving me a baby.

After Julie dropped me off, I burst into the trailer, eager to tell Dale I heard the baby's heartbeat. He was this baby's father. Maybe if I could explain how real this was, that a baby—our baby was growing inside me. That *I*—that *we*—were going to be parents. Maybe, that would change him like it did me.

But I stopped dead in my tracks when I found him in camouflage, passed out on the couch, the Winchester on the floor next to a couple of empty beer cans. Same scene, different day.

That question everyone kept asking me, *what is your plan*? I still didn't have an answer, but I knew it wasn't this. My baby deserved to come into the world to a mother ready for the job and I wasn't. But after today, after hearing my baby's heartbeat, even though I didn't know where to start, I was ready to learn.

CHAPTER TWENTY-FIVE

EDUCATION FOR TEENAGED MOTHERS

"Who can tell me why we sometimes cramp during exercise? Not that I've been exercising being nine months pregnant." Mrs. Van laughed, and her belly shook like a fake Santa's.

She was due to give birth any day. I'd often heard a pregnant woman's belly described as the size of a basketball, but Mrs. Van's was in oversized yoga ball territory. I touched my tummy and couldn't imagine it as big as hers.

Although she pretended to teach us about cellular respiration, it was as if her mind was elsewhere. I could relate. After hearing my baby's heartbeat, it was difficult to think about anything else. I didn't hate her as much as before.

During my first trimester, I toyed around with the idea of quitting school. But now, well into my second, like Dr. Patton said, my nausea and extreme fatigue had lessened. Being at school was much easier and more desirable than sitting in Dale's gloomy trailer all day until work at the laundromat.

A student messenger opened the door and told Mrs. Van that Mr. Givens wanted to see me. I'd been expecting and dreading this. He'd want answers to questions I still couldn't give.

"Angela," he smiled, a little more chipper than usual. "I'm glad to see you. Have a seat." He pulled the same worn-out chair for me he had a few weeks earlier.

My growing but not-quite-yoga-ball-size belly appreciated the gesture.

"I wanted to check in and see if you'd thought much about our last conversation. The one about your plan." The eyes underneath those bushy brows hinted that he was the one with something to tell me rather than the opposite.

"No, sir. Other than keep coming to school as long as I can. You know, until I can't." I placed my hands on my belly, visually reminding him of what was coming. My *no-plan* plan didn't do this baby justice. But I was trying. I was coming to school.

"Well, I have an idea. If you'd hear me out."

Since I hadn't come up with anything on my own, any idea was better than my non-idea. "Yes, sir. Of course."

He smiled and verbally jumped into his suggestion with both feet. "A former colleague of mine recently started a teen mother's program a few miles away at an alternative education school. I don't know a ton about it, but I thought maybe I could take you over to meet her, and we could check it out."

Skepticism challenged intrigue. Was his motive to get the token pregnant girl off the high school campus? Maybe. But he sounded genuine. There was no harm in checking it out. "Sure, that sounds great."

He stood. "Well, let's go, right now." Like Julie, Mr. Givens allowed me no time for procrastination.

He led me to a brown station wagon parked in the teacher's lot and opened the passenger door for me. Although the leather seats were worn and it had a musty old car mixed with cigar smell, it was immaculate.

Not knowing how to carry on a conversation with him, I was grateful he popped in a cassette tape of seventies classics that he quietly sang along to.

Even though I'd boycotted music since the lingerie encounter with Dale, the familiar tunes reminded me of listening to my father play the guitar and sing to me when I was younger. Especially when "Sister Golden Hair" by America came on. I almost wanted to join Mr. Givens on that one.

The small two-story brick campus was about a thirty-minute drive from North Lake High. When we arrived, Mr. Givens ushered me inside and into the office. Another guidance counselor met us there. "This is Mr. Demalina."

"Hi, Angela. Pleased to meet you." We exchanged a handshake. Unlike Mr. Givens who dressed in lose jeans and faded flannel, Mr. Demalina was polished in dark slacks and a crisp button-down. "This way." He pointed toward a door.

Skepticism dug its nasty little claws back in. This *program*? How could the two middle-aged men I followed know what was best for a pregnant teen girl when she herself didn't even know?

The second we entered the portable classroom behind the main campus, eyes bore into me. Eyes that already knew what mistake I'd made to wind up here because they'd made the same one. I wondered if this was how inmates felt the first-time guards ushered them to their prison cell. I half-expected heckling to start.

The eyes belonged to ten teenage girls of all colors, shapes, and sizes. Some were very pregnant, some were holding babies, and some were very pregnant and holding babies. This seemed like a place I didn't want to belong to but did anyway.

A petite woman, a no-nonsense Claire Huxtable look-alike, stood at the front of the room. The few episodes I'd seen of *The Cosby Show* made me wonder if any family was that put together. I also wondered, if like Claire Huxtable, this woman ran a tight ship with high expectations for her crew.

Captain Claire bounced over, and her crew followed. After she said hello to the men, she introduced herself to me. "Hi, you must be Angela. I'm Mrs. Keene."

The crew, rather than heckling, fired rapid questions. A dark-skinned girl holding a chunky baby in blue asked, "How far along are you?"

Before I could answer, a curly-headed blonde with a belly about the size of Mrs. Van asked, "Is this your first baby?"

Mrs. Keene held one hand over her other, making a T-shape. "Girls, time-out. Let's tell Angela a little about us first. After, she can tell us about herself—if she wants."

She pointed to the dark-skinned girl holding the baby. "Temeka's been here the longest. You start, and we'll go around the room."

"I'm Temeka, but you can call me Meka. I'm sixteen." She rubbed the top of her baby's fuzzy head. "This is Dante, and he's four months old." She held him on the crook of her hip with the confidence of a seasoned mother.

"He's adorable. Nice to meet you." I needed to learn how to hold a baby. I must've held my siblings, but that was so long ago.

"You, too. This class and Mrs. K, they don't suck." She smiled.

Curly Blonde rubbed her belly. "My name's Suzanne. I'm almost eighteen, and I'm seven months along with a baby girl. Welcome to Club Keene."

Club Keene. I liked the sound of it.

One by one, the rest of the girls told me their names and status. And as shocking as it was, a couple of them were pregnant with baby number two.

Afterward, curious gazes waited for me to speak. And even though my palms were sweaty, I wanted to share my story with them. Unlike everyone else in my life, these girls could relate. They were living the same life as me, at least part of it. "Hi. As Mrs. Keene said, my name is Angela. I'm seventeen years old and about five months pregnant."

The comments and questions resumed. But it wasn't the heckling I'd initially expected. It was more like getting to know someone you wanted to be friends with.

Mrs. Keene interrupted. "Girls, girls, go back to your seats, please. Finish filling out your nutrition journal. Oh, and mothers, don't forget to fill out your baby's feeding and diaper charts."

The girls dispersed and followed Mrs. Keene's directions.

"Gentleman, I'll send Angela back to the office when we're done." The two guidance counselors, likely relieved to be exiting a room full of teen girls and crying babies, complied.

I got the feeling people listened when Mrs. Keene spoke. And not like it was a bad thing. It was like if she told you to do something, it was the right thing to do.

"Follow me."

She led me to a large desk overflowing with textbooks and stacks of papers. On the top sat a thick manila envelope with my name on it. My name. On an envelope. Here.

"I'm sure you have questions but let me fill you in on a few things first. I started Education for Teenaged Mothers because I know what it's like.

I had my oldest son at sixteen. My goodness, that was thirty years ago." She paused and laughed to herself.

She handed me the envelope—the one with my name on it. "In there is your schedule. You'll be in here on Monday, Wednesday, and Friday from nine o'clock a.m. to three o'clock p.m. You'll take classes like money management, newborn care, and prenatal nutrition. You can read it all later. Then Tuesday and Thursday are the same times, but you'll be in the main building for your academic courses. Oh, and each Wednesday, the nursing students from North Lake Community College come to review your nutrition journal and to do a simple health exam on both pregnant students and babies."

The more she talked, the more I knew this was where I needed to be. This was where I *had* to be. ETM wasn't a school trying to pretend to help pregnant teens and new moms. Helping them was its entire purpose.

She said that when students deliver, they remain full-time in ETM and work on their academic coursework and assist each other in looking after the babies.

"I know that was a lot, and it's all inside that envelope. But do you have any other questions?"

The students clustered in groups around the room, laughing, working, and holding babies. Everyone kept asking me what my plan was. Maybe it was time I trusted that the right people had brought me to the right place.

"I only have one. When can I start?"

Mrs. Keene grabbed my hand and smiled. "Well, it's Friday. Let's take a little tour of the classroom. After that, you can go back to the office, and Mr. Givens and Mr. Demalina can complete the transfer and sign you up for the right academic courses, so you are on target for a May graduation. I see no reason why you can't start on Monday."

My heart leaped. "Mrs. Keene, I don't know what to say, except I really appreciate this opportunity. Very much." Finally, I belonged somewhere. Here.

"Of course. I didn't have anything like this when I was in your situation. That's why I do it. I want to see you girls have the support I wished I'd had."

On our tour, she first showed me the nursery. Nestled in one corner of the portable, several cribs housed a few sleeping babies. I couldn't believe in a few months mine would sleep there. In another corner, sat a small kitchen where a couple of girls prepared lunch following a recipe. In the middle of the room sat desks and a chalkboard on wheels. A few students were finishing up the assignments Mrs. Keene had told them about earlier.

Next, she opened a closet. "This is the 'Borrowing Closet.' It's full of maternity clothes for all stages of pregnancy. Take what you need and when you grow out of it, return it. Same thing for these baby clothes," she said as she pointed to the bins on the bottom.

"I take care of my girls. But I do have one huge ask. And it's non-negotiable. Before you sign on the dotted line, do you wanna know what that is?" Mrs. Keene glared at me with her soft, chocolate-brown eyes.

"Yes, ma'am," I responded without even thinking. Because, whatever she asked me to do, I'd do it.

She pointed to the portable door. "When you walk through that door, regardless of whatever else is going on in your life outside these four walls, in here, every single day, I expect you to be the best version of Angela you can be. That's it. Can you do that?"

Her ask echoed something my father had said to me when he told me I was going to have my own Number One. And even though I still didn't know what it was, I believed with Mrs. Keene's help, I could be the best version of me. "Yes, ma'am. I can. Thank you again."

This was it. This was where I would learn how to take care of me and my baby at the same time. The portable wasn't a house, but nonetheless, I'd finally found a home.

Chapter Twenty-Six

Fluttering Butterflies

"I'm going to miss seeing you at school every day," Julie said as we folded the laundry of a family who appeared to have at least three kids. Neon, floral tees—a pre-teen daughter, small firetruck pajamas—a toddler son, and a pink onesie—an infant daughter.

I took my time folding the onesie. When Julie had asked me before if I wanted a girl or boy, I hadn't answered. But I wanted a daughter. It was an opportunity to right the wrongs in my relationship with my mother. I wondered how the conversation with her and my dad had gone when he told her I was pregnant. I wondered if she thought about me. How sad I had to wonder.

"At least we'll see each other here every day," I replied. But truthfully, being at school with Julie was not fun anymore. Anytime Andrew was around they acted differently than before. I couldn't define it, but I could sense it.

"Oh, yeah about that. So next week is the last week before Christmas Break. My parents rented the whole family this gorgeous cabin up in

South Carolina. I've been meaning to ask you if you could handle the laundromat by yourself while I'm gone. You would make extra money. I figured it would help with all the baby things you'd need."

Sure, Jules. Have a great time on your family vacation while I stand on my feet for six hours folding the clothes of people who could afford to pay someone to fold their clothes. "Yeah, no problem."

"Perfect. Listen I gotta leave a little early tonight," she added, putting her last stack of clothes in a basket.

First, she blindsided me into working alone over Christmas Break and then she declared she was leaving early. "Okay. But what's so important?"

"Um...the annual Senior Skate night at Roll Air."

I grabbed another piece of laundry to fold as tears pooled behind my eyes. "Why didn't you say anything?"

"I don't know. I guess because it's not like you could go. I mean skating wouldn't be safe for you. In case, like, you fell or something."

"Well, you could've at least told me. Maybe I'd want to go watch." Even though I said it, not in a million years would I have gone and sat benched while teens skated around in a stupid circle, played pointless video games, and munched on over-buttered popcorn. "Never mind, just go."

"Ange, I'm sorry. I—"

I held my palm toward her to signal stop.

Without saying another word, she turned around and left. Even though she was my best friend, I was glad I'd never have to see her or Andrew ever again on the North Lake High School campus. Monday couldn't come fast enough.

After the trip to ETM and work at the laundromat, my feet were swollen, and my back ached. Dale wasn't home yet, so I laid down for a bit. Next to the bed on the nightstand sat the folder Dr. Patton had given me.

So far, I'd not been an active participant in this pregnancy. I just woke up each day, oblivious to what was going on inside my body. And although Mrs. Keene would teach me what I needed to know, it was time I also took some initiative.

I opened the folder and sifted through the contents until I found a pamphlet titled "Pregnancy - Month Five," which was my best guess at how far along I was.

"By month five, an embryo is about the size of a banana," the brochure read.

I went into the kitchen, grabbed a bruised banana, and put it next to my belly. I couldn't believe something that size was inside me. Mrs. Van's baby was probably the size of a watermelon.

Before it was too spoiled, I peeled the banana and took a bite. Then laid back down and kept reading. The brochure also said I should start to feel the baby kicking and moving. I read, "The first baby movements are called 'Quickening' and may feel like fluttering butterflies." I'd had that sensation all week. Was that the baby moving? I had thought it was indigestion.

I lay very still and placed my hands on my belly. A few seconds ticked by, and then, there it was. Although faint, I could definitely feel it. My baby was moving inside me. It was both exhilarating and strange. I wanted so badly to share this moment with someone. I would've called Julie, but she was at Senior Skate Night. No doubt she was rolling around the rink holding hands with Andrew.

This was probably the kind of thing most girls would share with their mothers. I didn't have that option either.

About that time, Dale came in. He'd have to do.

"Angela, where are you?"

"I'm in the bedroom lying down. Come here." I couldn't predict his reaction to anything. But I was still sharing this with him. This was too big to experience alone.

He bent down and kissed my forehead. Weird. "I swung by Mama and Daddy's. She sent these navy beans and ham for you."

My eyes widened as large as the plate. The banana had only awakened my hunger. And Dale rarely kissed me, much less brought me anything. Well, except for that gas station lingerie a few months back.

"Thank you. Something exciting happened today. For the first time, I felt the baby move. I had no idea that I'd been feeling it for a while. Do you want to feel it?"

"I don't know. Maybe." He shrugged.

I made the decision for him and grabbed his hand and placed it firmly on my belly.

He jerked away and wrinkled his face. "That's the baby?"

"Yes. A little person is growing inside of me. Our child."

His contorted expression transitioned into a smile. "My boy."

That was new. He hadn't shown any interest in the baby so far, boy or girl. Then out of nowhere, he wanted a boy.

"I don't care if it's a boy or girl as long as it's healthy." That wasn't entirely true, but I'd never say it out loud. I'd love this baby just as much regardless, but I did hope it was a girl.

I was about to change the subject and tell him about ETM, but he spoke up before I had a chance.

"I'm going out with Roger tonight. Today's his new girlfriend's birthday."

I didn't care. But I'd never known Roger to have a girlfriend.

"It's fine. Thanks for letting me know. I've got plans to finish reading the stuff Dr. Patton gave me anyway."

"Sounds good. Well, I'm gonna hop in the shower and head on over to his place. Don't wait up."

"No problem. I didn't plan on it." I tried to focus back on reading the brochures while the water from the shower sprayed down on Dale longer than usual.

After he got out, he put on a t-shirt without rips and a pair of jeans without holes. He even put on that cheap, strong cologne that made my eyes water. It was almost worse than his typical odor of stale ashtray. My intuition hinted at something, something that I'd rather not think about.

Alone, I scarfed down every drop of the navy beans and ham and read every piece of literature Dr. Patton put in that folder. Then read everything in the envelope Mrs. Keene had given me. The more I read, the more excited I was to start ETM. I had so much more to learn.

CHAPTER TWENTY-SEVEN

FORBIDDEN LIGHT

Early Monday morning, I roared my Ford Fairmont to life. I didn't want to be late. The last few months, I had dragged myself to North Lake High, but on my first day of ETM, I couldn't get there fast enough.

I parked, retraced my steps to the portable in the back and grasped the smooth doorknob. On the other side of this door was a real fresh start. I took a deep breath and forced my hand to open it. Inside, teen girls' laughter and babies' cooing filled the room. Sweet baby powder mixed with breakfast aroma.

I must've been standing awkwardly at the door for way too long. Meka and Suzanne waved me over to their table. I was wanted here. I removed my backpack and clutched it to my chest to navigate the maze of tables, desks, and pregnant bellies.

Since my hands were full, Suzanne pulled out a chair for me.

"Thanks." I dropped into it.

"You're welcome." She picked up a piece of crunchy bacon off a plastic tray. "When it's our turn to cook breakfast you gotta come in half an hour early."

Even if there was something breakfast-worthy at the trailer, I usually forgot to eat in the mornings. I wouldn't have either excuse now.

Meka bounced Dante on a knee. "I know how it is—being the new girl. You ever got questions we got answers."

"I appreciate it. This is all so new to me." Although I'd been there less than five minutes and didn't have any questions yet, clearly, Suzanne and Meka would be the ones I'd go to if I did. My stomach growled loud enough for them to hear.

"Go get breakfast," they both chimed.

I headed to the kitchen area. The breakfast duty group had already begun tackling their dishes. One of them handed me a tray of fluffy eggs, bacon, and toast. "Here, we saved this for you."

"Thanks." This place was too good to be true.

"For sure." Then she collected dirty trays from around the room.

While I inhaled breakfast, Suzanne and Meka chatted. Meka complained about her lack of sleep due to feeding a hungry Dante every few hours. Suzanne griped about her own sleep deprivation due to a kicking baby, adding her eagerness to be unpregnant to sleep like before. Based on Meka's comments, Suzanne wouldn't be getting much sleep after having her baby either.

As if she read my mind, she looked at me and said, "I'm giving my baby up for adoption, just so you know." She smacked her gum, blew a bubble, and popped it.

"Oh, okay." I wasn't sure what else to say. Choosing to give up her baby must have been tough. I didn't know her personal story, but I assumed she wanted a better life for her child—a better life than she could provide. I often questioned if my baby deserved a different mother than me.

Mrs. Keene grouped me with Meka, Suzanne, and another teen mom. After breakfast, we spent the first half of class in Mrs. Keene's lecture, "Budgeting For Baby." I knew I needed a crib, not just that roadside trash playpen Addis had brought over, but the list extended beyond that: bottles, pacifiers, and diapers, and more.

"I'll do what I can for you. But, ladies, this is also your responsibility. If you don't have a job, ask neighbors if you can walk their dog or babysit. Something. Your babies are gonna depend on you for a long time. Now's the time to prepare yourselves."

I felt grateful for the job with Julie. And next week, in her absence, I'd make extra cash. Mayflower had a Baby Superstore where I could likely find everything my baby would need. Although this was overwhelming, I wanted to make Mrs. Keene proud.

Groups rotated through centers the rest of the day—meal-planning, then infant care, and finally record-keeping. We had to write down everything, including what we ate, how much water we drank, how many hours of sleep we got, how much exercise—which I got zero except for the walk Mrs. Keene made the class take every day after lunch—things I'd never even given a second thought.

Girls who had given birth had a bunch of stuff to write down about their babies, like how many ounces of formula they drank or how many times they nursed, how much they slept, and detailed information about every diaper change. Poop had a significant role in baby record-keeping.

"Ladies, ladies, I need everyone's attention." Mrs. Keene snapped her fingers, and we all stopped what we were doing and gathered around her. "The North Lake Community College art class will be here Friday to do their annual holiday project with you. They're going to help you create a 'Baby's First Christmas' bib. Be thinking about what you'd like to put on yours. Trust me; they'll have plenty of ideas if you don't."

Meka nudged me. "Those art students. We did this last year. Be fair warned, whatever ideas you have, they'll likely override and over-deliver. Your baby's bib will look like it should be framed and hanging in an art museum." She laughed as she strapped Dante into his car seat.

Car seat—I'd need one of those—check. "I'll keep that in mind. Have a good night. See you Wednesday." I appreciated having an almost-friend here.

"See you later, AC." She looped her arm through the car seat handle, cradled it in the crook of her elbow, and effortlessly carried Dante away.

I moved my arm as if sweeping it through a car seat handle to carry my baby. At some point, I should probably ask her to show me how she does it. I'd heard someone say a maternal instinct kicks in all on its own when you have a baby.

Those same instincts must also fade. At least if you consider my mother's actions as a standard of measurement.

A bell rang. "Girls, have a good evening. See you Wednesday. And don't forget to write down everything in your nutrition journal for the nursing students to review."

Arriving home to an empty trailer, I threw my backpack on the table and pulled out the spiral notebook Mrs. Keene had given me to use as a nutrition journal. She'd told us to drink a gallon of water a day.

In the fridge sat a milk jug with about two tablespoons of milk swimming in a shallow pool of curds with an expiry date of last week. I poured the thick, putrid liquid down the sink and then rinsed it with the last of some laundry detergent I'd taken from the laundromat to use to wash dishes.

I grabbed a marker from my backpack and wrote "Water" on the label. Concerned Dale might drink out of it; I added the word "Angela's" above it.

The broken cabinet I used as a pantry resembled Mother Hubbard's cupboard and offered me nothing but a can of chicken noodle soup for dinner. Fortunately, the grocery store next to the laundromat stocked mostly generic brand foods, stretching my modest income slightly further. Sometimes I hid food in my dresser drawer. But because Dale was too lazy to heat a can of soup, it had remained safe in the pantry.

As the golden liquid boiled on the stove, I wrote in my nutrition journal. Because of ETM, I'd had eggs, bacon, and toast for breakfast. Lunch consisted of my usual bologna sandwich on two slices of stale white bread followed by a can of salty soup for dinner. Seeing it in writing, not the healthiest of days.

I popped the horse pills Dr. Patton told me to take and downed them with a large gulp from my water jug, gagging a little because the bitterness of sour milk still lingered. Then I read the label on the large orange bottle. I'd never done that before. "Complete Multivitamin for Mom and Baby, Folic Acid to support fetal development, DHA to support brain development, Calcium to support bone development." Hopefully, these would help make up the difference in my lagging diet. I needed to try and eat better. But to do that, I'd need more money from someone who didn't really like giving it.

About that time, I heard the trucks' rumbling engine. The back door swung open and in walked a very tired-looking and dirty Dale. Must have been a long day. While not the most consistent employee, he proved to be a hard worker when he showed up.

"Hey, looks like you had a tough day. Can I get you anything?"

"A different job. That new apartment complex we're framing is a killer." He sat down at the table with me and pulled off his work boots.

I looked down at my nutrition journal and decided this was about as good a time as any to go for it. "One of the requirements at my new school is to keep a nutrition journal. And the nursing students review it. I'd like to eat healthier; you know for the baby. But I don't really make enough to buy any more food than I already am."

He took off his ballcap and tossed it on the table. "Damn, Angela. I don't bleed money. The rent, utilities, expenses of my truck, I can barely make ends meet as it is. And really that's all you gotta cover is a few of your own meals. I'm doing everything I can." He lit a cigarette and went to the fridge for a beer. His two expensive vices would easily supply us with enough money for better quality food.

"I'm sorry. You're right. I appreciate that you pay for everything else."

He stood and took a worn leather wallet out of his back pocket. "Here. An extra ten bucks a month. That's all I can do." He threw the bill on top of my nutrition journal. Then stomped down the hallway, a trail of smoke following behind him.

A tear slid down my cheek as I took the bill off the table and stuffed it into my backpack. To him, our child's health amounted to a mere ten dollars.

The next day, I attended my academic courses, senior English and Algebra. The classes felt more like independent study, overseen by a teaching assistant. He provided me two textbooks, two syllabi, and pointed me to a study carol. "If you have questions, raise your hand; otherwise, this is a work-at-your-own-pace set-up. The quicker you work, the quicker you finish. Got it."

"Got it." I took my things to a study carol in the corner next to a sunny window. I kind of liked the idea of working on my own. If I paced myself well, I could make it on time to graduate with Julie and Andrew.

The baby kicked—a reminder that even if I finished by the time they did, I wouldn't wear a cap and gown with them and walk across a stage. The Adult Education Center didn't host a graduation ceremony. Everyone finished at different times—if they finished at all.

I opened Senior English and lost myself in the world of Kate Chopin's *Awakening*. I wanted an awakening like Edna Pontellier—to feel loved and have fun without the tragic ending. But so far, my life seemed to be hell-bent on breaking me. I read, "A certain light was beginning to dawn dimly within her—the light which, showing the way, forbids it." I knew I had a light in me, yet like Edna, at every turn, it was forbidden.

CHAPTER TWENTY-EIGHT

CHRISTMAS AT CLUB KEENE

BY FRIDAY, I HAD a good routine down. But when I walked into ETM, twice as many bodies filled the already full space.

A bubbly brunette in a paint-smeared smock, greeted me like a guest. "Hi. Welcome to the North Lake Art Class Bib Design. Here's a questionnaire to help the design team. You're working with team number seven. That's Kevin and Claire. The tables are marked. Bye." She waved at me as she looked over my head and greeted the next girl behind me.

I couldn't draw a stick figure, much less design a piece of clothing. Clothing—I need clothes for the baby. Luckily, I could get most of them here—check.

When I reached station seven, Kevin said, "Hi. Can you give me your questionnaire?"

I handed him my blank page. "There's nothing on it. Sorry, art just isn't my thing."

He and Claire shared an eye roll. Claire snatched it and started asking questions. "Do you like modern, renaissance, or abstract art? Or is there some other style you prefer?"

I had expected puff paints and glue on red and green pom-poms. I shrugged. "Sorry, I got nothing."

She snatched a pen off the table. "We'll go with"—eyes examined me from head to toe—"exaggerated realism. Next question, do you have a color palette in mind?"

"A what?"

Kevin interrupted. "Girl, have you ever seen a color wheel?"

Their condescending attitude irritated me. "No, why would I?"

He picked up a circular piece of cardboard lined with small colored squares along its edge. "This is a color wheel. A palette is when you... ugh, never mind." Then he turned to Claire. "Let's just pick it for her. She obviously doesn't get it."

Then he turned back to me. "Sorry, not that it's a bad thing. I mean, I couldn't do the whole baby thing. So, we're even."

I wanted to punch them both.

"Listen," Claire whispered. "We'll do it for you. Honestly, we get photographed with the final project for a competition. We just wanna win. So just stand there and act like you're helping, and we'll take care of everything else, kay?" She faked a smile as she awaited my response.

"Well, it's your lucky day. I excel at pretending." I snatched the paper from her and scribbled my name at the top.

I knew Mrs. Keene meant well. But this bib-making felt like a publicity stunt for North Lake Community College.

By day's end, my baby's bib resembled a mini version of a vintage scene straight from a Norman Rockwell calendar. After the obligatory photo with the very proud design team number seven, I hurried away.

Outside, I tossed the bib in the garbage can near the parking lot on top of about five or six others. Norman Rockwell's wholesome reflection of American culture could kiss my ass.

The rest of the week, I worked late hours at the laundromat. I used the extra cash to make some chicken and rice with canned veggies to eat on all week. My journal thanked me. Dale and I saw each other only in passing, a welcomed break.

Just as I'd settled back into bed after a middle-of-the-night bathroom visit, a loud knock at the back door startled me. The red glow of the clock radio's digits showed 1:00 am. I leaped out of bed, worried someone might be hurt, and peeked through the back door window—no one.

Then another knock followed by "Angela...open...." Dale had arrived and break time had ended.

I opened the door and the rancid smell of vomit hit me. Dale lay on the deck with puke streaking down his clothes.

"Where've you been? Let me guess, playing bingo at the American Legion?" I asked well aware that my sarcasm could have consequences.

"You're funny, you know that." He hiccup-laughed as he tried to stand, "Uncle Tuck's. Company Christmas Party," he mumbled, then fell onto me smearing puke onto my shoulder.

While leaving him outside in the December chill would be the sweetest of revenge, I couldn't bring myself to do that. "Let's get you inside." I gagged as I dragged him to the couch.

He slurred. "You don't like me. Why're you still here?"

Good question, Dale.

Like I'd done so many times with my mother, I pulled off his boots, the vomit-stained t-shirt, and pushed his jelly-legs onto the couch.

"Answer me. You're having my baby, and you don't even like me." He fumbled forward, failing at trying to light a cigarette.

If I lit it for him maybe he'd burn down the whole damn trailer.

Instead, I went to the kitchen and got him a glass of water from the sink, not from my cold jug in the fridge, and put it to his lips. "Here. Drink this."

He took a big gulp, then spat it in my face.

"Why did you do that? I'm trying to help you." I said as I wiped my face with the puke-free sleeve of my nightgown.

"Because you don't like me. You think I'm disgusting. You know what's disgusting? You—a pregnant teenager. That's disgusting."

Alcohol—the ultimate truth serum.

"Yeah, well, I didn't get this way by myself." I covered him with the Afghan off the back of the couch.

Pass out already, please.

"Mama says you think you're better than me. But I work hard for us. I do."

"You need to sleep it off. We can talk in the morning."

He reached his arms out toward me. "Come here. Come here. I'm sorry. Lie down with me. I didn't mean it."

"No, I'm not lying down with you. I'm going to bed."

He grabbed my hand and pulled me toward him. "Give me a good-night kiss. It's almost Christmas."

I jerked my hand away. "No. I'm going to bed."

Thankfully, his arm went limp by his side, and he started snoring.

I headed to the bedroom and changed out of my only nightgown that fit into a worn maternity dress. Then crawled back onto the lumpy mattress and stared up at the cracked ceiling. Dale was right. I didn't like him. His words should've hurt me. But they didn't. They terrified me. Because if this glimpse represented our future, I dreaded the rest of mine.

Chapter Twenty-Nine

A Stocking Full of Coal

The rapid ringing of the front desk's bell ended my bathroom visit pre-stream. I yanked the elastic waistband of my maternity pants over my bulging belly.

"Hello, hello. Is anyone here? Hello."

"Coming." When I turned the bathroom corner, I wanted to run back.

"Hey, I know you. Your name is—wait, don't tell me—Angela Carter? Am I right?" At the laundromat desk stood the captain of my cheer squad—my old squad—Erika Sterling.

I crossed my arms over my stomach and tried to suck it in. "Yep. It's me."

"I thought you were sent up North or something."

"Nope, still kicking it around good ole North Lake."

"And look at you with that big ole baby belly. Goodness. That's why I hardly recognized you." Her ice blue eyes scanned the laundromat. "Where's Julie? I thought she worked here."

"She's on holiday with her family. What can I help you with?" I wanted her gone.

"Oh, that's right. She did tell me she was going out of town. Cabin in the mountains, right? I totally forgot, duh." She smacked herself on the forehead.

My heart sank. Maybe she was my new replacement.

She tossed a couple of plastic-covered dresses on the counter. "Mom's been baking like all day. I really need these washed and ironed for Midnight Mass and Christmas Dinner. I'll even toss in a small tip." She winked. "I'm sure you could use it for baby stuff or whatever." Pearly whites sparkled behind glossy pink lips.

The nerve of her to bribe me so she could attend extravagant holiday events where everyone was over-dressed, over-gifted, and over-fed. But I swallowed my pride and agreed to wash her damn dresses.

It was five o'clock p.m. I'd barely have time to get to Dad's. I guess that didn't matter as much as the money did. "Sure. Come back in an hour."

"Thanks. Gotta bounce. Last-minute hair appointment. Bye."

"Your beautiful holiday dresses will be cleaned and ready to go."

I could cut one tiny thread. She'd never even know until it started unraveling at Midnight Mass. But instead, like the good girl I pretended to be, I meticulously washed and ironed her dresses as if they were mine and I had fancy dinner plans.

She was fashionably late picking up her garments. "You like?" She patted the tall mountain of blonde hair professionally twirled, twisted, and plastered into a gorgeous updo.

"It looks great." I pulled at my long brown mane tied back with a scrunchie. I hadn't even had a trim in nearly a year.

She slid a five-dollar bill across the counter. "Put the regular charge on Mom's tab, Sophia Sterling. Merry Christmas." She tossed the dresses over her shoulder and the doorbell jingled behind her.

I crushed the bill into a tiny ball and dug my fingernails into my palm. I wished five dollars didn't matter so much. But it did. Every dollar mattered. I unfolded the crushed bill and smoothed it out, then wiped my misty eyes.

I'd racked up nearly a hundred dollars. Earlier in the week, I spent fifteen on Christmas gifts for Amber, Levi, and Cole. But other than food and gas, I couldn't spend another dime.

"I'm leaving," I called out to Dale while he was in the shower.

"What? Where are you going? I told you we were going to Mama and Daddy's for Christmas Dinner." He yelled from behind a green shower curtain missing two hooks.

"Sorry, I already told my father I was coming over. I left Cole's gift on the kitchen table." I would've loved to see Cole open the coloring book and crayons. But after what Dale had told me, I wasn't ready to face Addis.

He poked out a sudsy head. "What about Daddy's Christmas? Don't I get something? You don't have to buy me nothing. Just a little appreciation."

Clearly, he had no recollection of the night before. The baby kicked and rolled, churning the bile in my stomach. "Sorry, I told my dad I'd be there like a half hour ago." I darted out of the bathroom before he could say anything else. I hoped he would drink too much at his parents to come home. There was nothing I wanted to give him for Christmas. He wasn't worth a stocking full of goddamn coal.

CHAPTER THIRTY

FULL BELLY, EMPTY HEART

I KNOCKED ON DAD'S apartment door.

"Sissy!" Amber wore red head to toe, including a crooked bow atop her light brown hair.

Good try, Dad. I smiled.

"I've got presents." I teased.

"I'll go put them under the tree." She grabbed the packages I held out. "I made all the decorations myself," she said as she skipped away singing Jingle Bells.

This wasn't a fancy holiday party, but I was with my family—most of them. That meant something.

A baking turkey led me to the tiny kitchen where Dad and Levi were chopping vegetables for the Carter Family's famous cornbread stuffing.

"Number One." Dad wiped his hands on his apron, wrapped his firm arms around me, and then returned to his chopping.

"Ange." Levi hugged me. For the first time in a long time, sharp lines weren't poking through his collarbone.

"I thought I was the only one gaining weight," I joked.

"This isn't just weight. It's fifteen pounds of pure muscle." Levi responded. He flexed his biceps. "I got back on the weight-lifting team."

"What! Levi, I'm seriously so happy!" I wondered if that had to do with Mom. This wasn't the time to ask, but it left me feeling hopeful—at least for Levi. The Coach would no doubt get him back on the straight and narrow. Something that was too late for me.

My rumbling tummy squashed my self-pity. "It smells delicious. I'm starved." I'd have another nutritious meal to write in my journal.

"Go check out Amber's handiwork."

Amber sat arranging presents under a Christmas tree covered in popcorn strings and coffee filter snowflakes.

"Great job." Although I was sure Amber enjoyed making the decorations, I couldn't help but wonder what had happened to all our family Christmas ornaments. Had Mom decorated a tree with them? Did they make her miss our family? Miss me?

I surveyed the other two open-doored rooms. Dad's bedroom barely fit a queen bed. A set of bunk beds filled another small room. No spot for a pregnant teen with a soon-to-be infant.

"Dinner is served." Dad carried a platter overfilled with turkey and stuffing to his small table. Dried sage and rosemary filled the air.

I pushed back thoughts of Christmas past and embraced the fact that at least I'd have a full belly tonight. Each bite of warm, soft stuffing and juicy turkey caused the baby to kick faster and faster. We both needed this meal more than I realized.

With a full mouth, Amber asked, "When can we open presents?"

"Finish your dinner first." Dad pointed his fork toward my baby sister. "And remember your table manners."

It had been a long time since something as trivial as table manners had mattered to anyone in my family. I slid my napkin off the table and placed it onto the sliver of my lap unoccupied by round belly.

After dinner, we gathered around the Christmas tree, and Dad passed out gifts. Amber loved the Strawberry Shortcake puzzle I got her. Levi also liked the ACDC t-shirt I'd found at a thrift store.

Dad passed me his gift. Inside a gold bag wrapped in glittery tissue paper was a brand-new soft maternity nightgown. "I love it. Thank you so much."

"I didn't know exactly what to get you, but I remember your mother lived in her nightgown when she was pregnant with you. I thought you'd like something cozy to spend the next few months in until we have a baby in the family."

Ignoring his comment about my mother, I clutched the nightgown to my chest, not only warmed by its softness but also by my father's words, *until we have a baby in the family*. For a fleeting moment, I thought everything would be okay.

Amber drew me a picture of her and me with a baby between us, and Levi gave me a tree ornament that read "Baby's First Christmas." Then Dad handed me my last gift, a Christmas card from my mother with a twenty-dollar bill tucked inside. She hadn't written anything on the card except for "Merry Christmas, Love, Mom."

No "Sorry I kicked you out of the house." "Sorry, you live in a trailer park." "Sorry, you are pregnant." Nope, she was sorry for nothing. A twenty-dollar bill wasn't a drop in the bucket compared to what she owed me—to the debt she never could repay. You can't buy someone's lost childhood back for them.

A decorated Christmas tree, a full tummy of holiday food, and my family—well, most of them—almost gave me the warm fuzzies. Almost. Instead, bitterness overtook me. It was all fake and temporary.

Amber and Levi laughed and pounded each other with rubber-balled paddleboards.

Unlike my siblings, that Christmas Eve I wouldn't sleep under my father's roof. Instead, I had to go back to a trailer that smelled like a pine air freshener, mold, and cigarette smoke. I had to sleep in bed with someone who wanted things from me I didn't want to do. I didn't get to sleep inside the home of someone who wanted to protect me.

I grabbed my gifts. "Hey guys, I'm really tired. I gotta go."

"What? We still have Christmas carols to sing and dessert. Can't you stay at least another hour?" Dad asked.

"I need to go. Sorry. Thanks for everything." I quickly hugged them all goodbye and hurried to my car.

Even with my own family, I was an outsider. Everywhere I tried to belong, I failed. As much as I loathed being in that trailer, it was the only place that I didn't feel less than. At least in that hellhole, I didn't have to pretend. The worse the version of myself that I became, the more Dale and the trailer dug in their claws.

When I arrived back at the trailer, it welcomed me with an eerie darkness—a darkness that lured me with the promise to protect my secrets. The things I did with Dale, that he did to me, the things I didn't protest. The things that made me the Slut, Whore, Pregnant Teen. The trailer wouldn't tell anyone.

Dale's truck wasn't in the driveway. Inside, I flicked on a small fluorescent bulb above a sink full of crusty dishes. On the kitchen table sat a not-so-well-wrapped gift from Dale. Totally unexpected. I hadn't gotten him anything. I unwrapped the loosely taped red and gold paper. Inside was a pair of slippers two sizes too large. Since the last thing he'd given me was a sleazy piece of lingerie, at least this gift I could use. I kicked off my sneakers and slid my swollen feet into the slippers.

I tucked the twenty dollars from Mom into my underwear drawer. I had one hundred and forty-five dollars to supplement my food budget and to buy things for the baby. Knowing I had that much money made me feel secure—ish.

Then, I ripped the tags off the nightgown and put it on. Before I hopped into bed, I pulled out the Christmas ornament Levi had given me. Next December, I'd be the mother of an eight-month-old baby. I hoped to God we weren't here. But even if there was a God, I doubted he was listening to me. I went to sleep with a full belly, but my heart was empty.

CHAPTER THIRTY-ONE

DAMN, IT'S A GIRL

"WE GOTTA GO. WE should've left five minutes ago," I shouted through the closed bathroom door. I'd been looking forward to this day for months. I wanted Julie to come too, but Dale had said no. Since he was finally showing interest, I didn't push it.

The toilet flushed. "I'm coming. Why'd you make the damn appointment so early?" Dale didn't like getting up before eight unless he was hunting.

But I wanted to get to ETM on time, so I ignored his comment. "Are you excited to find out if we are having a boy or a girl?" Conversations with Dale were more complicated and harder to come by these days. The farther my pregnancy progressed, the more he distanced himself from me, which wasn't the worst thing.

"Mama says the Simmons don't have girls. It's a boy. He'll be a deer hunter just like his daddy."

I rolled my eyes behind him. "I only want a healthy baby." I crossed my fingers because, secretly, I did prefer a girl.

As we walked to the clinic entrance, Dale said, "You go on in. I'm gonna have a smoke first."

Of course, he was. But at least he was here. At least he was attempting to do something for me. I had to give him credit for that.

I walked in alone, checked in, and sat in the waiting room. Dale came in a few minutes later, reeking of smoke. Pregnancy had heightened all my senses, and I could hardly stand the smell of tobacco anymore. I turned away and took a few deep breaths before facing him and saying, "Thank you for coming. It means a lot."

Although I usually avoided touching Dale at all costs, I wanted this moment to feel special. He was this baby's father. I slowly reached for his hand. He didn't jerk away. He actually smiled at me. It wasn't an *I'm so excited* smile. It was more like an *I'm so sorry* smile. But at least it was a smile.

"Angela Carter," called a nurse holding a folder.

This was it. I was about to find out the gender of my child. I let go of Dale's hand to push myself up. He stood and helped me. "Thanks."

"You got it." Then he shoved his hands into the pockets of his faded jeans and fell in line behind me.

"This way." The nurse pointed to a small room with an examination table and a large computer-looking machine and told me Dr. Patton would be in soon.

"Well, this looks expensive." In his dirty work boots, stained t-shirt and oversized flannel, Dale looked completely out of place in the pristine examination room.

"The Health Department is free. You don't have to pay anything. Pretty cool, right?" I hoped that made him feel more comfortable. I needed him to relax so I could.

"I'm paying for it in taxes."

We both knew he paid no taxes. His boss paid all the framers under the table. But I didn't say anything.

The door opened, and a grinning Dr. Patton entered. "Angela, nice to see you again. This is a big day."

He turned to Dale and extended his hand. "Hi, I'm Doctor Patton. You must be the proud soon-to-be father."

Dale shook the doctor's hand like it was his first time using the common greeting.

"So today, we're going to give Angela a sonogram. It's a non-invasive procedure for us to measure the baby to confirm if he or she is growing appropriately and to hone in on a more accurate due date. If your little one cooperates, we might also be able to determine the gender."

"The what?" Dale squinted as if he'd never heard the term before.

Humiliation consumed me. "The gender means if it is a boy or girl. I told you that."

Dr. Patton chuckled. "No worries. This is a new experience for you both. Then he patted the table. "Hop up here, and we'll get started."

I climbed onto the table, unbuttoned the middle buttons of the pink maternity dress, exposed my rounded belly, and settled back. I'd picked the dress out from the Share Closet at ETM, especially for today. As if the color choice could somehow influence the baby's gender.

Dr. Patton put a cold jelly on my tummy and moved the wand slowly over it. Although the footage was grainy, I could make out movement on the video screen.

"Look here. This is an arm. This is a leg." Dr. Patton pointed to different parts of the baby. "Your little one is very busy in there."

"I can feel it." As those tiny legs kicked on the screen, I felt movement inside me. Months ago, I didn't believe I was even pregnant. But watching my baby on the screen made it feel even more real. I wiped away tears so Dale wouldn't see. I hoped he'd get emotional during the sonogram. But he stood silently in the corner.

"Mom and Dad, your baby looks great. I'm going to take a few measurements, and then we'll see if we can find out if this busy little one is a boy or a girl."

Regardless of Dale's lack of enthusiasm, this was the most miraculous thing I'd ever experienced. I could see our baby—my baby— with my own eyes—the baby I'd hold in my arms in just a few months.

"Okay, little one, who are you?" Dr. Patton moved the wand meticulously over one area until, "Aha. Mom and Dad, are you sure you wanna know?"

Before Dale could say anything, I quickly replied, "Yes."

"Alrighty. You are the lucky parents of—a baby girl."

The news broke Dale's silence. "Damn, it's a girl! That has to be wrong. My family only has boys."

Dr. Patton laughed again. "Unfortunately, that's not how this works. The good news is, all indicators today appear that she's healthy, and the due date is accurate."

I was having a daughter. I wanted to scream with elation, but Dale's embarrassing comment infuriated me. I attempted to turn his sour mood around. "Isn't it great we know she's healthy? You're gonna have a sweet daughter."

Instead of responding to my comment, he said, "I'm gonna have a smoke. Meet you in the car." Then he left and shut the door behind him, leaving Dr. Patton and me alone.

I wanted to bolt out the door. Not with Dale, but away from the humiliation he'd left me with. But I was stuck on a table, half-undressed with a sonogram wand on my belly.

"Dr. Patton, I'm so sorry. He really wanted a son."

Dr. Patton must've wondered how I ended up with someone like Dale. I often did.

He wiped the jelly off my abdomen and put the wand away. "It's okay. I've seen it all. I'm sure he'll come around. I'll send the nurse in for a follow-up and to schedule your next appointment."

I buttoned my dress. I wanted to say, *No, he won't.* But I only said, "Thank you."

"You're welcome. And you're doing a great job taking care of both yourself and the baby. You could stand to gain a few pounds, but other than that, keep up what you're doing."

As I walked to the car, I couldn't help but think of my mother. I had a connection with her now; we both had daughters. Anger and hurt—mostly hurt—still lingered at what she'd done to me, but I wanted to forgive her. I needed to forgive her. I needed to be able to call her and talk about pregnancy and babies. She would be my daughter's grandmother. If being a mother wasn't enough to inspire her to turn her life around, maybe being a grandmother would.

I opened the car door to a red-faced Dale white-knuckling the steering wheel. I slid into the passenger seat and tried to think of something to say to lessen his brewing outburst.

"I'm really glad you were here today." I hoped the lie sounded sincere.

He slammed the steering wheel. "That damn doctor don't know jack. You can't tell anything from that crappy machine."

"You're right. It could be wrong. But I really don't care if it's a boy or girl as long as we have a healthy baby." I hoped I hadn't pushed it too far.

"In case you didn't get the memo, I ain't too happy about you railroading me into a relationship by getting yourself knocked up. And with a girl." He cranked the car and spun out of the clinic parking lot, leaving skid marks behind. "At least if it was a boy, I know what that's like. I figure I'd know how to be a daddy to a boy."

So that was it. Dale was scared he wouldn't know how to parent a daughter. At least he was thinking about being a parent. But I wasn't going to let him place all the blame on me. "This was an accident. We're both to blame, but we need to make the best of it for our child."

He sped up and raised his voice. "You wanted this, and you never asked me. You're lucky I'm taking care of you."

"Yes, I know I'm lucky." If he knew what the word meant, I'd tell him what he said was hyperbolic to the nth degree.

"Please, please slow down. The last thing we need is a speeding ticket." I begged. He was driving at least fifty miles per hour in downtown North Lake where the speed limit was thirty-five. The local cops were tough on traffic violations. But it wasn't just a ticket I was worried about. The way Dale drove was a good indication of his mood.

The fear of a speeding ticket must have worked. As the vehicle slowed, so did his breathing. Then much to my surprise, he spoke. "Sorry. This is just all new to me. It's gonna take me some time."

I let go of the grab handle above the door I hadn't even realized I was clutching. "I know. There's plenty of time. For both of us. And thank you for slowing down." I rested my head against the window, placed my hands on my belly, and closed my eyes. I was having a daughter. I smiled a little. I'd won this one.

Back home, I sat at the kitchen table to finish up some homework before heading to school. Dale plopped on the couch, crossed his boots on the coffee table, and lit a cigarette. He exhaled the smoke louder than usual.

The hairs on the back of my neck stood on end. He should've already left for work.

" I shouldn't have acted like that. I'm sorry. Come here?"

No way I was moving out of my chair. "Everything's okay. Thanks for apologizing. I need to finish this assignment." I replied without turning in his direction.

"Angela, baby, come here." A sickening attempt at seduction dripped off his words.

I ignored him. But I feared where this was headed. A tear splat on my algebra homework, smearing the answer to $2x - 3y =$. And algebra wasn't easy for me. I wiped another away. I crossed my legs. Tight. My breathing shallowed. I'd avoided doing this with Dale for weeks. Apparently, my streak would end today.

The couch creaked as he rose, and boots clunked on the floor behind me, an unpleasant reminder of that first night Dale kissed me at his parents' place. I wish I could go back and tell myself, *Run. Get away from him. Dale Simmons will not be your hero. He'll be your captor.* Here was another chance for me to run, yet I didn't. Instead, I sat frozen solid. Easy prey.

When he was right behind me, he leaned down and whispered, "You gotta girl. You should be happy. Let's celebrate. It's been so long."

I unfroze and put my hand over my nose to avoid inhaling his hot, humid, smoke-tainted breath.

He grabbed my hair and pulled my head back. Not enough to really hurt, but enough to get my attention.

"Let go. Please leave me alone. I told you I need to finish this assignment."

He yanked a little harder before dropping my hair and moving his hands to my chest. "Baby, I only need a few minutes. You've got time."

"Dale, please, no." I pushed his hands away and like the flip of a switch, Dale went from coaxing boyfriend to angry abuser.

He kicked my chair almost knocking me over. His voice thundered and his limbs flailed. "You wanna know why I'm pissed? I don't get you. You live here with me by your choice. I pay all the goddamn bills for us both. We're having a kid together. If we're together, we're together. And this is part of it."

To avoid risking getting him angrier, I accepted his terms. "I'm sorry. You're right." I rose from the chair. Tears streamed down my face at the ease of my defeat, at how broken I was.

In the bedroom, he shoved me on the bed and yanked up the maternity dress.

Terrified he might hurt the baby; I swallowed my tears and forced my body to go limp. I let Dale do what he wanted to do.

The day most expectant parents found out their baby's gender, they would talk about baby names and nursery colors. They might celebrate the good news with family and friends at a fancy restaurant.

But not for me. The day I found out I was having a daughter, I allowed her father to rape me.

After he was done, he buttoned his jeans. "See that wasn't so bad." Then he pulled a five-dollar bill out of his wallet. "Here. Take yourself out to lunch. I gotta get to work."

Five-Dollar-Whore That's who I was. After the door to the trailer slammed shut, I screamed into the pillow until my throat was raw and let the tears flow.

When I had no tears left to cry, I pushed myself up. I didn't know how, but I had to get out of here. What I did know was I'd never let Dale Simmons do that to me again.

CHAPTER THIRTY-TWO

A HONEY OAK CRIB

SCALDING WATER BEAT DOWN on me in a too-long shower. I soaped myself from the waist down and rinsed at least five times. I'd have to shift some money from our food budget to make up the difference in what I'd just cost us in gas to heat the water. But even when I got out, I still felt dirty. Some filth wouldn't wash down a drain no matter how hot or long the shower.

I slipped on elastic-waisted pants and a maternity smock. Even though I hadn't eaten that morning, and I should've been hungry, Dale had crushed my appetite. And I wouldn't give him the satisfaction of using the five bucks for lunch.

But I refused to let him spoil everything about this day. I refused to let him take this from me. Despite what had happened earlier, I'd celebrate in my own way.

I picked the pink dress I'd borrowed from ETM off the floor and threw it in the garbage. That dress would never again see the light of day.

I called Mrs. Keene and told her I felt unwell. After what had happened with Dale, I needed some space before I faced anyone. But I did tell her I found out I was having a girl. She congratulated me and said she'd see me later in the week.

Next, I called my father at work. With each ring of the phone, Dale faded into the background and my excitement about having a daughter grew. By the time I was transferred to his office, I couldn't help but blurt it out. "Hi, Dad. I wanted you to be the first to know. You're going to have a granddaughter."

"Well, hey, Number One. That's the best news I've heard all day."

"Thanks. It's good news to me, too. I'm going to go window shopping today. I mean, I can't buy anything, not yet, but I can look and plan."

"Why aren't you at school?"

If he knew the truth, he wouldn't want me here. Maybe he'd get a bigger apartment with enough room for me and a baby. But I didn't dare tell. Fear of Dale—and fear of what people would think of me—kept the truth buried deep. So deep that sometimes I just pretended it wasn't real.

"I had my doctor appointment this morning. By the time I got to school, I wouldn't have had but a few hours." The lies formed without hesitation. So easily, even I almost believed them.

He mumbled something to a co-worker. "Sorry about that. Got a sales meeting in a few."

"I know you have to go. I can't wait to tell Amber this afternoon. But will you tell Mom for me?"

"Of course. And just so you know, I hope my granddaughter turns out just like her mother."

I didn't want her to be anything like me. At least not now, but maybe one day. Maybe that's what he meant. "Thanks. Bye. Love you."

"Love you, too, Number One."

Now that she was back from her trip, I'd tell Julie in person at the laundromat. She had already been calling herself "Aunt Jules" for weeks. She would be so excited that she could start buying all the pink.

I drove a half-hour to the closest baby superstore. The sweet smell of baby powder greeted me. This was exactly what I needed.

A smiling lady staffed a desk at the front entry. "Hi, are you here to open a registry?"

"A what?"

"A baby registry. Here, fill this out, and I'll get you started."

She handed me a clipboard with a questionnaire. It included information about me, which I filled in, and the father, which I left blank. Other questions included baby's gender, due date, and baby shower date. Girls like me didn't have baby showers. But I could pretend. I picked a random date in April and handed it back.

"Perfect. Take this device and scan the barcode of the items you want. Bring it back to me, and anyone that comes in shopping for you will know what to buy. Here's a list of the most common items new babies need. Any questions?"

"No, thank you." Finding the items on the lengthy list felt like a scavenger hunt.

The first section on the list was "Feeding." I followed a large sign hanging from the ceiling. There were three or four aisles of shelving full of baby bottles, tiny dishes, cutlery, and bibs. I picked up a box of bottles, found the barcode, and scanned them. *Beep. I bet Mom will get me these,* I pretended. Next, I scanned a cute pack of bibs decorated with pastel farm animals. These were much more baby-friendly than that ridiculous creation Claire and Kevin made. *Beep.* I scanned a few more items in "Feeding" before moving on.

The next section was "Nursery." Roughly thirty beautiful cribs fitted with gorgeous baby linens sat on display. I walked by several and ran my hand along their smooth railings and caressed their plush bedding.

Then I saw it—a honey oak crib with elegant pastel bedding. A rose-colored skirt brushed the floor. A plump mattress wore paisley-printed sheets. A matching change table and paisley diaper stacker flanked one-side of the crib. On the other, sat an over-sized cream-colored glider with a footstool. I sat down on the glider and put my feet up.

I closed my eyes and pretended the scanner was my newborn daughter. I rocked her as she wound down for the night. Then I looked at the price tag on the glider—more than double what I'd saved. Next, I checked the price tag on the crib. It was nearly triple what I had hidden in my underwear drawer. I wouldn't have a glider to rock my daughter in, and she wouldn't have a crib to sleep in, much-less beautiful bedding.

My daughter would sleep in the hand-me-down playpen from Addis that looked like she'd dug it out of someone's trash.

I bet Mrs. Van registered here for her baby shower. Nathan would sleep in one of these gorgeous cribs with some expensive fire truck-themed bedding. His nursery wouldn't have anything second-hand. My daughter's nursery would have nothing new.

I delivered the scanner back to the woman at the entrance. "Sorry, I just remembered, I have an appointment. I'll come back and finish later."

"No problem, but don't wait too long. Your family and friends need time to purchase you all the latest and greatest baby gadgets."

I wanted to be excited about this baby. But the mundane tasks of picking Amber up every day and folding laundry with Julie became less of a distraction and more a reminder that soon that would be my permanent life—taking care of kids and doing laundry. And I wanted more.

CHAPTER THIRTY-THREE

THE APPLICATION

ETM SOMEWHAT MADE UP for the misery I endured in my home life.

The three days a week in Mrs. Keene's class, I learned practical things that would matter once the baby was born.

I also got lots of time with babies. I helped Meka with Dante and any other student who needed an extra pair of hands with their little one. Each day my confidence grew that I would have the skills I needed to take care of my daughter when she was born.

During the two academic course days, I was flying through both the senior English and algebra coursework and my grades had significantly improved.

Mr. Demalina opened the door to the ETM class right as I was changing a diaper of one of the student's infant sons. He asked to chat with me in his office. I finished the job, passed the little guy back to his mother, and followed him out the door.

When we arrived at his office, he gestured to me to sit and took his place behind his desk. "Your grades here are really good. You're quickly progressing through the curriculum. Have you thought about what you're going to do after high school? What I mean is, have you thought about college?"

That fantasy had evaporated months ago. "Before, yes. I'd thought about going to college, to become a teacher. But now, I don't know how that would all work."

"Well, I talked to Mrs. Keene and told her I want to take you over to North Lake Community College and have you speak with an academic advisor there. Just to be sure that if you do decide to go down that path, you'll know how to navigate it. We could head over there now and be back in time for dismissal."

Talk about déjà vu. Guidance counselors ushering me off to the next thing like I was the poster child for *This Girl Has More Potential Than She's Tapping Into.*

The difference was this current thing, ETM, was possible. It didn't cost money. My baby could come with me after she was born. But college seemed so out of reach for someone like me.

Even though it was pointless, I agreed. Mr. Demalina could go home tonight and brag to his wife about this pregnant teen he helped guide toward a college degree. He could boast that he probably spared her from a life of poverty. Once I left ETM, he'd never think about me again. But for today, I'd let him believe I was savable.

Mr. Demalina's crisp suit perfectly matched his sleek black sedan. Shiny leather seats boasted meticulous care.

Thankfully the drive to North Lake Community College from the Adult Education Center was only about ten minutes. Just long enough for him to quiz me about ETM, what I liked and what I thought could be improved. I told him that I liked that we could learn about taking care of babies and take academic classes all in one place without having to worry about childcare. The only improvement I mentioned was that a bigger building would be nice. It was only small talk, but Mr. Demalina seemed to care about the success of the program.

Mr. Demalina parked in the Visitor Parking lot next to the quaint campus where Julie would attend in the fall.

As we walked toward the campus, clusters of students littered a gorgeous courtyard with a circular fountain. They laughed as they threw heavy backpacks over their shoulders. Their carefree lifestyle taunted me.

I followed Mr. Demalina into the Admissions Office. He told me to wait for him, then disappeared down a hallway. Several chairs filled the small room. But I didn't sit. Might as well not get too comfortable.

A sign read, "North Lake Community College, Your Future Starts Here." Instead of "Your" it should have read "Everyone Else's." The baby kicked. She was my future. North Lake Community College wasn't.

A few minutes later, he returned with a stunning, middle-aged woman in a sophisticated black pantsuit, a floral blouse peeked from underneath a form-fitting blazer. "Hello, Angela, I'm Mrs. Tibbals." She held out a manicured hand, a large diamond sparkled.

My cheeks flushed as we shook. Peeling nail polish and swollen fingers were another reminder of why I didn't belong here.

"Let's go chat in my office." She held an arm toward the same hallway she and Mr. Demalina had emerged from.

"Yes, ma'am." I trailed behind her scent of expensive perfume.

In her office, a tall lamp sat in the corner and bathed the space in soft light. The room's walls featured framed degrees and college memorabilia. Family photos, including a handsome husband and two teenage sons, filled the edges of a mahogany desk. I tried to imagine having a mother like her, but I couldn't. Her sons probably had no idea how lucky they were.

She opened a folder and flipped through some documents. "I've looked over your transcripts. Impressive. You've pulled your grades up since transferring into the ETM program. I work closely with Mr. Demalina. One of our initiatives is identifying students at his campus who we think would be a good fit here at mine. Then we provide scholarships for students to attend. We like what we see in you and want to offer you the opportunity to apply. If you're interested."

"Excuse me?" I couldn't believe these words were being spoken to me.

"It's okay, I'm sure hearing all of this for the first time is a bit overwhelming. Mr. Demalina and I think you would be a good applicant for our Non-Traditional Student Scholarship Program."

This incredible opportunity had fallen into my lap, and I had no choice but to decline. "I'd like to say yes. But, when the baby's born, I either need to find a full-time job to pay a sitter or not work and take care of her myself. I appreciate the offer. I really do. But I don't know what's going to happen yet."

She pushed a folder toward me. "You don't have to make any decisions today. Here's the scholarship application and admissions information. My contact information is also inside. If you have any questions, feel free to call me."

I slid the folder that I felt unworthy to touch off her desk.

"Angela, both Mrs. Keene and Mr. Demalina have spoken with me at length about you. They have faith you can do this. People believe in you. It's okay to believe in yourself, too."

"Thanks." I'd already disappointed everyone in my life who knew me. Time to add Mrs. Tibbals and Mr. Demalina to the list.

———

Later that day, I sat at the kitchen table in the trailer, the packet in front of me. I thought about Miss Jones. Had I not gotten pregnant, I'd be volunteering in her classroom this year. I would've had my college plans laid out. Something she'd said to me on the last day I saw her stayed with me. *You can still have a career. You just may have to work a little harder to make it happen.*

I wanted to have the faith in myself that Mrs. Tibbals said Mrs. Keene and Mr. Demalina did. I wanted my daughter to one day look up to me as a role model. If I stayed on my current path, she wouldn't.

I pulled the documents out of the manila envelope. With a shaky hand, I put pen to paper. At first, it was all the usual information, name, date of birth, address, and expected major. I wrote Elementary Education, just like Miss Jones.

Next was an essay. The prompt: "In 500 words or less, How Will This Scholarship Help You Achieve Your Personal, Academic, and Career Goals?"

The leaning floors, nicotine-stained walls, and broken cabinets in this run-down trailer wasn't the home I wanted my daughter to grow up in. But it wasn't only the condition of the trailer. Life here with Dale would never be the family I wanted for her or for me. I picked up the pen and wrote.

How This Scholarship Will Help Me Achieve My Personal, Academic, and Career Goals

By Angela Carter

Thank you for the opportunity to apply to the North Lake Community College's Non-Traditional Student Scholarship Program.

Ever since I was a little girl, I envisioned walking across the stage at my high school graduation then heading off to a college campus. And after working with an after-school tutoring program, I realized teaching was the degree I yearned to pursue. But after a positive pregnancy test my senior year, that dream seemed out of reach.

Although my grades suffered at the beginning of the year, after transferring to the Education for Teenaged Mothers program at the Adult Education Center, I've found the support I needed to pull them back up. And once again, college and my dream of becoming a teacher seems like a possibility for me.

This scholarship will help me personally because financially, it will be challenging for me to work and pay school tuition as a young mother. It will help me academically because I can focus on school without having to worry about money. It will also help me achieve my goal of earning a degree in Elementary Education.

There is one more thing about me I'd like you to know. I want to be a good mother and be able to provide for my daughter. I want to be a role model for her and show her that you can still follow and achieve your dreams even when life doesn't turn out as you'd planned.

I appreciate your consideration,

Angela Carter

I tucked the application and essay into the enclosed self-addressed, stamped envelope. I was headed to the mailbox when the rumble of Dale's truck sent me sprinting back inside. I ran to the bedroom and shoved the envelope under the mattress. Maybe I wouldn't mail it anyway. It was probably stupid to even think I could go to college.

I then scurried to the kitchen and pretended I'd been doing dishes.

He walked in and started down the hall toward the bedroom. "I'm taking a shower."

"Okay." I hoped he was going out with Roger and his new girlfriend, again. The last thing I wanted was to be alone with him. Even though he'd tried nothing since the rape, I felt it was a temporary reprieve.

As I swirled a cup around in the soapy water, my mind floated from Dale to the application. I had to mail it. What if I got the scholarship? What if I figured out a way to go to college? I could leave Dale and this trailer behind me. While he showered, I pulled the envelope from under the mattress, ran outside, and placed it in the mailbox. Then I vowed to never think about it again.

CHAPTER THIRTY-FOUR

THE PARTY

DALE WORE HIS NEWEST pair of stiff Wranglers, a crisp white button-down, and freshly shined cowboy boots. For a moment, he almost looked like a good guy. But I knew different.

"Where're you going?" I asked. Not like I cared. I'd rather be alone.

"It's not where I'm going, it's where we're going," he said as he walked past me and grabbed a beer out of the fridge. He never drank water.

Aftershave filled the kitchen. He'd even shaved. Odd.

"There's a party after the football game tonight at Roger's house, and you're going to be my designated driver. Plus, it'll do you some good to get out. All you do is go to school, work, or stay here."

He wasn't wrong. The last thing I wanted to do was go anywhere with him. But the fact that he wanted a designated driver. That was a good thing. As much as I personally despised him, he was my daughter's father. I wanted him safe. "Sure, I'll go."

I was relieved he didn't also want to go to the football game. I didn't want to watch Julie and the rest of the team cheer.

A few minutes later, we pulled up to Roger's trailer to a party in full swing.

Inside the smokey living room, I spotted Andrew. I hadn't seen him since I transferred to ETM. I had no choice but to face him.

Dale said he was going to find the beer keg. Out of the corner of my eye, I saw him and Roger dart behind long, blonde hair into a back room. *Whatever. Have fun tonight.* Maybe whatever he'd find in that room would deter him from needing anything from me.

I made my way through the crowd to Andrew. "Hey. How are you?"

"Oh my gosh, Ange, it's so good to see you. "He wrapped his arms around my neck, then backed away and looked me up and down. "Wow. You're definitely pregnant."

"Thanks for pointing out the obvious." In the tent of a dress I wore, I must've looked huge compared to the last time he had seen me. "What're you doing here? Not that it matters. I've just never seen you around this crowd."

"My brother. I'm the designated driver. Trust me, I'd rather be hanging out with Julie. She told you, right?"

His words blindsided me. "Told me what?"

"We're going to prom together. Crap, I'm an idiot. I guess I just put a proverbial foot in my mouth. Sorry."

"No, it's okay. That's great—the two of you." Even though I'd long ago decoded they were together, it would've been nice if Julie had told me rather than hearing it from him. Not a cool best friend move.

Andrew broke the awkward silence. "Yep, so I'm the DD tonight. I guess the same for you, for Dale?"

I nodded. I was glad to see Andrew was only here to babysit his older brother. He'd really turned things around this year, escaped the party scene. Apparently, he'd also turned up the romance with Julie. I was an outsider again.

Dale stayed out of sight the entire night, and I had no interest in looking for him. Andrew and I spent the evening catching up. I didn't tell him about the scholarship application. I wouldn't tell anyone. I'd just look stupid when I didn't get it.

After a few hours, someone gripped the back of my arm. "We're going—now." The stench of beer filled my nostrils. I guess he'd found the keg.

"Hey, Dale. What's up? Remember me, Andrew? I'm Aaron's younger brother. I think you guys played football together back in the day."

Dale shot him a look of death. "Yeah, punk. Stay away from Angela."

"Man, we're just friends." He held his hands up in surrender.

I wanted to melt into a puddle on the floor. Every damn opportunity he got, Dale humiliated me. I didn't care if he was angry with me. I was used to it. But I didn't like him treating a friend like that. "Andrew's been a friend since we were kids. He's dating Julie." I hoped connecting Andrew to Julie would cause him to back off.

Without saying another word, Dale pushed me away from Andrew and out the door. I mouthed *sorry* to Andrew. He started to follow us, but I shook my head to stop him.

"Let go of me. I'm going with you."

But he kept a tight grip on my arm as he pushed me out the door, down the wooden steps, and toward the car. Then he flung open the passenger door and threw me in. My left hip smashed into the gear shifter. Pain shot down my leg. "You've been drinking. I need to drive. That was the whole point of me coming." I couldn't let him start the car.

But he climbed into the driver's seat and demanded, "Give me the keys."

I clutched my purse to my chest. "Please, no."

"You don't wanna do this. Give me the damn keys."

A small crowd, including Andrew, had gathered on the front deck, but no one stopped Dale. He was an angry drunk. Everyone knew that—including me.

I dug the keys out of my purse. He snatched them away from me. I buckled the seatbelt, closed my eyes, and wrapped my arms around my belly.

Dale accelerated fast, and the car swerved over the bumpy, dirt road. I opened my eyes right before the car hit a mailbox. I leaned over to grab the wheel and steer us out of its path.

"You're scaring me. Please, slow down. You almost hit that mailbox."

He yanked my hand off the wheel and shoved me toward the passenger side of the car. My head slammed into the window. A metallic taste erupted in my mouth.

"Oh, now you're scared. I should've just left you at the party with him. Is he the real daddy of that baby?"

"What? No, no, I swear this is your baby. Andrew is only a friend. Please, slow down."

But he didn't. Instead, he started punching the windshield with each breath. Screaming, cursing, accusing. "You were all over him. Do you think anybody really wants you now? Seventeen years old and pregnant. I'm all you got. If I were you, I'd remember that."

His words punched me in the gut. "We were only talking." I didn't want to believe Dale was all I had, but he was right. "Please, just slow down and we can talk."

The car continued to accelerate. Dale continued to scream.

I had to fix this. My swelling belly was a physical reminder that soon I'd need what little stability he offered, even though it came at a great price.

Use a different approach. Be apologetic. Take the blame. Passive-aggressive was my signature personality trait, so this was easy for me. "I understand how it might've looked. Please, just let me drive us home."

It didn't work. Dale swerved the car with one hand and shattered the windshield with the other. I was surprised that as drunk as he was, he could do both. Then, as if it had been his goal all along, he lost control of the wheel and the car spun violently. I closed my eyes again and cradled the baby girl in my belly who I wasn't sure I'd ever hold.

Chapter Thirty-Five

Nosedive

It was only seconds, but the car spun for what seemed like minutes before coming to an abrupt halt. The front of the rusty Ford Fairmont, now with a busted windshield, took a slight nosedive into a shallow ditch. I was thankful to be alive.

Drunk and incoherent, Dale moaned. But other than a bloodied and mangled fist, he seemed okay. I pushed the door open and got out. Although a little stiff, I was able to walk.

I moved toward the driver's door with plans to push him to the passenger seat and attempt to back the car out of the ditch. But, when my hand touched the cool metal of the door handle, I froze. Then I backed away from the car.

Fueled by adrenaline I ran, away from Dale, away from the miserable, disgusting thing called my life. Six months pregnant and running like my life depended on it, as if somehow, I could escape.

"Come back. I'm hurt. Please," he begged.

But I didn't go back. I didn't want to help him. I only wanted to run.

I didn't stop until I couldn't see the car anymore. I bent over, and the quick, shallow breaths slowed. I took a deep inhale and cradled my heavy belly.

Guilt flowed through my veins. *What if Dale was hurt?* Then panic shoved guilt to the curb. *What would Dale do to me the next time he saw me?* He'd be enraged both for me talking to Andrew and leaving him on the side of the road.

I was only a mile or so from Dale's parents' place. I had nowhere else to go. It was my only option.

I dragged heavy legs up the steps on the Simmons' front porch. My back ached. I desperately needed to go to the bathroom, and I couldn't stop shivering. February had been a chiller this year, and I was pretty sure the temp was in the low thirties. I raised a clenched fist. I was afraid to knock, afraid of what to say, but more afraid of staying outside all night alone.

"Hold on a minute. It's one o'clock in the morning. Who is it?" Wispy hair stood on end and a stern eye bore into me through a small crack. "Angela. Where's Dale? Is he okay?"

"We got into a little argument. He dropped me off. That's all. Can I come in?"

She stepped aside and opened the door wide. "I guess. What was the fight about? You know not to make him mad when he's drinking."

Of course, Addis would blame me. "It was nothing. If you don't mind, can I crash here tonight? I'm sure he'll pick me up in the morning."

"Fine." She opened a closet and tossed me a flat pillow and a thin blanket then slammed the door to her bedroom.

I collapsed onto the sweat and cigarette smoke reeking lumpy sofa. Then I wedged the pillow under my swelling belly and rested my head on folded arms. Once I finally got as comfortable as I could, the baby started kicking. As horrible as most of my life was, when it was quiet, I loved every moment of feeling her come alive inside me. *Baby girl, mama's going to take care of you. I don't know how, but I promise.*

———

The faint rays of the sun invaded the Simmons living room and nudged me awake from a restless sleep. I had to pee badly, and my body was sore. Everything hurt. From the bathroom, I heard the phone ring. I finished up in time for the last of a one-sided conversation.

"Uh, huh. Yeah. Dale Simmons is my son. Yeah. Okay. Can we see him? Yes, sir. Thank you."

"John, what's going on?" He spoke so slowly that I wanted to lasso the words out of him.

"Well, it looks like Dale might get a DUI. After he dropped you off, he was on his way home to sleep it off. A damn deer ran out in front of him, and the impact busted the windshield. Right outside the trailer park, a cop pulled him over." He shuffled his way back to his throne, a worn-out recliner in the middle of the kitchen.

I guess that meant Dale wasn't too hurt, and he was able to start the car and back out of the ditch. But seriously. Hit a deer. That's how he explained the busted windshield. Not that he shattered it himself as he assaulted his pregnant girlfriend.

Addis ran out of the bedroom and cursed at John for hanging up the phone. She mumbled under her breath while she dialed the number she knew by heart—the jail. She rapid fire questioned the poor person unlucky enough to answer.

John and I faded into the background as Addis drilled the police station. She scribbled notes she'd no doubt later share with the family criminal defense attorney, sleazebag Michael Graves.

John knew his place. "You need a ride home?"

And I knew mine. "Yes, please."

I heaved into the cab of his old black Ford. John didn't talk much, so the ride was quiet. Part Cherokee Indian with thick, jet-black hair and nearly black eyes, he probably had been handsome in his youth. But now, a lifeless beer belly spilled over the seatbelt, and his forehead bore deep lines of a hard life.

We pulled into the crumbling asphalt trailer park driveway. John got out, opened my door, and helped me down. "Thanks for the ride."

He grunted and tilted his head. Then climbed back into the cab and waited until I made it safely inside before backing out. Unlike his son, John at least tried to be a good man. It wasn't his fault he didn't know how.

The inside of the trailer was hazy as the late morning sun peeked through the dusty windows and beige curtains. Even when Dale wasn't here, smoke hung in the air like smog. Oppressive and heavy. But I was alone. For that, I was thankful.

Dale was in jail. For at least one day, I could relax. He wouldn't be coming in drunk. He wouldn't demand things from me I didn't want to do. He wouldn't curse at me. I wouldn't have to be afraid. For at least one day, I could experience what my life would be like if Dale Simmons disappeared.

Chapter Thirty-Six

In Prison

I LAY IN A contorted heap. My head throbbed. The baby had kicked all night, and I'd barely settled in by sunrise. But a ringing phone forced me to abandon all hope of getting any more sleep.

Maneuvering my ever-changing body out of bed was more difficult each day. But I managed to answer the phone before whoever was calling gave up.

A recorded voice spoke. "Hello. This is a collect call from..."

"Dale Simmons." His name, in his voice, chilled me to the bone.

"...an inmate at the North Lake County Correctional Facility. All calls are subject to recording. To decline this call, hang up now. To accept, remain on the line. By accepting, you agree to all charges."

I remained on the line, even though the urge to hang up was tough to ignore.

"Hey. They gonna keep me until I see a judge Monday. Then I don't know." His scratchy voice indicated a well-deserved hangover.

Good, both for him feeling like shit and for him sitting in jail.

Except I needed what little he provided. "What am I supposed to do? The windshield is busted. The rent is due next week and food."

"Mama's already retained that same attorney that got me out of the last DUI. She also talked Aunt Joan into waitin' a couple weeks on the rent. Daddy's got a friend who owns a junkyard. They're gonna come fix the windshield. You know, cause of that deer."

Really? This was the story he was sticking to? "The deer?" I said through clenched teeth and a tight jaw.

"Yeah, the deer. Anyway, we gotta pay for parts. Somewhere around eighty bucks or so. You're gonna have to figure that one out on your own. Not much I can do sittin' here. Maybe time yo' daddy stepped up."

I collapsed onto the floor at the realization that Dale's drunk tirade was going to cost me nearly every dime I'd saved up for the baby. His mama was fine fronting her baby boy's lawyer. But helping me fix something of mine he broke—she drew the line there. And I had no choice. I had to fix it, or I couldn't go to work or school.

My only other choice was to ask my father for money. I knew he'd help me, but I also knew he'd have questions I didn't want to answer.

The conversation with Dale ended abruptly. No sentiments or affections, a simple "later" followed by a click and a dial tone.

I forced myself off the floor and hung up the phone. I couldn't control it any longer. I threw myself on the couch and screamed into a cushion then punched it until every muscle in my body ached. I hated Dale Simmons. Hated. Hated. Hated.

Eventually, I dragged myself to the kitchen and picked the receiver back up. Might as well get this call with my dad over.

"Number One," he said as soon as he knew it was me.

Stop calling me that. I don't want you to say that to me ever again.

I twisted the yellow coiled cord of the phone around my fingers as my stomach twisted in knots. "I need to ask you a favor." I bit my lips to hold back the sobs that threatened to tell my father just how bad things were.

But Dad's voice was chipper and unaware of the hell his daughter was enduring. "Sure, I'm all ears."

No use wasting time with small talk. Might as well dive into the lies head on. "Dale got into a little bit of trouble before we got together and has been on probation. Last night, he was driving my car, and a deer ran out in front of him, and the impact busted the windshield. As he was driving home, a cop pulled him over and took him in. He should be out soon, but I may need to borrow a little money until then."

I held my breath the several seconds it took before my father spoke.

"I'm pretty sure you aren't telling me the whole story."

And I wasn't going to, but I needed to say enough. "He was drinking."

More silence, more thinking. "Anything you ever need, I'm here for you. But me giving you money is by-proxy allowing Dale to spend money he should be spending on you and his soon-to-be-born daughter. So, no. I won't give you money."

My heart sank.

"But, until he gets out, you're welcome to come here and eat three meals a day."

I hated how things were, but I understood. I thanked him for the gesture and promised I'd be over for dinner the next day.

I hung up the phone and absorbed my surroundings. This wasn't a home. Dale may have been the one in jail, but I was the one in prison.

Chapter Thirty-Seven

Surprise!

I expected in a day or two I'd find out when or if Dale was getting out of jail. Until then, I'd try my best to enjoy the solitude. Even if it was inside this run-down trailer.

I called Julie and filled her in. She offered to come to stay a few nights with me, but I wanted the alone time. Even though I didn't bring it up with her on the phone, I planned to talk to her in person at some point about what Andrew told me at the party. I just needed to find the right time.

Dad called me again to confirm dinner. He was going to make gumbo. My stomach growled all morning in preparation for my favorite dish. Amber and Levi were also going to be there. More than anything, right now I needed my family.

The rest of the day, I worked around the house. Since Dale wasn't here smoking up the joint, I opened the windows and let in some fresh air. I put the clean sheets on the bed I'd washed at the laundromat. It was a slight improvement.

Lastly, I walked into the tiny room where the baby would sleep. There wasn't much in it. The old playpen Addis brought over and a change table I found at a thrift store. I opened the closet and ran my hand across the tiny garments. Because of ETM, thankfully my daughter wouldn't lack clothing.

I'd been so busy all day the time snuck up on me. I only had a few minutes to get ready to go to Dad's. I changed into a cute floral maternity dress, also from ETM, grabbed my keys, and headed out the door.

Even though I had to hand over my hard-earned cash, I was grateful that John and his friend fixed the windshield; otherwise, I'd be going nowhere. I still didn't know why the police hadn't questioned Dale further about it. He had a bloody fist and there wasn't a dead deer anywhere in sight. But I'd given up hope long ago that people in authority did their due diligence to keep criminals away from victims.

When I parked at Dad's apartment, a car that looked like Julie's sat in the space next to his. Strange. I knocked.

Amber greeted me with a warm embrace. "Close your eyes and hold my hand."

"Hello to you, too. What's going on?"

"I said, close your eyes and hold my hand."

"All right." Her tiny fingers laced mine and she led me inside.

"Okay, open them."

"Surprise!" Dad, Levi, and Julie gathered around the small kitchen table; a pink cake sat in the center.

Amber announced, "Welcome to your baby shower."

Confusion swarmed in my brain. "My, what? What's going on?"

"Your Dad and I've been planning this for weeks, and with what's going on, we thought now was the perfect time."

My body trembled and I covered my mouth in a poor attempt to contain my disbelief.

Julie swooped in and squeezed my neck.

"Jules, I don't know what to say. Thank you."

Dad hugged me next. "I'm gonna be a grandpa soon. You didn't think I wouldn't want to celebrate?" My father's shirt absorbed my tears. "Hey, this is a happy occasion." He said as he pulled me away.

Levi placed a muscular arm across my shoulder in a side hug. "Uncle Levi," he said. "I like the sound of it."

I wiped my eyes and then rubbed my belly. "I'm so happy that you all are as excited as I am to meet my daughter. It means more than you'll ever know."

"Can we eat cake now?" Amber pleaded.

"First dinner, then cake." Dad had always been quick to bust out what he called, "Grandma's Rule." I needed to put that one in my future parenting skills toolkit.

The gumbo, my best friend, and my family nearly filled my empty emotional tank. Mom was the only thing missing. Amber told me she had a new boyfriend. I hoped he was a good guy.

After the gumbo and a slice of cake, Amber asked, "Is it present time yet?"

"I believe it is," Dad said. Then they all left the room.

In the few seconds they were gone, I thought about how alone I always felt. But I wasn't really. I had the best friend in the world and my family. Maybe it had been me shutting them out, not the other way around.

Dad and Levi returned carrying a huge box.

"What is that?" I walked toward it. As soon as I was close enough to see the picture on the front, I stopped dead in my tracks. I couldn't believe it. It was the honey oak crib from the baby superstore. I fanned my eyes, failing at keeping a second round of tears at bay. "How did you know?"

"You can thank your best friend." Dad nodded in Julie's direction.

"You'd described it in such great detail to me that when Amber and I went to go look for it, we knew exactly the crib and bedding you wanted."

"The bedding?"

Julie handed me a gift bag. I removed the tissue paper, inside was the rose-colored skirt and floral paisley quilt. I hugged the quilt to my chest. "Jules, thank you so much. I love it."

Amber handed me two more bags. Inside were the matching sheets and diaper stacker.

"You're the best little sister in the whole world. Thank you."

"Here, this one is from Mom and Dad."

Julie's parents. I hadn't seen them since I'd been pregnant. Shame had prevented me from lots of things. Inside the bag wrapped in pink tissue paper, were diapers, receiving blankets, and several baby toys.

"And last but not least, there's one more. It's from your mom." Dad gave me an envelope and a small, wrapped box. "Wait until you get home to open that one."

The overwhelm was almost too much. "Guys, I'm beyond grateful."

"Levi and I will bring the crib over sometime in the next couple of days and set it up for you." Dad offered.

Amber added, "Julie and I will come and help with everything else."

The rest of the evening, we examined all the gifts and talked about baby names. Amber insisted on Cinderella. Later, Dad took center stage and recounted our family's birth stories. There was so much laughter. I didn't want the night to end. For the first time in months, I felt loved, supported, and excited to welcome my baby girl into the world.

With Dale out of my life, joy was possible. For all I cared, he could rot in jail for the rest of time.

CHAPTER THIRTY-EIGHT

A LETTER AND A CIGAR BOX

I BROUGHT IN THE bags from the baby shower and placed them in my nameless daughter's room. But I was too distracted to think about baby names because something else had my full attention.

At the kitchen table, I sat still—the envelope and package from my mother in front of me. As much as everything my dad, Julie, Levi, and Amber had done for me that night, it was this I'd waited months for. I knew where I stood with them. With Mom, I didn't.

I rubbed my fingers across my name. She had the most beautiful cursive handwriting. As a young girl, I tried to emulate it, always with a fail.

The off-white stationary inside held the faint scent of Giorgio. I clutched it, closed my eyes, and reached far back in time. Mississippi. I was about nine years old. Good grades came easy. The day I failed my first spelling test, I had rushed off the school bus and hid in the garage, the evidence crushed into a ball in my palm.

Mom found me shivering and sobbing. She didn't ask questions, just held me. Each inhale of Giorgio on her satin blouse had calmed me.

Once the tears stopped, she said, "Honey, whatever got you this upset, it's in the past. You can't do anything about it. But what you can do is handle it differently next time. And I know you well enough to know that's exactly what you'll do."

I never told Mom about the spelling test, but I suspected my teacher had called her in advance. I also never failed another one. I wished I could cry into her chest and inhale Giorgio in person rather than smelling it on a piece of paper. I needed my mom. I unfolded her words. Words I desperately hoped would mend the broken pieces inside me. Mom's words used to be able to do that.

Dear Angela,

Hey, Baby Girl. I want you to know I am so sorry for so many things. I was in a bad place. But it's no excuse for me neglecting you kids. The last day with you when you told me I'd turned out like my mother, that hurt deeply because I knew you were right. Only I wasn't ready to admit it.

I expected you would have gone to your dad's. Not in a million years, even in the state I was in, was my intention to kick you out with nowhere to go. I'll never forgive myself.

But ever since that day, I couldn't forget what you said. And when your dad called and told me you were pregnant, I went to AA that very same night, and I haven't had a drink since.

I also have news of my own. I met a nice man at AA, Bob. He's been sober for more than 15 years. He has been a real big help to me during my recovery. And it may seem soon, but we are getting married in a small ceremony at the courthouse. If you're ready, I'd love to have you there. I've changed. I hope you believe me.

After the wedding, we are moving to the Panhandle. Bob's mother needs some help and I need a change of scenery. Levi and Amber are coming, too. They will visit you and your dad during vacations and summers. He and I have talked at great length about this. We believe a fresh start is also good for them.

Enclosed is a little cash. I'd like you to use it to buy your daughter, my granddaughter, her coming home from the hospital outfit. The gift, it's just an old cigar box with a collection of things I saved since you were a baby. I hope you enjoy having them and maybe adding your daughter's things to it.

I love you,

Mom

The clock's minute hand circled its face at least twice before I could collect my thoughts. Every emotion a human could experience ripped my soul to shards. That day, my clothes in garbage bags, she thought I would go to Dad's. It was all a misunderstanding.

Part of me wanted to hold on to anger. She should have written me a note then, instead of waiting months. She should have told me to go to Dad's. Problem-solved. The last several months of my life wouldn't have been absolute hell. And I wouldn't be pregnant. But I was pregnant. I was about to have a baby, a daughter. I'd heard her heartbeat. I'd seen her image. I'd felt her move. I was already in love with her.

I unwrapped the package. I'd explored the contents of this old cigar box many times over the years. Inside was my tiny hospital baby ID bracelet. My daughter would wear one like it in a few months. My mother's was there, too. I picked up one of several *It's a Girl* cigars and sniffed. I imagined my father proudly smoking one after I was born. I doubt Dale would be excited enough about his daughter's birth to pass them out to his friends. But my dad had been. There was the deck of cards Dad told us about at my baby shower. The ones he bought in the hospital gift shop. He had played Solitaire for hours in the waiting room while my mom was in labor with me. Fathers weren't allowed in delivery rooms seventeen years ago.

Underneath a tiny pair of socks were some of my newborn baby pictures. The one that caught my attention was one of the three of us. Mom and Dad looked so young. Like me, they'd become parents before they had grown up themselves.

I was a little blindsided. Mom was moving with both my siblings to the Panhandle. It's not like I had been forthcoming about my life to anyone, either. But knowing she went to AA because of me, that alone made everything worth it.

I put the box and letter in a dresser drawer. It was already eight thirty at night. I didn't care. I was going to see my mother.

CHAPTER THIRTY-NINE

FORGIVENESS

As I drove, I thought about what I'd say to Mom. So much had happened over the last few months. I wanted her, someone, to know it all. I'd kept so many secrets. Who was I kidding? I was still keeping secrets. But this was about repairing our relationship, not me unloading what was going on in my life. That would come later. If ever.

I parked in front of my childhood home. When I reached the front door, I smiled as I stepped on a new welcome mat. She had changed. I knocked. It didn't feel right barging in.

Mom opened the door. She looked beautiful in a pale blue robe. "I was hoping you'd come." She hugged me, I inhaled Giorgio. I never wanted to let her go. All these months without my mother, it was over.

Her eyes watered. "Honey, I'm so sorry. I never meant—"

I interrupted. "I read the letter. You never need to apologize again. What matters is now. And I'm so proud of you."

We embraced again and forgiveness flew through me, leaving no room for anger or pain.

"It's been a long day, but I'll come over soon and we can catch up and I can meet Bob. I just needed to see you tonight."

"I'm so glad." She stood back. "Look at you glowing."

It was hard to believe I hadn't seen her since I'd been pregnant. I wanted to spend as much time with her as possible before she moved. We had a lot of lost time to make up.

"Baby Girl, you go home and get some rest and drive safe. How about next weekend? Then we can talk about the baby and the wedding and everything."

"That's perfect. I love you."

"Love you, too." She paused for a moment. "Before you go, one last thing. In AA, part of recovery is making amends to those we've hurt. But we can't expect forgiveness. I want you to know how much I appreciate yours."

"You're welcome." But forgiving her was also for me. Resentment is a heavy burden to bear. "I'll see you next weekend."

By the time I got back to the trailer, my mind reeled. This had been one of the best days in a long time, but worry consumed me about what I'd find out tomorrow. As much as I wished I never had to speak to or see Dale Simmons ever again, nothing between us had changed. I still lived with him. I was still having his baby. The nightmare was far from over.

CHAPTER FORTY

THE ARGUMENT

As I BACKED OUT of the driveway, Addis pulled in, blocking my exit. I braked inches away from slamming into the front end of her already beat-up Corolla.

News about Dale would be the only reason she was here. I wasn't about to get out of my car. This was my turf. If she wanted to talk, she'd have to come to me.

She beeped her horn several times before realizing I wasn't heeding to her demands. Dressed in a shabby robe and slippers, she marched toward me. A mom on a mission.

I cranked down my window and she jutted in her pointy chin. "Dale just called. He has a hearing later this week. He told me to tell you if anyone asks, you know what to say about the windshield."

I knew what she meant. But I was going to make her say it. "I don't know what you're talking about."

"Please. That's my baby boy. I don't want him locked up."

"I need you to be more specific." The sarcasm felt so good.

Her approach shifted from demanding me to lie to begging me to. "The deer, Angela."

I started to roll the window up. "I need to get to school."

She pushed down the glass, sobbing. "He wants to be there when his baby girl comes."

The nerve that she pulled my unborn child into this made my blood boil. But Dale was my child's father. And even though I didn't want to lie for him, I also was afraid of the potential consequences if I didn't. "Fine."

"Promise me. Say, you promise," she pleaded.

"I promise." I hoped it wasn't a promise I'd regret.

"You better not be lying. I don't much care for a liar." Then she tightened her robe and stole away to her car.

What she said—I was a liar either way.

After school, I headed to the laundromat. Julie sat at the desk flipping through a prom dress catalog. After all she did for me with the baby shower, I didn't want to bring up the Andrew thing. But it was now or never.

She shoved the catalog in a drawer as soon as the bell on the entrance door jingled. "Hey, how was school?"

"Jules, I saw what you were looking at."

"I'm sorry."

"No need to be sorry. I saw Andrew at Roger's party on Friday night."

"He told me. I feel bad."

"About what?"

"You're my best friend, but I feel like I can't talk to you about normal teenage things anymore, like boyfriends and prom and stuff like that."

"Of course you can. You're being ridiculous."

"Every time I try, you change the subject. You may not realize it, but you do."

My heart was about to beat a hole in my chest. "I do not. Name one time."

"I don't want to argue. And you're the one who brought it up. But I have feelings, too."

"Excuse me. I seriously cannot believe what you're saying. You know what, how about you fold the fitted sheets by yourself tonight?"

"Ange, don't leave. You're taking this all the wrong way."

"How you feel is how you feel. I'm sorry I'm such an inconvenience in your normal teenage world. Maybe it's time you get a normal teenage best friend." I stormed out.

As I drove home, I replayed the argument with Julie. She was right. I didn't want to hear about prom and college from her. Maybe that was selfish. But it felt like she was living her life at me. It was a constant reminder of all the things I couldn't or wouldn't ever be able to do.

All the plans we'd made as kids, cheering our senior year, color-coordinating our prom dresses, me going with her family in an RV to tour the Midwest after graduation. None of that would ever happen. She'd make those memories with someone else. And it was time I gave her the permission to do it.

CHAPTER FORTY-ONE

THE INVESTIGATION

SITTING IN MY SENIOR English class, I couldn't focus on my reading assignment, *A Tale of Two Cities* by Charles Dickens. Even though I liked the story, reading about true love was depressing. To me, it only existed in fiction.

Several days had passed since the argument with Julie. I hadn't gone back to the laundromat either. Eventually, the money would run out. Addis had told me Dale would probably only be in jail for maybe a few weeks. I could stretch what I had and make it that long. I bent my head down toward the open book sitting on my desk and tried again to escape to London.

I'd hardly read a word when a touch to my shoulder startled me.

"Sorry to interrupt, but someone's here to see you. I need you to come with me," said Mr. Demalina.

"Oh, okay." I'd never had a visitor at school. My mind raced as we neared the office.

When he opened the door, a young woman in a dark blue uniform stood in the middle of the room. She wore a badge on her chest and a gun on her hip. Blonde hair was pinned into a tight bun, not a single strand out of place.

Mr. Demalina's introductions confirmed my worst fear. "Officer Cresswell, this is Angela Carter."

"Hello, Miss Carter. It's a pleasure to meet you." She offered a thin smile and held out a hand. But the intensity in her eyes indicated this visit was anything but friendly.

Her firm, confident grip grasped my sweaty palm. "You, too."

"Mr. Demalina, is there somewhere Miss Carter and I can speak in private?"

"Sure, you can use my office." He pointed to a room across from the main lobby.

Officer Cresswell closed the door behind us. "Miss Carter, please have a seat."

I complied.

She remained standing, legs slightly more than hip-width apart, spine straight. She grabbed a small notepad out of her back pocket and a pen out of her front.

"Miss Carter, the reason I'm here is I need to ask you a few questions about the incidents surrounding a DUI concerning Dale Simmons. You do know Mr. Simmons?" She peered down at me, poised to write each word I spoke.

I laid a shaky hand on my belly. "He's my baby's father."

"Were you with Mr. Simmons on the night of Friday, February twenty-eighth?"

This wasn't about the windshield so I could answer it. "Yes."

"And where did you and Mr. Simmons go that night?"

A ton of people saw us, so I had to tell the truth. "We were at a party at his cousin Roger's house."

"Can you provide me the address?" She scribbled ferociously in her notepad.

My thoughts bounced all over the place. "336, no, 337 County Road 88, North Lake. I think."

"And approximately what time did you and Mr. Simmons leave that address?"

I stared at the scuffed floor, trying to remember the details of that night while wishing I could forget. "Around twelve-thirty a.m., I think?"

"Who was driving when you left?"

My breathing shallowed. "He was—Dale." The night I had thought I was going to die.

"The vehicle." She flipped through the pad and read through some previous notes. "The Ford Fairmont, it's registered in your name—correct?"

She would know the answer to that question. "Yes, ma'am." I wanted this over.

"And, Miss Carter, before you handed Mr. Simmons the keys that night, were you aware he was intoxicated?"

My heart pounded as she hammered me with question after question. "Yes, ma'am, I did give him the keys. But we weren't together most of the time at the party. I was talking to a friend. I can't confirm if or how much he'd been drinking." Shock tore through me at the thought that maybe I'd be in trouble for handing him the keys.

"And what happened between the time that you left the party and when Mr. Simmons was pulled over for the shattered windshield?" Officer Creswell shifted her steely gaze from her notepad to me.

To avoid looking at her, I closed my eyes and recalled how terrified I was that night as Dale punched the windshield and the car spun off the road. I remembered leaving him in the car and running in the cold to his parents. I also remembered what I'd told Addis when I showed up on her doorstep. I opened my eyes and met Officer Creswell's gaze. Terrified more of the consequences at home than with the law, I knew exactly what to say.

"Dale and I got into an argument at the party. He dropped me off at his parent's place so we could each have a little space. Then he went home. The next morning, we got a call that he got pulled over because of a shattered windshield. He said a deer ran out in front of the car and he tried to swerve, but it was too late, and he hit it. And since he had been drinking, the officer that pulled him over, took him to jail." Although I hoped I was wrong, I knew what the next question would be.

"And what, Miss Carter, can you tell me about the condition of the windshield on your Ford Fairmont before Mr. Simmons dropped you off? Please be very specific."

Here it was. Up until this point, I'd technically told the truth. But now, she was about to put in writing every word of the lie I was about to tell.

I wanted to tell her the truth. About everything, not just about that night. She was a police officer. She was supposed to protect people. But right then, I didn't feel protected. I felt vulnerable and exposed.

I thought about Addis saying my baby needed her daddy there when she was born. As much as I didn't think Dale was worth it, my baby was. I didn't want her to open her eyes in the world for the first time fatherless. I filled my lungs with deceit, then exhaled the lie. "I don't remember."

"You don't remember anything about the condition of the windshield?"

Here was the opportunity to tell the truth. The truth about the abuse I'd suffered at the hands of Dale Simmons.

But instead, the words, "No, ma'am, I'm sorry," stumbled out of my dehydrated mouth.

She nodded and put the notepad and pen back in their respective places. Then reached into her front pocket, the one underneath her badge, and pulled out a business card. "Miss Carter, if you happen to remember any more details about that night, anything, please give me a call at the station."

I took the card and doubted I'd ever use it. "Yes, ma'am."

"Thank you, Miss Carter. Best of luck to you if I don't see you again. And I do very much, appreciate you telling me the—truth—and helping to shed light on Mr. Simmons' case."

"You're welcome." Even though it was Spring, my lie hung in the air like the sticky humidity of a miserable Florida summer. It was hard to breathe, and a warm, moist layer of sweat covered me. Although she didn't know the truth, I was certain Officer Cresswell knew what I'd told her was far from it.

CHAPTER FORTY-TWO

DADDY'S GIRL

I PUSH-PINNED THE WHITEST sheet I could find over the window in the baby's room. Then pulled the oak-spindled change table I'd found at the thrift store under it. The sheet would not only block the sun but also the scenery. I didn't want to have to look at other mold-streaked trailers every time I changed a diaper.

A knock at the door alerted me that my guests had arrived. For the first time, my deplorable living conditions would be on full display for my family.

I opened the door and Amber skipped inside. "I'm so excited to help you with the baby's room today."

"Me, too." Amber didn't react to the trailer's appearance, but I was certain my father would.

Dad and Levi carried the large box up the rickety wooden steps and through the back door.

"Point the way," was all Dad said.

While the guys built the crib, Amber and I went outside to take the linens off the clothesline I'd hand-washed in the kitchen sink. Julie was supposed to be here, but that was before our argument. She was probably glad she didn't have to deal with me and my problems anymore. Our lives were so different now. I doubted we'd ever speak again. As much as it hurt, I had a new reality now.

"Sissy, have you thought of a name yet?" Amber's question jerked my thoughts away from my former best friend and toward the harsh reminder that my daughter remained nameless.

"I haven't. Nothing's really come to me. Is your vote still for Cinderella?"

"No, I changed my mind. I was thinking Ratrisha. Do you like it?"

Despite my circumstances, I couldn't help but smile. Amber had always had that effect on me. "Well, it's unique. That's for sure."

"When I have kids, I'm naming them all Ratrisha, even the boys." We both laughed.

I was so going to miss them. Amber was my little sidekick. My reminder that innocence still existed in this world. And Levi, I'd just started building a relationship with him. I regretted I hadn't done more.

"Girls," Dad called from the open window. "Come take a look."

I grabbed the laundry basket, and Amber and I raced back inside to check on Dad and Levi's progress.

I stopped in the doorway of the baby's room and almost dropped the basket. "Guys, it's even more gorgeous than I remembered."

Amber and I added the linens. The sparkling new crib with the floral beautiful bedding sat in stark contrast to the rest of the room. The worn shag carpet, walnut paneled walls, stained ceiling, and rusting metal closet doors looked even more dilapidated. If I noticed it, so did my father.

"We're probably moving out of here when the baby's born and I get a job. Dale's company has been framing some really nice apartments. He's got an inside connection."

Dad didn't say a word. But he didn't need to. The way he pursed his lips as he shook his head and looked around the room told me everything I needed to know.

"Can we go? I'm going to a movie later with some guys from the weight-lifting team," Levi said.

I was glad he was back with his weight-lifting team. I now held the honor of sole recipient of the Carter Family Disappointment Award.

"Amber, Levi, I'll meet you in the car." Once alone, Dad said, "I know this"—he pointed around the trailer—"isn't a reflection of you, but I'm not a big fan of this setup. When Dale gets out, he and I will be talking. It's long overdue. Understand?"

"Yes, sir. I understand. And thank you."

"You might not be thanking me after my talk with Dale." Then he hugged me and left.

I wanted to run after him. Tell him everything. How Dale really treated me, what happened the night of the party, the interrogation by the police officer. Those things scared and confused me. But I also didn't want him to think I was a total disaster. I couldn't have it both ways.

I ran my hands across the crib's smooth, pristine railing. This was the life I wanted my daughter to have. But other than her crib, everything in her life, including me would be garbage.

CHAPTER FORTY-THREE

GETTING CLOSE

"ANGELA, YOUR TURN." CATHY, one of the nursing students who visited ETM each week, called me into a corner of the classroom. My favorite part of Cathy's visits was hearing my baby's heartbeat. My least favorite was that she reviewed our nutrition journals.

"Honey, I talked with you about this last week and the week before. You aren't eating enough. You should be at around two thousand plus calories a day, and sometimes you barely crack a thousand. And you aren't gaining enough weight. At this point, I would have hoped you'd gained at least twenty pounds, and you've only gained fifteen. What's going on?"

My daughter wasn't even born, and already I was failing at motherhood. The only requirement at this point was eating and I couldn't even manage that. "I'm sorry, my baby's father's in jail, and I've been trying to make what little money I have last until he gets out, which should be soon."

She patted my shoulder. "There's a program called Women, Infants, and Children, or WIC. I want you to apply. They can help you get food stamps. I'm surprised the Health Department hasn't already enrolled you. I'll get you an application before I leave."

I didn't tell her they had tried several times, but with so much going on in my life, I kept forgetting to apply. "Yes, ma'am. I appreciate it."

"I usually recommend breastfeeding, but because of your low weight, I'm concerned. WIC will pay for infant formula. So, I think that's the route I'd like you to go. Are you okay with that?"

"Yes ma'am. Whatever you think is best." I hadn't even considered how I'd feed this baby. Especially since I wasn't even doing a great job feeding myself.

"When is your next appointment with the Health Department?"

"Monday. I go every week now. Why?"

"Your measurements today indicate your baby has dropped lower into your pelvic cavity, which means labor might be soon. How are you feeling?"

While I assumed she meant how I was feeling physically, it was emotionally where I was a mess. But she wasn't here for that conversation. "Well, I can breathe a little easier. For a while, that was tough, but I do feel more pressure down there if you know what I mean. And my belly gets tight a lot, but it always stops."

"Those are Braxton-Hicks, false contractions, but they are doing something. What did the doctor say when you were there last?"

"He said everything looked good." Her questions worried me.

"Okay. I'm going to call and ask them to get you in by the end of the week. Just to see if you've dilated. Do you know what that means?"

I was a little offended. She knew labor and delivery was a huge part of our curriculum, which I'd done well at, thank you very much. "Of course. No, Dr. Patten said nothing about dilation on Monday."

"I want you to be ready. Have your bags packed. If your water breaks or you get consistent painful contractions you can't talk through, not like the ones you have now, go to the hospital immediately. Understand?"

"Yes, ma'am." I knew Cathy meant well, but she was a little annoying.

The phone rang as I walked into the trailer after school. I sprinted inside as fast as my growing frame allowed.

It was that same North Lake County Correctional Facility recorded call. Again, I accepted.

"Hey, Attorney Graves did his thing and Mama and Daddy posted bail. I'm coming home."

"Great. When?" Mixed emotions clashed in my head. For me, Dale coming home was not good. But, for our baby, it was. At least that's what I told myself.

"It'll be soon. I'm glad. To be getting outta here. I didn't want to miss the baby being born."

Maybe sometimes lies are meant to be told. What he said made me hope mine to Officer Cresswell was one of them.

CHAPTER FORTY-FOUR

THE WEDDING

THE UNEXPECTED BLARE OF a truck horn caused my hand to flinch. "Dammit." I grabbed a Q-tip, ran it under the faucet, and tried to remove the mascara from my eyelid. I had to leave in a few minutes to be on time for Mom and Bob's wedding.

The impatient driver blared the horn again. I gave up on perfection, tossed the Q-tip into the trash, and shouted toward the bedroom. "Dale, get up. Roger's here, and I'm leaving."

"Tell him to come back and get me at noon. I'm tired." Dale had been out of jail for two days and had yet to work a full one. He'd been acting sick or depressed or a combination of both. More than likely, it was the lack of drugs and alcohol. His lawyer said to lay low until his arraignment. I didn't think he liked laying low.

I delivered Dale's message to Roger. He mumbled something I couldn't hear, then backed out and left. Roger seemed irritated. That was a first.

Mom, Bob, Levi, and Amber were standing in front of floor-to-ceiling glass that overlooked a small pond surrounded by deep green foliage. The ornate wooden ceiling of the room where the courthouse weddings took place complimented the deep, rich red tones in its carpeting.

The bride glowed in an off-white sundress. The groom beamed in dark jeans and a black button-down, his long grey beard and hair neatly combed.

"You guys look great," I said as I entered the sunny space.

Bob greeted me with a warm hug.

"Thanks for what you've done for my mom."

He put his arm around her. "She's a special lady."

"Baby Girl, I'm so glad you could come." Her eyes sparkled and she wore a genuine smile.

"I wouldn't have missed it for the world." My afternoon doctor's appointment lingered in the background. Cathy's insistence I see him before the weekend left a simmering concern.

But I pushed it aside when Amber grabbed my hand and said, "Sissy, Mommy's getting married, and you're having a baby."

"Yep, and you're way too smart for your own good." I did my best to pick her up and swing her around like I used to do. But the second I lifted her; a sharp pain flew across my abdomen. I placed my hand on it and winced.

"Ange, you okay?" Levi put a firm hand on my arm.

"Yeah. Totally. Just pulled something."

A man in a suit carrying a clipboard entered. "Well, are we ready?"

"We are," Mom and Bob replied in unison.

Levi, Amber, and I stood next to Mom.

In that moment, watching them get married I realized, just because my parents' relationship had ended, it didn't mean it was a failure. It was good until it wasn't, and that's okay. Quitting something that isn't working meant you had the chance to start something that could.

After the short and sweet ceremony ended and the groom had kissed his bride, Mom asked, "Are you sure you can't squeeze in coming to lunch with us?"

"Sorry. The nurse at school wanted me to see the doctor before the weekend. You guys go on. And congratulations."

"Please call me as soon as you get finished and give me an update."

"I will." I wanted to go with my family. Be a kid at the table with a children's menu and crayons. Shoot spitballs through straws with Levi. But I wasn't a kid anymore. I was almost a mother. I hugged everyone, then left and headed toward the Health Department to find out just how soon before I officially claimed the Mom title.

Dr. Patton removed his gloves and tossed them in a red bin. "Well, since Monday, things have progressed quickly. You're dilated four centimeters. Are you not feeling your contractions?"

The news caught me off guard. "I mean a little. But I thought they were Braxton-Hicks like the nurse at school said." I sat up and tucked the paper sheet covering my bottom half under my thighs.

"From what I can tell, I think you're having a baby this weekend. You're a couple of weeks early, but that's still considered full-term so no need to worry."

A million thoughts rushed through my head. I hadn't bought the baby's coming home outfit. I hadn't packed a bag. I hadn't even picked a name. And most importantly, I hadn't made up with my best friend. I couldn't have this baby without her.

"What do I do next?" Suddenly I'd forgotten everything I'd learned in ETM.

"You're in early labor. It could last a couple of days. For now, go about your normal activities. Walking can help things progress. You're young and already partially dilated. When your contractions increase in intensity to where you have difficulty speaking, or your water breaks, whichever comes first, head to the hospital. Do you have any other questions?"

My mind blanked. "Not right now."

"You're going to do great. I'll see you soon."

After Dr. Patton left, I fell back on the examination table. *I'm about to have a baby. I need to get busy.*

Chapter Forty-Five

Obstinate, Headstrong Girl

I walked into the baby superstore for the second time. The sweet smell of baby powder hit me with urgency. It was time to put the money Mom gave me to good use and find my daughter a coming home outfit.

For about an hour, I sifted through racks of ruffly pink newborn dresses. They all looked the same. Nothing grabbed me. I gave up. Rather than waste the money on something I didn't like, I'd select something for her to wear from the clothes I already had.

Near the exit, an older woman sat behind a table stacked with embroidered onesies.

"Did you make these?" I asked.

She put down the book she'd been reading. "I did. Looking for anything special?"

"A coming home outfit." I put my hands on my belly. "For my daughter."

"Okie dokie. Most people go for something a little fancier than a onesie, but your choice. The phrases on these are reading-inspired. It's a fundraiser for the nonprofit, A Book for Every Baby. A portion of the proceeds goes toward sending each newborn from our local hospital home with a book. Looks like you'll be getting one soon."

The phrases read, "Future Bookworm," "Mom's Reading Date," "The More You Read The More You Know," "Little Prince," and then I saw it. A onesie that read, "Obstinate, Headstrong Girl." Oh my gosh. I knew what I'd name my daughter. I'd name her Elizabeth—after one of the strongest and most independent women I'd ever read about in any novel. She was a woman who refused to live a life that wasn't true to herself. That's the kind of role model my daughter deserved and if it couldn't be me, it would be Elizabeth Bennet.

I pointed to the pale-yellow onesie my daughter, Elizabeth, would wear home from the hospital. "I'll take that one."

"Oh, you're a Jane Austen fan? *Pride and Prejudice* is one of my favorites." She wrapped the garment in pastel tissue paper, slipped it into a gift bag, and passed it to me.

"I read it last summer." I paid, thanked her, and dashed out. I still had so much more to do.

Back home, I called my parents and alerted them to be on baby stand-by. Mom wanted to rush over, but this was her wedding night. Besides, I knew who I wanted to see.

I picked up the phone and dialed the number to the laundromat, she'd still be at work. So many times I had wanted to call. Stupid stubbornness. But Julie was as big a part of Elizabeth's story as me. She had to be there.

"Hello, Spin City Laundry. How can I help you?"

"Jules, it's me." I held my breath.

"Angela? Is everything okay?"

"Yes, everything's fine. I called to say I'm sorry. Can I blame it on pregnancy hormones?"

She didn't respond right away, but when she did, I knew once again that she'd be my best friend for the rest of my life. "Yeah, I guess if you mix teenage and pregnancy hormones, that's one heck of a recipe for disaster."

We both laughed and just like that it was over.

"I also called to tell you something else. Today, Dr. Patton said I'm almost ready to have the baby and walking would help progress the labor."

She wasted no time volunteering. "I guess I'm coming over after work for a little stroll."

"And one more thing, she has a name—Elizabeth Julie."

"Seriously! I love it. I'm going to be the best aunt in the history of aunts."

Of course she would.

After we hung up, a methodical urgency kept my panic at bay, and I continued my to-do list.

In the baby's room, I straightened the quilt inside the crib and re-tucked the pink towel around the pad on the change table. Then I added a few more diapers to the paisley diaper stacker. Elizabeth's room was ready.

I emptied my school backpack and put in it the nightgown Dad had given me along with the too-big slippers from Dale. With no idea what my postpartum body would look like, I picked out a loose-fitting maternity dress to wear home. I also put in the onesie I'd bought and a receiving blanket Julie's parents gave me. Then I sat it by the back door of the run-down trailer my daughter would call her first home.

Dale came in as I was writing names and phone numbers to give to Julie to call when I did go to the hospital. "Hey, how was work?"

"Long."

I wanted to ask, *How was it long when you only worked half a day?* But I restrained myself. I didn't want to fight, not tonight.

"Julie's coming over. Dr. Patton said the baby's coming soon and that I should walk."

Maybe knowing his daughter would be here soon would stir some emotion, but no.

"That's fine. I'm gonna lay down. I'm tired."

"Okay." His post-jail demeanor was complicated. Booze and drug-free didn't make for Dale a happy boy.

But his issues weren't mine. I was focused on something bigger. I couldn't wait for Julie to get here. I had a feeling a long night awaited us. And I was looking forward to every moment.

Chapter Forty-Six

Memory Lane

Julie knocked on the door as I attempted to reach over my belly and tie my sneakers. "Come in." I gave up. "Can you do this for me?"

"Is this what I have to look forward to one day to if I ever get pregnant? Not that I'm planning on it anytime soon."

"Not being able to tie your shoes isn't the half of it. Speaking of, how are things with Andrew?"

"I'd hardly call pregnancy a transition into Andrew."

I nudged her. "I didn't mean it that way. Like in general."

"Good. We're taking it kinda slow, but I like the direction we're headed. How about you and... Dale?" She always paused before she said his name.

I waited until we got outside and started walking to answer.

"Before he went to jail, things were, let's just say, not great. But since he's been home, he's like a shell of his former self. We don't really talk. And when he's not working, all he does is sleep. It's weird."

"I won't ask you tonight what 'not great' means. But one day, even if it's not me, you need to tell someone."

Walking down the crumbling asphalt streets of the trailer park, I couldn't imagine ever telling anyone the things that had happened with Dale. Those nightmares I'd take to my grave.

I was done talking about him. "Do you remember the day we met?"

She flung her head backward. "Oh gosh, yes. I was such an idiot."

"I thought you wanted to fight me. You were like this sixty-pound twig standing with your legs apart and hands on your hips demanding to know who we were and why we were there." I stopped in the middle of the street and mimicked her stance.

"I was the unofficial city pool sentry. I had to personally vet anyone who entered, like a bar bouncer."

We laughed so hard we were almost crying. "Stop it. Unless you want me to have this baby in the middle of the street. I gotta sit down."

"Here, let me help you." Julie grabbed my arms as I lowered myself awkwardly to the side of the pavement. I remembered that day at the pool like it was yesterday. It was the summer my family had moved to Florida. Levi and I begged Mom to give us money to go to the pool. Julie and I had been inseparable ever since.

After our laughter wound down, she asked, "Are you nervous?"

"A little. I mean not so much about the birth process. I know that like the back of my hand. But, after. The other side of motherhood is a dark abyss."

"Ange, you've got this. Don't put too much pressure on yourself. The only thing you need to worry about right now is bringing Miss Elizabeth into the world. You'll figure out the rest."

Figure out the rest. People said that like it was doing something. But it wasn't. It was only an excuse to not do anything. "Yeah, I'll figure it out."

"Hey, it's getting dark, and you probably should get some rest in case our walk was productive. Let's get you back."

Julie stood and then helped me up.

When we got back to the trailer, I gave her the list of names and phone numbers.

"The second you go into labor, call me. I don't care if it's the middle of the night."

"I will. Thanks for coming. I needed this."

"I did, too. All right, rest. Let's hope we have a baby soon."

After she left, I took a warm bath. Reclined in the tub with my belly protruding like an iceberg, I couldn't imagine not being pregnant. I had grown so used to feeling her inside me.

I moved my hands around trying to figure out which body parts were where, and that's when I felt it. The muscles in my abdomen tightened like a vice grip. I grabbed the sides of the tub and held my breath. It was time.

CHAPTER FORTY-SEVEN

LABOR INTENSE

As I DRESSED, A brief calmness washed over me. Then the shooting pain of another contraction swept the calm far, far away leaving nothing behind but a brewing storm.

"Dale, Dale, you asleep?" I shook him lightly.

"I was. Damn. If you can't sleep, go to the couch."

"I haven't been sleeping. I think I'm in labor."

"Do you know for sure?"

I put one hand on the door frame and the other under my belly and bent over. The discomfort started low and then spread around my entire torso before receding.

"I'm pretty sure. I'm having contractions, and both nurse Cathy and Dr. Patton told me to go to the hospital when I couldn't talk through them. It's close to that."

"Call Mama. I can't drive anyway, and I gotta work tomorrow." He tugged at the comforter and rolled over.

So much for wanting to be there when the baby was born.

"Addis, it's me. Can you take me to the hospital? I think I'm in labor." Another contraction. I tried to breathe through it like I was taught in ETM. With each one, the muscles in my stomach tightened a notch more, forcing me to hold my breath instead.

"Of course. I'm on my way. Hang on." Addis was more ready for this baby than me.

Next, I dialed Julie's number. "The walk must've worked. Addis is taking me to the hospital. Can you call everyone? I'll have Addis keep you updated on when to come up."

"Are you kidding me? I'll probably beat you there. We're having a baby tonight. Good luck. You've got this."

"Thanks. I'll see you on the other side."

I laid on the couch, closed my eyes, and placed my hands firmly on my belly. Starting at my back, the muscles tightened and ripped across my entire torso hardening it like stone.

Headlights flashed through the living room window. Addis must've sped the entire way. I waited for the contraction to recede, then pushed myself up, grabbed my backpack, and waddled outside. The next time I came back to this trailer, I'd have a baby with me.

The first thing Addis said when I opened the passenger door was, "Where's Dale?"

"Sleeping. He said he had to work in the morning." Honestly, I could care less if he came. All that mattered to me was meeting my baby daughter.

"He's not missing his baby's birth. I'll be right back."

I was in labor, and Addis was more worried about her son. At least she was consistent.

Through the car's open window, I choked on the moist night air as another contraction erupted. I did my best not to tense and to allow the pain to do its job.

A few minutes and contractions later, Addis emerged. Dale trailed behind her. He slipped into the back seat and lit a cigarette.

Nice of you to join us. I leaned the seat back, closed my eyes, and focused on my breathing.

Addis talked nonstop about her labor and delivery experiences and offered me what sounded like mostly terrible advice. "And make sure, no matter what, you don't push too hard, even if they tell ya. You'll split down there. They can pull the baby out with them forceps if they need to."

I wished she'd shut up. At least Dale was content, silently smoking one cigarette after another.

Addis pulled up to the Emergency Room entrance and let Dale and me out. "Go sit over there." I pointed. Without debate, he complied.

I checked in with a nurse at the ER desk. She brought around a wheelchair and said she'd take me to Labor and Delivery. I took off my backpack to sit and Dale took it from me. That was about as useful as he'd been during my entire pregnancy.

She pushed me into the elevator. When the doors closed, the intensity of cigarette smoke weakened my pain threshold. "It hurts."

"I know, hold on," she said. "We're almost there."

"Is Doctor Patton here tonight?" I asked as the elevator door opened.

"Yes, he is."

Relief flooded through my body as a contraction released.

"Dad, you wait here. We'll set Mom up and then come get you."

"Where can I have a smoke?"

The nurse pointed to a door.

He handed me my backpack. "Later."

Dale was a man of priorities. But I didn't care. His presence wasn't helpful anyway.

The nurse wheeled me into a room filled with three beds separated by thin curtains. Moaning women filled all but the one in the back, which was now mine. She helped me into a hospital gown, took my vitals, and asked me a bunch of questions while writing everything down in a chart. She then slid a thick elastic band up my torso to my belly and placed two circular objects connected by cords to a large machine underneath. "One of these is to monitor the baby's heartbeat, and one is to monitor your contractions."

"When can I get something for pain?"

"Dr. Patton needs to examine you first, and he'll let you know."

The curtain moved. "Hello, Miss Angela. I thought I'd see you soon, but I didn't think it'd be this soon. Let's see what's going on." He slipped on a pair of rubber gloves. "You're about six to seven centimeters dilated. How are you feeling?"

I white-knuckled the hospital bed railing. "Sorry, it hurts."

"We're going to get you a little relief. Don't you worry. You're in good hands. This is one heck of a team." He dropped the gloves in a red bin and left.

Relief couldn't happen fast enough.

The nurse inserted an IV into my left arm and added some medication. Seconds later, my eyelids grew heavy, and a welcome drowsiness washed over me.

"I'll be back to check on you in about a half hour. If you need me sooner, press this button."

Alone, whirring machines lulled me into a dream-like state. I was on a balcony at the beach—crashing and receding waves far below me. With each one, I drifted farther and farther into a peaceful calm—the ocean waves a distant white noise.

But then my senses turned acute when the smell of ashtray yanked me from an ocean-front balcony and back to a hospital bed.

"Hey." The sperm donor had arrived.

"Is anyone else here?"

"Yeah, Julie, your Mama and Daddy, Levi. Mama. Bob's home with Amber."

A warm liquid filled the bed. "Go get the nurse."

"What do I say?"

"To come here. Go." I arched my back to avoid the wet sheets.

He stayed in the hallway while the nurse checked me. "Honey, your water broke. It's okay. Totally normal."

Maneuvering my awkward body around like a pro, she changed both my gown and the sheets and re-attached the elastic bands and monitors. Then she studied the long receipt-like paper a large machine kept spitting out. "Now that the amniotic sac is no longer intact, labor should progress nicely. I'll have Dr. Patton come check on you soon."

After she left, Dale shuffled in and dropped onto a stool.

I lay on my side gripping the bed rail. Labor pains squeezed, twisting my stomach muscles into knots, and wringing out the last of any relief from the medication.

"Sorry 'bout the last couple a days. This is all so different for me. Not drinking, having a baby. You have it all together."

My back stiffened, an ominous warning another contraction had readied its claws. My jaw clenched and I hissed. "I don't have it all together. The only difference between the two of us is in the last few months, I've tried."

Dr. Patton appeared. Dale slipped out when the doctor said he was going to check my dilation.

"All right, Miss Angela, let's get you to the delivery room. It's time to meet your baby girl."

CHAPTER FORTY-EIGHT

ELIZABETH JULIE

EVERYTHING HAPPENED FAST. Two nurses wheeled me into the delivery room and transferred me from the bed onto a delivery table. They strapped my legs in stirrups, framing Dr. Patton, who now wore a headlamp, in a perfect triangle between my shaking knees. Blinding bright light blurred my surroundings. "It hurts so bad." I cried.

One of the nurses said, "I know. But you're doing great. When I count to three, grab under your knees, tuck your chin into your chest, and push."

A Fear Beast extended its claws, ripped out any confidence, and left nothing behind but excruciating gashes of self-doubt. "I can't do it."

"Yes, you can. We're going to lift your shoulders and help you."

They lifted my dead weight, and I gripped myself behind sweaty knees.

"All right. While I count, take a deep breath, then push. One, two, three. Push."

I channeled my disintegrating energy and pushed as hard as I could. Then fell back onto the delivery table. "I can't do it. Make it stop."

"Yes, you can. We're going to do the same thing again."

"No. Please. It hurts too bad." I begged.

"Honey, once the baby's born the pain will stop. And for the baby to be born you have to push. You can do it. Come on. One, two, three. Push."

I dug into a place in my soul I didn't know existed. With each push, sounds I'd never heard from a human filled the room. The Fear Beast retreated into a shadow.

"You're doing great. Her head has crowned. One more push like that, and she'll be out." Dr. Patton's voice was calm, encouraging.

"Okay." I cried as fire erupted between my legs.

The nurses lifted me again. "Here we go, give it all you got. One, two, three. Push."

A guttural scream harnessed the final fragment of energy within me.

Dr. Patton asked the nurse for a bulb syringe. "You did it. Her head is out. Now don't push until I tell you to. Keep breathing."

Rapid, shallow breaths couldn't fill my lungs with enough oxygen. My vision blurred and the room spun. The Fear Beast snarled.

"Okay, Honey, it's time," said a nurse.

"I can't. I can't."

"Yes, you can. You're so close. One, two, three. Push."

I had to find the strength to keep going outside myself because there was nothing left inside—inside where my daughter was. Elizabeth. *Obstinate*—I dug my chin into my chest. *Headstrong*—I took a deep breath. *Girl*—A final burst of adrenaline and it was over. The Fear Beast was gone.

I fell back on the table—raw throat and cracked lips. But none of that mattered when the most beautiful sound filled the room—my daughter's cry. Uncontrollable tears spilled. "Can I see her?"

A nurse wrapped her in a receiving blanket, then placed her in my shaky arms. Elizabeth was really here.

"Dad, you can come over and see your baby girl," a nurse said.

Dale emerged out of a shadow.

Dr Patton said, "Angela, you did it. She looks great."

I looked down and studied Elizabeth's tiny face. She was the most gorgeous thing I'd ever seen, and she was mine.

"You're gonna be a good mama," Dale said with an out-of-character tenderness.

Regardless of how he'd treated me over the last few months, I took advantage of the moment. "She also needs a good dad."

He placed a hand on top of her tiny head full of medium brown hair, the same color as his.

"Dad, you can head to the waiting room and give your family the good news. We need to get the baby to the pediatrician in the nursery and mom to recovery. You'll be able to see them both again in about an hour." The nurse took Elizabeth from me. I didn't want to let her go.

"Can you tell everyone thank you for waiting and that I can't wait to see them and for them to meet Elizabeth?"

"Elizabeth?" Dale stopped in the doorway and turned around. "I didn't know you'd picked out a name. But it's a good one. See ya." Then he left.

The nurse placed Elizabeth in a rolling cart and pushed her out the door. My arms already felt a void in her absence. As I caught a last glimpse of my daughter, I knew I would do anything to provide her with the best life possible. And to do that, some things needed to change.

CHAPTER FORTY-NINE

HAPPY "BIRTH" DAY

AFTER DR. PATTON AND the labor and delivery nurses wrapped up the not-so-pleasant post-partum procedures, they admitted me to my hospital room. The nurses transferred me from a wheelchair to the bed and told me a pediatric nurse would bring Elizabeth in soon. New motherhood euphoria kept my exhaustion at bay.

A nurse pushed in the same small rolling cart. "Dr. Carson said Miss Elizabeth looks perfect. Six pounds even and nineteen inches long." She picked up the swaddled bundle and handed her to me. It already felt like I'd held her a thousand times.

Her tiny eyes were closed. I could have stared at that face for eternity.

There was a knock at the door. The nurse opened it. Dale and our families poured in. Julie carried in a small pink cake with a zero candle in the center. Quietly, they all started singing, "Happy Birthday to you. Happy Birthday to you. Happy Birthday, Dear Elizabeth, Happy Birthday to you."

My eyes watered.

"Thanks. I hadn't thought about that. Today being her actual birthday." I turned the swaddled bundle to face them. "Elizabeth, meet your family."

"She's beautiful." Mom said through sobs only a grandmother could muster.

"I can't believe I'm an aunt." Julie sat the cake down on the side table next to a plastic pitcher of water and kissed Elizabeth on the forehead.

Addis pushed her way through. "Let me hold my granddaughter."

"Sorry, not yet. I just got her. I promise you'll get your turn, but not today." I wasn't about to hand her over to anyone yet, especially Addis.

The nurse interrupted. "Okay, everyone, now that you've all had a chance to see Mom and baby, let's give Dad a few minutes alone with his new family. Then it's time for them to get some rest."

I was so proud Julie wanted to be a nurse. I couldn't have done this without them.

Dad kissed me on the cheek and whispered, "Just now had that talk with the father of my granddaughter. Love you, Number One."

"Love you, too, Dad."

Levi waved goodbye from the door. I'm sure this whole baby business was awkward for an almost sixteen-year-old. I'd get time with my family later. Right now, all I wanted was to get to know my daughter.

After they left, Dale sat on my hospital bed's edge. "She's a cutie, all right. You did good in there. I can't imagine what that was like for you."

"It was the hardest thing I've ever done in my life. But she was worth it." I appreciated his compliments. But I was still ready for him to leave.

"Your daddy and I talked. I'm sorry for some of the shit I've done. I'm gonna do better. Got a daughter now." He gave me a soft smile.

"Thank you. We can do this. She deserves it." I covered the top of her head with kisses.

"What's next?" Dale asked.

I was grateful he picked up my cues and was also willing to do what I said needed to be done. It was about time.

"We need to get picked up in the morning after we get discharged. Since I don't have insurance, we have to leave the hospital within twenty-four hours."

"Okay. I'll be at work. Call Mama. She can come get me, and we'll pick you both up."

"The car seat Mrs. Keene gave me is in Elizabeth's room. Don't forget it."

"I won't. See you tomorrow." He touched the top of Elizabeth's head one last time, then left.

Finally, I was alone with my daughter.

I bent my knees and placed her on my thighs. "Okay, Miss Elizabeth. It's time Mommy gets to see what you look like under all this."

Her eyes were still closed tight, and her tiny body swaddled in the hospital receiving blanket. She looked like a baby burrito. I unwrapped her. I'd have to ask one of the nurses to show me how to wrap her back up. I pulled off her pink and blue knit cap; she had so much hair. One by one, I counted each tiny perfect finger and toe.

I pulled her into my chest, overwhelmed with the gravity of the moment. I never wanted this feeling to end. I had no idea what would happen to us after we left this hospital. It felt so safe here. And that's all I wanted, for us both to be safe. I was afraid when we left, that feeling wouldn't come with us.

CHAPTER FIFTY

DISCHARGED AND CONFUSED

A KNOCK AT THE door woke me from a restless sleep.

"Discharge time." A nurse entered, pushing Elizabeth in her rolling cart.

The night before, they'd brought her to me every four hours so I could feed her a bottle and to check on my recovery. Then they'd take her back to the nursery for me to rest. But resting in four-hour increments wasn't easy. I now understood what Meka had said about being tired. Mom-exhaustion was on a level of its own.

The nurse placed Elizabeth in my arms—arms that would never tire of holding her.

"Good morning, Baby Girl. We're going home today." Only I wished her home wasn't in a smoke-filled run-down trailer. I wished I was taking her to a home in a neighborhood like Julie's with a nursery as fancy as her new crib. She started crying, and the nurse passed me a bottle. I wanted so much better for her than I could provide.

"Mom, I'm going to go over the discharge notes with you now while you feed her."

The notes contained about twenty bulleted items on newborn-related topics such as how often they should eat, how to burp them, everything you'd ever want to know about baby poop, how often they should sleep, where they should sleep, how they should sleep, how to take care of an umbilical cord, and car seat safety.

She also reviewed my post-partum care, such as avoiding baths and only showering to prevent infection. And that I could expect to bleed for up to six weeks. I'd learned much of this in ETM, but getting answers correct on a quiz was way different than putting that information into practice.

"Honey, are you okay?"

The blank expression on my face must have hinted at my overwhelm. "I'm a little nervous, that's all." I looked down at Elizabeth, drinking the last of her bottle. I didn't know how I'd take care of her when I hadn't done that great of a job taking care of myself. Cathy said I shouldn't nurse since I wasn't consuming enough calories, and I hadn't applied for WIC yet. How could I afford formula? As reality slowly kicked in, confusion and fear crept up my emotional meter.

"It's okay. You can do this. You have this beautiful baby girl here that needs you. Your mothering instinct will kick in. I promise. How you're feeling is totally normal for first-time mothers." She patted my shoulder.

I signed the bottom of the page with a shaky hand. I couldn't believe they would let anyone walk out with a baby.

"Here, in this bag is what you'll need for the first few days, some extra diapers, formula, the medication to prevent breast engorgement since you aren't nursing, all kinds of other goodies, and a bunch of literature explaining everything you need to know." She put a pale green diaper bag on the bed.

"Thank you." I peeked in. Inside was a board book version of *Goodnight Moon* with a sticker on the front that read "A Book for Every Baby." Despite my nerves, I smiled. I'd never forget that woman at the Baby Super Store and how I finally decided what to name Elizabeth.

"You're welcome. And if you have any questions after you get home, feel free to call us."

I unwrapped her swaddle, took off the tiny hospital t-shirt, and carefully dressed her in her going-home onesie. I hoped that's how she grew up, like Elizabeth Bennet—stubborn enough to follow her own heart.

There was another knock at the door. Addis and Dale walked in. He was carrying the car seat. "How was the rest of the night?"

His concern sounded oddly genuine. "It was good. I mean, I barely got any rest, but she's been eating great."

"Come here, Miss Elizabeth, so Grandma can put you in the car seat." Without asking, Addis took Elizabeth from me. I didn't mind this time since I had no idea how to work the complicated contraption.

Addis read the onesie out loud, "'Obstinate, Headstrong Girl.' What on God's Green Earth does that mean? You're supposed to put her in a cute pink dress for her coming home outfit." She mumbled something else as she strapped Elizabeth in.

I ignored her question. "Thanks for buckling her in." Addis' actions and attitude were a crystal ball into what I assumed would be a rocky relationship for us. And although I didn't want her help, I needed it.

Dale grabbed my arm as I swung my legs off the bed to get into the wheelchair the nurse would roll me out in. "Here, let me help you."

He didn't seem like the same person. When I was pregnant with Elizabeth, I'd already felt a change inside me. Maybe now that she was here, that change would happen in him.

Addis went to lift the car seat, and the nurse said, "Grandma, why don't you carry mom's bag? Dad can do that."

Ha. I wanted to laugh out loud. Addis rolled her eyes and snatched my bag from me. Dale lifted Elizabeth and scooped his arm through the handle. Not with the finesse of Meka, but more like a new father nervous he'll do something wrong but hopes he won't.

After the nurse helped me into the backseat, and Dale figured out how to pop Elizabeth's car seat into its base, I grabbed her tiny little hand. Slowly the hospital disappeared into the rearview mirror. My daughter's soft skin, Dale's change toward me, and even Addis' annoying desire to help made me think that maybe we would be okay.

I struggled walking up the steps into the trailer. Dale held on to me until I got up and into the bedroom. "Do you need anything?"

"I'd like some water. And my daughter. If you don't mind."

Addis held Elizabeth captive in the living room. Her high-pitched annoying voice rang through the trailer. "Hey there, Grandma's little girl, who loves you? Grandma does. Who's Grandma's little princess?"

Dale and I locked eyes. For a brief moment, and that didn't happen often, he and I were on the same page. "Gotcha. I'll be right back."

I slipped out of my shoes and put my feet on the bed. Every muscle in my body ached.

A few minutes later, Dale returned, carrying Elizabeth in one arm and a glass of ice water in the other. That was the first time he'd held her since she'd been born. "Here, little one. Go to your mama." He gently placed her in my arms. "Sorry about that. Mama always wanted a girl."

"I know. Can you go ask her to make a bottle? Maybe that'll make her feel useful." I didn't care how much Addis always wanted a girl; Elizabeth wasn't hers. I'd accept her help, but I wouldn't let her overstep.

"Good idea." He left for the kitchen again and was back in a jiffy. "Here, she said anything you need, just let her know."

"I need her to leave." We shared a quiet laugh. For a moment, I wondered if he realized the bad things he'd done to me were actually bad. Maybe he really didn't know.

"She's about to. I'm going with her. She's gonna drop me off at work. Got another mouth to feed now. You gonna be okay?"

"Yeah. We'll be fine." I hoped I could manifest that maternal instinct everyone kept talking about.

He kissed Elizabeth on the top of the head. "Bye. See my girls later."

"Bye, Daddy." I picked up her tiny arm and pretended she was waving.

I'd never love Dale. That was a given. But I wanted my daughter to have her father's unconditional love. She deserved that. It was up to me to make sure it happened, and I was willing to sacrifice my happiness for hers.

CHAPTER FIFTY-ONE

REALITY CHECK

I CAREFULLY PLACED ELIZABETH on the change table and smiled at the yellow onesie. Even though she was less than twenty-four hours old, I already had so many hopes and dreams for her. Dreams bigger than a trailer park.

With a pair of infant nail clippers, I snipped off her baby bracelet and slipped it into the pocket of my dress. Then I changed her diaper, cleaned her umbilical cord like the nurse told me, and did my best to emulate the nurse's swaddle. Not half bad.

Her tiny eyes were shut tight, so I placed her in her crib on top of the soft, paisley sheets. A few nights ago, the empty crib reflected how I felt. But now, seeing my daughter sleeping inside it, I felt empty no more. I was full. Full of more love than I'd thought possible—maternal instinct had officially kicked in.

I took the cigar box my mother had given me out of the dresser. I dropped Elizabeth's tiny ID bracelet in it. Then I cut mine off and added it to the contents. Maybe one day, I'd pass this box on to her like my mother had passed it on to me.

Since I had a few hours before I'd need to feed a hungry baby, I called my mother. "Hi, Mom. We're home from the hospital."

"I want to hear about my granddaughter, but first, how's my Baby Girl doing?" Grandmothers were still moms first.

"Good, I mean, other than being really tired and feeling like I was hit by a Mack truck. After having a baby, I can see why. I'm certainly not ready to do that again anytime soon. But she was worth it."

"She's beautiful. I'm sorry we're moving. I won't be around to help you."

I would have much-preferred Mom a mile down the road than Addis. But I didn't want her covered in any more guilt. She'd carried enough of that around for a lifetime. "Don't feel bad. We'll visit. It's not that far a drive. I definitely plan to come with her this summer."

"That would be great. Hey, Julie and I are making a schedule to get meals to you and Dale for the next week. Any special requests?"

"Do you even have to ask?"

"Your Dad's gumbo?"

My stomach rumbled to life as soon as she said the word. "I could eat three bowls of it."

"Do you want me to bring you something over now?"

As much as I wanted the gumbo, exhaustion had a bigger hold on me than hunger. "No, I'm gonna rest today. But tomorrow'd be great."

"I'm sure your dad would love to make some 'Welcome Home, Elizabeth' gumbo."

"Thanks for being there. I know it was a long night."

"I'm so proud of you. You're going to be a great mother."

I hoped her confidence in me would help me build my own. "I'm going to do my best. Well, I'm going to take a nap before she needs to eat."

"That's exactly what I was about to say. The best advice I ever got was to sleep when the baby sleeps. Love you. I'll bring over some food tomorrow."

"Thanks. Love you, too."

I went into the kitchen to find a snack to at least curb my hunger pains so I could nap. But when I opened the fridge, I lost my appetite. Inside it I spotted a twelve-pack of beer box, half empty. Laying low didn't last long. I wanted to be angry. But he'd been oddly nice. And drinking wasn't breaking the law. I just didn't like who it turned him into.

I slept the rest of the day when Elizabeth slept and fed her every four hours as instructed by the hospital discharge nurse. At six o'clock p.m., she'd fallen asleep. I set my alarm for ten o'clock. I planned to take one last nap with her before Dale came home. For now, I wouldn't mention the beer. I needed to focus on myself and Elizabeth exclusively for the next week because in seven days, I had to be back in school to meet my graduation requirements.

The alarm woke me to darkness. Elizabeth cried in the pillow cradle I'd made for her on my bed. I fumbled around on the nightstand and turned on the lamp. "Come here, Sweetie. Let's go make a bottle."

Cradling my newborn, I turned on the hall light to lead me safely to the kitchen.

After I made the bottle, I sat on the couch to feed her. Headlights shone through the open window. I coughed as the exhaust from Roger's truck sifted through it.

Dale stumbled in, barely able to shut the door behind him. "There's Daddy's girls." He collapsed on the couch next to me.

I stood with her. I refused to allow my new daughter to inhale her father's booze and tobacco-infused breath. "I thought you said your attorney told you to lay low. This doesn't look like laying low."

"I didn't tell ya. My attorney's gettin' me off on a technicality." He fumbled taking off his boots. "Happens all the time. If you got a good one."

"Where've you been? I've been here all alone on my first day with her. I would've thought you'd want to be with us."

"Roger and me and some guys went for a few celebratory drinks in honor of my baby girl. I'm a daddy now." He hiccupped through his excuse, then leaned back and shut his eyes.

My fresh maternal instinct cloaked me in courage. "The first day your new daughter is home from the hospital, you go out and party and don't even bother calling. That's unacceptable."

I started down the hall. "You're sleeping out here. Do you hear me?" But he was already snoring.

I carried Elizabeth into the bedroom and shut and locked the door behind me. I didn't know if I was locking us in or him out or both. The truth was, whether Dale made the decision to be a good father or not didn't really matter. Because I'd decided to help him, Elizabeth deserved that. He just wasn't making it easy. Mothering instinct was a bitch.

CHAPTER FIFTY-TWO

CROSSING A THIN WHITE LINE

I DIDN'T UNDERSTAND HOW a month of pregnancy could feel like an eternity, but a month of motherhood could fly by in the blink of an eye.

"She's already gotten so big," Suzanne said as she held Elizabeth while I helped prep the ETM breakfast. Although she'd already given birth and the baby had been adopted, Suzanne would finish out the rest of the year.

"I know. She's already grown out of her newborn clothes." As I scooped the scrambled eggs onto trays, Mrs. Keene approached me.

"Mr. Demalina called and would like to have a word soon."

Ever since that visit by Officer Creswell, a call to the office always made my heart race.

"Go now. I've got Miss Elizabeth. It looks like she's ready for her nap." Suzanne said as she turned toward the cluster of cribs.

I wondered if holding Elizabeth made her miss her baby. But she'd already started applying to colleges and making plans. Plans that would be difficult as a new mother. Plans I tried not to envy.

Mr. Demalina opened a folder and scanned a document. "In reviewing your transcripts, you've completed everything you need to graduate."

For the last several months ETM had been my safe zone. But I'd done it. I'd graduated. The news was bittersweet at best. "That's great. I was a little worried because of the week I missed when I had the baby."

He tucked his reading glasses into his front pocket. "What's next for you?"

He wouldn't like my answer, but I had to give it. I squared my shoulders and forced a smile. "I got a job at a daycare. Elizabeth can come with me for free."

"And..." His glare asked for information I couldn't provide.

"I'm sorry. Right now, I can't do the college thing."

"Please tell me you at least filled out the scholarship application?"

I'd almost forgotten about it. But I probably wouldn't get it, and if I did, I couldn't use it, so I lied. "No, it's not the right time. But I appreciate everything."

I felt terrible disappointing him. But this was my life. And I had to make the best decisions for me and Elizabeth for now. Maybe down the road things might be different—unlikely, but maybe.

He nodded in defeat. "I understand. You'll receive your diploma in the mail in a few weeks. I wish you the best."

"Thank you." We shook hands, and I headed back to ETM. The dread of my future pretty much depleted the euphoria of new motherhood.

Tonight, Julie and Andrew would walk across the North Lake High School gym stage and receive their diplomas. Mine would come in a mailbox. After graduation, they'd go to the senior lock-in and stay up all night eating pizza and dancing.

Today, my official last day of high school, there'd be no party. But there would be a lock-in—in a trailer. And I would be up all night—feeding a hungry infant.

I didn't regret Elizabeth, not even a little. She was the best thing that had ever happened to me. But the rest of my life: one colossal regret.

Back in class, I checked on Elizabeth. She was fast asleep in one of the cribs. I thanked Suzanne for keeping an eye on her. Early on, I'd tried to bond with Meka, Suzanne, and a few other girls. It's not like I didn't like them. I just didn't have the mental bandwidth to do it. And I knew I'd probably never see them again after I left—another regret.

Mrs. Keene approached; a huge grin exposed pearly white teeth. "You did it. You graduated."

"I really appreciate everything you did for me. I probably would've dropped out of school if it hadn't been for ETM."

"You're not limited by this season of your life. It doesn't define you. And I hope, more than anything, one day you'll have the faith in yourself that others have in you."

Here was another person I'd let down. "Thank you." I hugged her one last time and said goodbye to the other girls. Then I buckled a sleeping Elizabeth into her car seat and, because of what I'd learned here, effortlessly slipped my arm through the handle and carried her out the door. Outside an afternoon Florida shower ensued. I tossed a blanket over Elizabeth and quickly popped the car seat into its base.

I sat in my car and allowed the rain and my tears to pass. Mrs. Keene had said she was proud of me, but how could she be? I'd finished high school—big deal. Graduating was supposed to be the start of something bigger—not the end of something small.

When the storms inside me, and out, let up, I headed to my graduation party at the Sunshine Estates trailer park.

Dale and Roger were inside drinking and watching TV. They always loved a good ole storm. You can't frame houses in the rain.

"Hey, Miss Angela. Ain't seen you in a while," Roger said as he popped a can.

He'd always been nice to me. Maybe not the smartest guy in North Lake, but nice. "Hey, Roger. Busy with the baby and school, which today, I found out I'm done." At least I had someone to personally share the news with.

"Congrats. You can put all that crap behind you now," he replied.

"Yeah, thankfully, that's over. Good riddance." Like them, I was now the highest version of myself, which was pretty low.

"How's Daddy's baby girl?" Dale got up to rub Elizabeth's head.

I pulled the car seat away so he couldn't. "She's good, out cold."

He pointed toward her room. "Why don't you put her to bed and let's celebrate your graduation."

Celebrate? I didn't feel like I had anything to celebrate.

Julie and Andrew were probably at the school by now rehearsing. Julie told me the whole senior class devised this plan for each student to give the principal a marble as he handed them their diploma. By the end of the ceremony, he'd have one hundred and fifty marbles in his pocket. No, make that one hundred and forty-nine.

"Sure, why not." I carried Elizabeth's car seat into her room and carefully unbuckled her. When I placed her in her crib, she wriggled and let out a soft cry. I froze. Once she settled, I pulled her door almost shut and tiptoed out.

Back in the living room, Dale held a beer toward me. My initial reaction was to say "Thanks, but no thanks." Instead, I took it.

Roger stood. "To the beautiful Angela. Not only are you a new mama, but you're also done with high school and free to live the rest of your life on your terms. Congrats." We clicked our cans together.

Then I popped the top and chugged the beer. It was time to stop fighting the inevitable. As the pungent liquid raced down my throat, I realized this is who I am now. I didn't stop until the can was empty.

Dale shouted, "Go, Baby, go." Then handed me another.

Roger pulled a small container out of his pocket. "Miss Angela, this is extra special—just for you." He dumped out a white powder on the coffee table. Then took his driver's license out of his wallet and formed the fine powder into three equal lines.

Dale rolled a dollar bill into a thin tube. Then he bent down, put the bill up to his nose, inhaled, and one line vanished. He handed the tightly rolled bill to Roger.

Line two—poof—gone. Roger offered the bill to me.

I didn't take it.

"Baby, do you know how proud I am of you right now? Do it. There's nothing to be scared of. You deserve to celebrate how hard you've worked."

Julie and the rest of the seniors had college plans and curfews. Every single one of them would trade places with me if they could. I could have a real celebration—like an adult. I snatched the rolled bill from Roger. Then, I bent down toward the table and crossed a fine white line.

Chapter Fifty-Three

Fake a Smile and Say Cheese

My throbbing head rested on a tingling arm. Dale must have taken my pillow. I reached out for it—nothing.

A baby cried—Elizabeth. My eyes shot open to darkness. *Oh my God!* I was on the floor of her bedroom.

I propelled my stiff body up and almost tripped at the shorts and underwear around my ankles. Shock forced me to act rather than think. I yanked them up, turned on the night light, and grabbed her. Her little face was beet red, and arms and legs flailed inside drenched footed pajamas.

"Hey, Sweetie. Mommy's here." My hands shook as I placed her trembling body on the changing table. Her full diaper told me I'd been out for hours.

After I slipped her tiny limbs into a clean diaper and fresh pajamas, I picked her up and held her close. A thousand worst-case scenarios raced—some of which I feared were true. "I'm so, so, sorry." As her heartbeat against my chest, her body calmed, and her cries slowed.

Everything was so damn hard. Things that should have been easy. All of it. Just keeping her fed and in a dry diaper for one night. My mothering bar couldn't be any lower and yet I still couldn't reach it.

She nibbled on my finger. I was terrified to witness what I'd see when I walked out of her room. But I had to feed her. I had to fake strength that didn't exist.

A shirtless Dale lay passed out on the couch. Roger, thankfully fully clothed, was slumped over in one of the green chairs. Beer cans littered the floor. Bits and pieces of the afternoon started coming back to me. The flashbacks filled in a hazy picture of a horrible scene. I pushed the nightmare deep into my dark soul so I could focus on Elizabeth.

I scooped out powdered formula from a nearly empty can. Great. I'd have to ask Dale for money. I was still waiting on the WIC approval I'd finally applied for.

Back in the bedroom, as I fed her, I thought about Suzanne giving her baby up for adoption. I should've done the same thing. Elizabeth would have a better life with any mother that wasn't me. And any father that wasn't Dale. Maybe it wasn't too late.

But she was here and in my arms. It would kill me now to give her up. I was the only mom she knew. I laid her on the bed and wrapped myself around her as sobs tore my emotions to shreds. I had to do better. I had to be better. I wanted to be a good mother. It was just so hard to be good here.

Hours later, sour body odor woke me from a restless sleep. Dale had made it to the bed. Light filtered through peeling plastic shades that covered dirty windows. I didn't want to follow him down his path of destruction. But I had no other path to follow. And I didn't have the means to forge my own.

I pulled Elizabeth to me and inhaled her soft, sweet scent. "Come on, Baby Girl. We have things to do today." I couldn't get out of the trailer fast enough.

———

Bob and Levi were loading the moving van. Mom and Amber ran outside toward my car. When I got out, they almost knocked me over with hugs.

"Sissy, where's Elizabeth?"

"She's in the backseat." My head throbbed. I hadn't had a hangover since before I got pregnant. Even after a shower, I still felt dirty and disgusting.

"I'll get her." Mom opened the door and took her out of her car seat. "You're growing so fast. Nana's gonna miss you."

"I checked my calendar. It's only four weeks until we come." Four weeks before my hell reprieve.

Amber jumped up and down. "I'll have my dog by then." Bob had insisted she have a furry best friend to help her adjust to the move.

We walked toward the boys. "Hey, Sis."

"Happy almost sixteenth birthday." I'd pulled away from so many people the last year. I regretted Levi had been one of them. "I'll see you in a few weeks and we can celebrate."

Bob shut the moving van's door. "That's the last of what's going in here. The rest will have to squeeze into the car." Then he turned to mom, "Hey, Nana. It's my turn to hold the little one." He held out tattooed hands; each finger bejeweled with silver and turquoise rings.

"Of course, Poppa Bob." She passed Elizabeth to him then turned to me. "I have something for you inside."

"You guys go on. I got Elizabeth," Bob said. Levi and Amber encircled him, and goofy baby talk erupted.

I followed Mom inside and the shame of last night followed me. Our footsteps echoed in the empty space. Erased of any evidence of the Carter family, it was if a criminal had cleaned up a crime scene. A sadness I hadn't expected tugged at my slow-beating heart—all the things that could've been.

Inside, she picked up a bag off the kitchen counter and handed it to me.

"What is it?"

"Open it."

Inside I found a camera and several rolls of film. "Thank you."

"I don't want to miss a thing. Take tons of pictures. I'll pay for them to be developed and send you new rolls of film each month."

"This is perfect." I opened the camera and popped in the film. "Let's get some before you guys leave."

She smiled. "Great idea."

As we headed toward the door, I stopped. "Mom, I wanna take one last walk through the house."

"Sure, Baby Girl. Take your time."

When we moved from Mississippi, Dad and I had taken one last tour of our empty home. In every room, we shared a happy memory allowing our hearts to take those with us.

In this house, happy memories would be more difficult to recall, but I had to try. I looked over at the stove, easy—gumbo. This kitchen wasn't the chef's dream like the one back in Mississippi, but Dad's gumbo always tasted just as delicious. Although I'd helped him make it many times, I'd never paid enough attention to make it on my own. I'd ask him to show me so I could make it for Elizabeth when she got older.

I walked down the short hallway. On the right was the bathroom—Julie. At fifteen, we pierced a second hole in our ears in there.

We froze our lobes with ice cubes and pushed needles through our frigid flesh. We got into so much trouble. I ran my index finger over one of our silver matching studs. She and her family were gone on their Midwest RV trip. The one I was supposed to take with them.

Levi's room sat across from the bathroom. It was always full of half-taken-apart toasters and hair dryers. Anytime an appliance died, he disassembled, reassembled, and even fixed some of them. We always joked he'd be an engineer. There was a great college in the Panhandle.

I peeked into Amber's hideous purple room. Mom had let her pick the color. On painting day, we had as much of the color on us as the walls. So much laughter. Purple would always be my happy color.

The last room on the right was my parents'. I squeezed my eyes tight and searched until I found what I was looking for. It was a Saturday morning, and they were still in bed. I was about thirteen or fourteen, but I climbed in with them like I'd done when I was little. I don't remember what we talked about, but I do remember how I felt sandwiched between them, safe and loved.

Finally, I walked into my old room. I laid down between the indentations on the carpet where my bed once sat. There were eighteen openings in the AC vent on the ceiling, sixteen panes of glass in the window that faced the front of the house, nine in the one that faced the side, and one hundred and twenty slats in the louvered closet doors. I knew those things because I used to lie here and count them when I was bored. Back when I was innocent enough not to have a care in the world.

I couldn't recall any of those details about the trailer because I never laid in that bed bored and innocent. In that bed, I was nothing like the girl that lay here. And no one knew the things I'd done and that had been done to me. Being in my childhood room for the last time, I decided I'd do everything in my power to make sure no one ever did.

I got up—time to go fake a smile and say cheese.

CHAPTER FIFTY-FOUR

SMALL STEPS

"Good morning. As soon as you drop off Elizabeth, I'd like your input on the rest of the summer activities," said Alison, my new boss at Small Steps.

"Sure, I'll be right back." My prior experience landed me the job at the only daycare in North Lake. It was only for the summer, but at least it was a temporary reprieve from asking Dale for money.

"There's my little sunshine." Ms. Debby, Alison's mom, ran the infant room. "How was Elizabeth's night?"

"Good. Slept eight hours straight. That's a first. She refused her bottle this morning, so she might be hungry. Already getting a little stubborn."

Ms. Debby took her from me. "Miss Elizabeth, that's too long for a growing girl like you to not have something in that little tummy."

My shoulders dropped that I didn't pick up on the things Ms. Debby did. My mothering instinct still wasn't up to par.

"I'll keep an extra eye on you today, honey." Ms. Debby walked away, covering the top of Elizabeth's head with soft kisses.

Alison and I spent about an hour planning the rest of the summer. She agreed I could read a chapter book to the older kids. I picked *Island of the Blue Dolphins,* about a twelve-year-old Native American girl stranded alone for years on an island off the coast of California. I'd always admired Karana's resilience in the face of adversity. It was a message all kids needed to hear. It was a message this kid needed to hear.

We wrapped up when parents started dropping off their kids. I collected my group. "Danielle, you are the line leader, and William, you are the caboose. Everyone else, line up by the colors of the rainbow based on what you're wearing." Last week I'd taught them about Roy G. Biv, so this was their quiz. I'd taught the same thing to a student at the after-school program, the memory rubbed my raw wound.

The children switched places until the line was perfect.

"Nice job, let's go."

At the playground, most of the kids hit the swings or the monkey bars. But a few always lingered behind. Playground time was also interrogation time.

Olivia, a little blonde who always wore dresses, grabbed my hand, and asked, "Can you be my teacher next year?"

Another rub. "I'm not a teacher. But I'll be here with you all summer."

"I think you'd make the bestest teacher." Then she skipped away and joined another kid playing hopscotch under a tree.

My mind drifted to Miss Jones. I thought about calling her in August to visit her classroom. Just for fun. I still hadn't heard anything from the school about the scholarship. It's not like college was even an option for me but being here made me long for it again.

After recess, I was passing out art supplies when Alison entered. "Mom said she thinks Elizabeth has a fever."

My heart raced and the walls closed in. "What? Can I go check on her?"

"That's why I'm here. Go."

I sprinted to the infant room. Ms. Debby cradled Elizabeth in a rocking chair while her assistant tended to the other infants.

"How is she?"

"After you left, she got fussy and still refused her bottle. Then she felt a little warm."

I picked her up and instinctively pressed my cheek to her warm one. "I'm gonna take her to Dr. Carson's office. Will you tell Alison?"

"Of course. Keep us posted."

Even though I wanted to speed directly to Dr. Carson's, I first pulled into the gravel driveway of a partially framed apartment complex. Elizabeth's father needed to know where I was taking her. Roger and some other guys were carrying two-by-fours and nail guns. I didn't see Dale.

But I did see a car I didn't recognize. Dale sat in the front seat talking to the driver—a familiar female. I took off my sunglasses.

Are you kidding me?

I backed out before anyone saw me.

Suspicions crept into my thoughts and reached back into things he'd said, things he'd done. Times he hadn't come home. Intuitively, I knew what I'd find if I looked. As much as I wanted to be angry, I pushed the thoughts aside. Elizabeth was the important one now.

Dr. Carson took his stethoscope out of his ears and zipped up Elizabeth's footed onesie. "It's only a viral infection. Very common and not surprising since she just started daycare. Over the next few months, she might catch a few as she builds up immunities. For the fever, keep her hydrated, and give her a few lukewarm baths. And no daycare till she's fever-free for twenty-four hours."

The news returned the color to my cheeks. "Thank you."

"You bet. If anything changes, give us a call. But she should be fine in a day or two."

I took Elizabeth home and called Alison to tell her we wouldn't be in tomorrow. As Dr. Carson suggested, I gave her several lukewarm baths and offered her fluids, but she refused. By early evening, she finally started drinking.

After her last bath, I put her in cozy pajamas and in the center of my bed. She'd sleep with me tonight. I wrapped my body around her and closed my eyes. Her breathing, her sweet scent; they were intoxicating. Being her mother was the only high I needed.

CHAPTER FIFTY-FIVE

DO SOMETHING DIFFERENT

THE SLAMMING OF THE back door woke me. I reached out and felt for Elizabeth. Her skin was cool to the touch. Her fever had broken. I glanced at the clock—one in the morning. I got out of bed and tiptoed toward the bedroom door.

Dale was on the phone. "Roger just dropped me off. Yeah, she's asleep. You coming to get me? Okay, I'll wait outside."

He hung up the phone and then walked toward the bedroom. I jumped back into bed and pretended I was asleep. He stood at the threshold of the door and stared at us. I held my breath and tried to be as still as possible. My lungs were about to explode.

Please go.

After the longest minute of my life, he turned around and left. I exhaled. I knew who he was going to meet, and she could have him.

The next morning, thankfully, Elizabeth was completely back to normal, drinking her bottles and cooing. That allowed me to focus on my other issue—Dale.

It's not because I loved him, I didn't. But the fact I was ninety-nine percent sure he was cheating on me still hurt. I was the mother of his child. I did everything in my limited power to help us build a family. Dale put nothing in. He only took whatever he wanted out.

After a few hours of investigatory digging, I had her phone number. The girl, who months earlier Dale had said Roger was dating, I now knew he'd been the one dating her all along. Even that night at the party, it was to see her. I'd driven him to see her the same night he accused me of cheating. But that's the thing about cheaters, they accuse you of their bad behavior allowing them to hide behind your clamoring defense.

My hands trembled as I dialed her number. I didn't even know what to say. Maybe I'd hang up. But I was done doing nothing. It was time for me to do something.

"Hello." Darlene answered in a deep, hoarse, smoker's voice.

I took a couple of breaths to calm my quivering one. "Hey, I'm Angela Carter. Dale's girlf..." I did not want to call myself his girlfriend—because I no longer was. He just didn't know it yet. "We had a baby together. Please don't hang up."

For all I knew, Dale was in bed next to her. She'd been a pretty girl back in high school, with long, shiny blonde hair and a porcelain complexion. But now, in her late twenties, she bore no resemblance to her yearbook photo. Drugs don't only damage you on the inside.

"I've been expecting your call. I'm surprised it took you this long to figure it out."

"So, it's true? You and Dale?" I knew the answer. But I still wanted to hear her admit it.

"I ain't gonna lie. We've hooked up a few times. But he's nothing I want long-term. I'm surprised you do." She exhaled as if she'd just taken a deep drag off a cigarette. "Listen, Pop Tart, you didn't ask for my advice. But you're getting it. Back when I was your age, I had my first kid, too. Now I have three. All of 'em got different daddies. Do something different with your damn life." The harsh tone of her voice hinted at both regret and warning.

"What do you mean?"

"I don't know. Just do something different than, you know, than what I've done. I gotta go. Baby's crying."

"Darlene, thank you." I'd just thanked the woman who had been sleeping with my daughter's father. My life couldn't be any more messed up.

I wanted to punch something or someone. But Dale wasn't the sole recipient of my fury. I was much angrier with my naivety.

But I had no other options. Like it or not, a way out of here was way out of my reach. I couldn't support Elizabeth with my meager income from Small Steps. For now, I had no choice but to share a bed with a man who was also sharing someone else's.

I wasn't supposed to go to Mom's until tomorrow. But I couldn't face Dale. I'd confront him about Darlene and the fallout could have devastating consequences. He hadn't hurt me, at least physically, in a long time, not since Elizabeth had been born. I'd do everything possible to keep it that way.

I threw some clothes for me and Elizabeth into a duffle bag and tossed the hideous playpen Addis had given us into the car. Not that he deserved it, but I scribbled Dale a note to tell him we left a day early to visit Mom since Elizabeth was feeling better. Then I called her and said we were coming today. She was thrilled. I wished I shared her excitement.

The mailman blocked me as I tried to pull out of the driveway. He put something in the mailbox. After he left, I checked it to be sure there wasn't an overdue bill or something important I'd need to take care of before I left.

I cranked down the window, grabbed the stack of mail, and sifted through it. Of course, a power bill—marked late. I'd sent Dale to pay that weeks ago. A few pieces of junk mail. Then my heart stopped as I held an envelope addressed to me from North Lake Community College.

I put the car in park. My hands trembled. I thought about not opening it. It could be a scholarship rejection. After just finding out Dale was cheating, my emotional tank couldn't handle any more bad news. And if it was an award, I didn't see how I could even make that work since I had to have a job and couldn't afford daycare.

But maybe I could. Maybe I could make it work. I held my breath as I carefully peeled open a piece of mail that could change my life.

Inside were a couple of pieces of paper and a self-addressed stamped envelope. I slowly unfolded them and read a letter written directly to me.

Dear Ms. Carter,

North Lake Community College is pleased to inform you that you have been selected as the 1988 recipient of the Adult Education Center for Continuing Education Foundation Scholarship.

This scholarship will cover tuition and books for up to four academic years or 120 college credit hours, whichever comes first.

Recipients of this scholarship are required to maintain a 3.0 GPA and complete at least 30 hours of community service per semester.

If you choose to accept this award, please sign the enclosed Letter of Intent and return

on or before August 1, 1988. You can send the
Intent via the self-addressed stamped envelope
or deliver it in person to our Admissions
office.

Congratulations on this excellent achieve-
ment!

Sincerely,

The Adult Education Continuing Education
Foundation

I'd won the scholarship. Never, not in a million years, did I expect this. An entire group of people whom I'd never met believed in me. I wiped away a tear, then opened the glove box and tucked the letter safely under my car's owner manual.

As I drove away, the trailer faded in the rearview mirror. The letter in my glovebox could be my golden ticket out of there.

CHAPTER FIFTY-SIX

THE PANHANDLE

ON THE SEVERAL-HOUR DRIVE from Central Florida to the Panhandle, I ran through various scenarios, but each one had holes. If I went to school all day, I couldn't work full-time at Small Steps. Elizabeth's childcare wouldn't be free anymore. I'd have to get a job where I could work nights and weekends to afford it. Then she'd also need someone to watch her when I worked. And there was no way I was leaving her with Dale or Addis. Even a free ride to college wasn't free.

A few miles from Mom's, I stopped to gas up. At the station, I tugged a poorly folded map out of the glovebox to check the last of the directions. The corner of the envelope from North Lake Community College poked out from under the car manual. For now, I'd avoid thinking about my future, or lack thereof, and just enjoy my family and distance from the life I never wanted.

I fed Elizabeth a quick bottle and changed her diaper and outfit. Then strapped her back into her car seat and pulled up to the payphone outside the gas station. I dug a quarter from the bottom of my purse and dialed Mom's number. "Hey, Mom. I think I'm about twenty minutes away."

"I can't wait. Drive safe."

Maybe I'd share with my mom some of what was going on with Dale. Not all of it. Anything I told her couldn't be untold. And she'd tell Dad. I'd be forced to act.

No, I'd probably say nothing. Just keep up the façade that life was picture-perfect. But the thought of going back to Dale in that disgusting trailer filled me with an all-consuming dread.

I pulled into her new neighborhood, Palm Gardens, which featured few gardens. Instead, most of the lawns were full of pebble beds and tropical plants. Not uncommon in Florida; definitely saved on the water bill. Two motorcycles were parked in the driveway in front of the modest home. Mom's blue Chevy Cavalier sat in the street. The last car Dad had bought her.

I hadn't seen my father much lately. He'd been busy moving in with his new girlfriend, Paula. When I got back, maybe I'd go see him and tell him about the scholarship. He was a problem-solver. Maybe he'd help me find a solution I hadn't thought of—one without as many holes as Swiss cheese.

I parked behind Mom's car. She ran out of the house dressed in all black. A curly perm replaced her signature pixie cut. I chuckled at her fully embracing this new biker lifestyle. It suited her.

"Oh, Baby Girl. It's so good to see you." We embraced briefly before her attention diverted to the back seat. "Oh my gosh. Look at how big you've gotten already. Come here to Nana."

My heart warmed as I got Elizabeth out and handed her to my mother. I hadn't realized it until then, but Elizabeth had been the catalyst for her getting sober. At three months old, my little girl was already changing the world.

The door swung open again. A grinning Amber sprinted toward me, followed closely by a large black dog.

"Sissy, this is Sammy. He's a lab."

I opened my arms wide. Amber filled them. I picked her up and twirled her around. "I won't be able to do this much longer if you keep growing."

After I put her down, I patted the pup. "Welcome to the family, Sammy."

Bob came out next, wiping his hands on a worn apron. Mom had already told me he planned to make me his famous spaghetti. Besides the few snacks I packed, I hadn't had a real meal all day.

He reached for my bags. "I'm sure you're pretty worn out. Let me carry in your luggage."

Relieved for the help, I handed them to him.

Their house was similar in size to our simple one back in North Lake. Except here, framed family photos filled walls, even some with my dad, and potted plants filled shelves. It wasn't just a house. This was a home.

Levi and his new girlfriend rose from a cozy-looking leather sofa. "Good to see you."

He side-hugged me. Thick biceps indicated he was still lifting weights—a good sign he'd stayed on the right path and found a tribe. My little brother wasn't so little anymore.

"You, too, sis. This is Stephanie." He called attention to the petite dark blond next to him.

"Nice to meet you." I extended my hand for a shake, but she reached in for a hug instead.

"I've heard so much about you and Elizabeth." Then she darted over to Mom and gushed over my daughter.

Amber grabbed my hand. "Sissy, come outside. I wanna show you some of Sammy's tricks." I'd so missed my little sister.

"Go on. Let me have some time with my granddaughter."

It was still a little hard, but I needed to trust my mother.

Amber led me through the oregano and garlic-infused kitchen and out a door into a grassy fenced-in backyard.

"Watch this." She threw a stick a few feet away. Sammy retrieved it in his large mouth and brought it back to her.

"That's impressive. Did you teach him that?"

"Sammy had a trainer for a few weeks."

A trainer? A very put-together thing for Mom.

"You like it here?"

"Yeah, duh. They let me get a dog." She grabbed a frisbee, threw it like a pro, and Sammy caught it mid-air. Amber pulled a treat out of her pocket and praised her pup.

Mom may have changed her appearance, but she was again the mother I remembered from my childhood. I relaxed, knowing their circumstances wouldn't force Levi and Amber to grow up as quickly as mine had.

"Girls, time for dinner," Mom called.

———

"Oh my gosh. That literally was the best spaghetti I've ever eaten." It wasn't hyperbole. Mom must have picked her husbands through her pallet.

"Why thank you," Bob said as he wiped some sauce from his beard. "You guys should go watch my brother play pool tonight. He's pretty entertaining. Give Nana and I some time with Elizabeth and you a break."

"Oh, heck yeah. Jim's a legend here in Milton. Can I drive your car?" Just like any newly minted-driver, Levi jumped at the opportunity to get behind the wheel.

"Sure, just be careful. And make sure you get Stephanie home by her curfew."

I would've much rather stayed and talked to Mom than watch my new stepfather's brother play pool. But I also wanted to spend time with Levi and get to know Stephanie.

"Sure, let's do this." Instead of spilling my guts to my mother, I'd spend the evening in a smoky billiard room.

CHAPTER FIFTY-SEVEN

THE DANCE

BALL BREAKERS LIVED IN a dilapidated strip mall flanked on one side by an ice cream shop and the other by a thrift store. I'd much rather go to either, but Ball Breakers it was.

A bouncer stopped us at the door and checked our IDs. Then he put bracelets on our wrists to indicate we were underaged. Sometimes I forgot I was still a kid.

When I entered the pool hall, the scent of beer and cheap perfume replaced oxygen. Sweaty men surrounded pool tables, and scantily dressed women lingered close by.

A guy who looked to be about my age emerged from the crowd. He fist-pumped Levi. "What's up, bro? Hey, Steph." He hugged her and then turned toward me. Dark, messy hair swept to one side. Thick eyebrows framed striking hazel eyes, and an unlit cigarette dangled between full lips.

Levi introduced me. "This is my sister, Angela."

"Nice to meet you. Name's Harley." He smiled and nodded in my direction.

"You, too." I forced myself to scan the rest of the room. But when he spoke again, my eyes took on a life of their own and locked with his.

"You guys wanna come over to my table and watch the last of the tournament? With each beer Dad only gets better and he's currently about a six-pack in." His hands rested in the back pockets of perfectly fitting jeans.

I wished I'd changed out of my faded denim shorts and the baby spit-up-stained t-shirt.

"That's why we're here," Levi answered. "Jim's the Man."

We followed Harley to a corner high-top and set up shop. "You guys want something? As shocking as it is, they do serve non-alcoholic drinks here. I suggest Barq's root beer. This is as far South as you can get it."

"Seriously? I haven't had a Barq's root beer since we moved from Mississippi." I wondered if Harley and I would have anything else in common. Not that I cared. Or maybe I did.

"Cool. I'll be right back." He smacked the table and darted toward the bar.

"You're staring at him." Stephanie teased; a girlish grin plastered across her face.

"Uh, no, I was just stretching. A little sore from the drive." My cheeks warmed.

She doubled down. "Oh, and stretching in that direction is helping?" She pointed toward the bar at Harley, who'd just pulled out a stool for a guy on crutches.

Dale wouldn't have even noticed.

I rubbed my neck. "It sure did. Feels much better now." When a crisp, musky scent washed over me, I knew Harley was back before I saw him.

"Ice cold." He sat the bucket of root beer in the center of the table.

Levi grabbed the bottle opener attached by a piece of string to the bucket, popped a top, and passed it to Stephanie. Harley popped a top and passed it to me. We probably looked like two couples on a double date. If he had a girlfriend, he probably treated her like a guy should treat a girl—pull out a chair, buy her a drink.

"Cheers," said Harley, and we clinked our bottles.

The sweet earthy liquid slid down my throat and washed away a little of my bitterness at life. Rather than being forced to live like a grown-up, I was a kid pretending to be one. I'd missed this phase of my life.

We watched Jim play pool for the rest of the evening. We clinked our bottles and cheered each time he sank a ball.

Instead of familiar hunger pains, my belly hurt from laughing. The last time I'd laughed this hard was when Julie and I were walking to induce my labor.

Harley looked a lot like Jim, except his dad was shorter with an emerging beer gut. Harley was tall and slim, and his white shirt clung to his toned chest like a wet suit.

After his dad sank the eight ball and won the tournament, he threw his arms in the air. The entire joint erupted in cheers, including me.

As he went to put his stick away, he stumbled.

"That's my cue. Better get the old man home before he can't walk to the car. I'm strong, but not that strong."

I stopped laughing at those words. He was leaving.

Although he faced Levi, I felt his gaze on me. "I'll come back if you guys are gonna stay. I'll just be a few minutes."

I crossed my fingers under the table in anticipation of Levi's answer.

"You bet." The boys clinked the necks of their root beers together again.

Harley wrapped a tan arm around his dad and led him out.

"I think he likes you," Stephanie said when Levi went to the bathroom.

I fanned my cheeks to cool them. She'd called me out for gawking at him earlier, but had she also noticed him returning the stares? "Stop it. Anyway, it's not like I'm single."

I'd offer my left arm to rewrite the last year—erase Dale like a dull pencil. The only trace of him I wanted on the pages of my life was Elizabeth.

"Well, you can be friends. Really good friends." She giggled.

The boys returned about the same time. "Since the tables are open, you guys wanna play a round?" Harley asked.

Stephanie spoke first. "Yes. Let's play teams, us versus you two." She pointed to Harley and me.

Our eyes met and two voices replied, "Okay." He handed me a pool stick and my skin tingled when his fingers brushed mine.

My experience playing pool was in the never-have-I-ever range. Harley did his best to coach me. Toward the game's end, our only ball left was the solid blue two. I was up, and the shot was tricky. He leaned in close and helped me line it up. Distracted by him gently pressing against me, I missed, and we lost. It was totally worth it.

"You guys want to play again?" he asked.

"Sorry, it's too close to my curfew," said Stephanie.

I wasn't ready to leave.

"Yeah, I gotta get Steph home." Levi grabbed her hand.

Harley said, "I can take Angela home later if she—if you—want me to."

I shrugged. "Why not? It's not often I have a babysitter for Elizabeth."

"Later." Levi and Harley fist-pumped again, and he and Stephanie left.

Harley was the first guy other than Dale who I'd been alone with in a long time. He was the first guy I'd *wanted* to be alone with in a long time. "I need to make a quick call. Where's the pay phone?"

Harley put our pool sticks in the rack. "It's down the hallway across from the bathrooms. "Here." He pulled a quarter out of his pocket and tossed it to me.

I caught it.

He flashed a wide grin. "Nice catch."

"Not so good at pool, but I guess I'm a good catch." I hadn't intended the insinuating pun.

Harley nodded. "No, I think you're a great catch."

He wouldn't think that if he knew me. "I'll be right back."

I dropped the quarter into the pay phone and dialed. "Hey, Mom. How's Elizabeth?"

"Sleeping like an angel. I put her playpen in my room. I hope it's okay. I didn't know when you guys would be back. You can sleep in tomorrow."

"For sure, thanks." The last thing on my mind was sleep. "Levi took Steph home. Harley, you know Jim's son, is gonna bring me back later. If that's okay?"

"Absolutely. Have fun. You're in good hands. And don't worry about Elizabeth. We're loving every minute."

"Awe, I'm so glad." I was also loving every minute of my night. "Thanks, again."

Before I rejoined Harley, I slipped into the bathroom. I dug in my purse for my strawberry lip gloss and brushed my long, brown hair. I wasn't the prettiest girl in the room; well, maybe at Ball Breakers I was. In general, I was average. Nothing about me stood out.

But at that moment, away from Dale, I felt pretty. I felt desirable. I felt hopeful. I walked out of the restroom with my head held slightly higher than when I went in.

Harley nodded in the direction of a jukebox. "Wanna play some music?"

"Okay. But I get to pick." Someone dropped a coin into the machine before I had a chance to. A woman's voice came out of the staticky speakers, and a slow, sensual melody filled the room.

Ball Breaker's few late-night customers congregated around the jukebox in pairs, bodies close, swaying to the music. It was that time of night when the beer buzz ignited the desire not to go home alone. Even though we weren't drinking, I still felt that buzz and didn't want to go home alone.

"Miss Angela, may I have this dance?" Harley reached his hand out to me like a real gentleman. I took it. He pulled me toward him and wrapped his arms tenderly around my waist. I placed my head on his chest, and we moved slowly in a melodic circle.

I closed my eyes and was no longer in a smokey pool hall. Instead, I was dancing to classical music in a gorgeous ballroom robust with the scent of fresh flowers. The train of my flowing white gown brushed across elegant parquet flooring. Surrounded by our closest family and friends, my new husband twirled me around the room. By the song's end, I knew, without a doubt, I'd never spend another night with Dale.

CHAPTER FIFTY-EIGHT

A NUMBER ON A NAPKIN

WE STOPPED MOVING WHEN the song ended. But we didn't separate. Harley rubbed my head, and I breathed him in.

Then he whispered, "Let's get you home." He put his hand on the small of my back as natural as if he'd done it a thousand times and led me out the door.

"My car's over there." He pointed to a sexy, black El Camino. He opened the passenger door, and I slid into its smooth leather seat.

He turned on the radio and lowered the volume. I placed my hand on the center console inviting him to grab it—he did. Our fingers comfortably laced. Palms pressed together sparked an osmotic emotional pathway of untold stories. Even though we knew little about each other, we'd already shared so much. When we got to Mom's, he turned off the engine. The night wasn't over yet.

"I had a great time tonight. You have no idea how much I needed this."

"I kinda figured. Levi's told me a little. I saw a picture of you and your daughter over there a few weeks ago. And you, a thin smile, and empty eyes. I couldn't stop wondering why this gorgeous girl holding this beautiful baby looked so sad."

What he said made me feel like he could see right through me—but not like I was exposed—like I was safe. Tears spilled down my cheeks.

He pulled me toward him. "Any chance you'll tell me what's behind those tears?"

I pulled away and dropped my head. "I'm worried about what you'll think of me. Some bad things have been done to me, but I've also made some really bad choices."

So many times, I had wanted to tell Julie, Dad, Mom, or anyone really, what was happening in my life. But I always held back. I was afraid. Afraid they'd judge me or pity me. I wanted everyone to think I was stronger than I was. But with Harley I felt the one thing I hadn't felt in a long time—secure.

He lifted my chin. "You don't have to tell me anything. But if you do, it won't change the fact that I think you're incredible."

We'd only known each other for one night, but I believed him. I trusted him.

Hiding behind lies had become my primary defense mechanism. *Pretend everything is great and maybe you'll fool yourself that it was.* But every time Dale came in drunk, every time I had to clean up his vomit, every time I had to skip a meal so I could afford formula, every time I walked into that trailer, all of it was a reminder there wasn't a lie big enough.

About an hour later, I had no more stories left to tell and no more tears left to cry.

He sat quietly for a few moments. "I'm not gonna lie. A lot of that was difficult to hear. But here's the thing. You don't have to be that person anymore. You have a choice." He paused. "My mom died a few years ago."

"I'm so sorry."

"I'm okay now. But it was a tough time. Dad's still processing it."

It was my turn to listen.

"I was about Levi's age. I had big plans to go to college in Jacksonville for landscape design like the old man wished he would've. But after Mom passed, I didn't go to school for weeks. Dad stayed drunk. One night, I took a bunch of pills. I just wanted the pain to stop."

I squeezed his hand, encouraging him to go on.

He choked back tears. "I woke up in a hospital bed, Dad crying over me. I never wanted to put him through that again. But I also realized it wasn't just about him. It was about me, too. And no one could save me but me. Sometimes you've got to be your own hero."

His words lay heavy on me. At the beginning of the night, I pictured he had lived this typical teen life. But like me he'd also had to grow up fast. "I can't imagine how hard that was for you and your dad. But I understand what you mean. Like you did, I have to rescue myself."

"There's one more thing I wanna tell you. People who hurt others, like Dale, need to be held accountable."

He was right. I needed to stop protecting Dale, and I was ready.

The faint light of the morning sun peeked from behind a palm tree. "Elizabeth will be up soon. I don't want to, but it's time for me to go inside. Thanks again. For everything."

He scribbled his phone number on a napkin. "I wish we lived closer. But, whenever you head this way again, give me a call."

He got out of the car and opened the door for me. We embraced one last time. As hard as it was to say goodbye to Harley that morning, it didn't feel like I was walking away from anything. It felt like I was walking toward something—my future.

CHAPTER FIFTY-NINE

DEAR DALE

URGENCY DROVE ME TO pack to leave in record time. "I'm gonna miss you guys." The original plan was for us to stay another night, but I had to leave today to make this work. Dale framed houses on Saturdays, not Sundays.

I squeezed my mother's neck. "This was a good move. I promise I'll be back soon. Until then, I'll keep the pictures coming." I popped Elizabeth's car seat in its base and hung a couple of toys from the handle, hoping they'd keep her content between the quick stops I'd have to make to feed her.

"I love you, Baby Girl." She poked her head in the back seat and kissed Elizabeth one last time. I didn't want to rush her, but I only had a small window of opportunity, and I wasn't going to miss it.

My family stood outside and waved. I watched until they disappeared from my rearview mirror. Once the dust settled, I'd return. That was a given.

On the drive back to North Lake, powered by the adrenaline that filled the gap my lack of sleep left, I mentally mapped out my plan. After all this time, I was finally leaving Dale Simmons.

Deep shades of orange bathed the horizon when I returned to the trailer. Dale could walk through the door any minute. I had to work fast. My exit had to go exactly as planned to escape with as little blood on my hands as possible or to have as little of mine on his.

I strapped Elizabeth into an old baby swing Alison had given me from the daycare. It sat in front of the back sliding glass door. Outside, I'd placed a birdbath a neighbor had put on the curb. Elizabeth loved watching the birds and the occasional squirrel stop for a visit. Hopefully, the nature scene would hold her attention while I hustled.

Then I quickly compiled a list of what I needed to accomplish.

1) Pay bills and take receipts

2) Pack half of Elizabeth's clothes and toys

3) Pack ALL of my clothes

4) Pack ALL of my personal items

5) Call Dad

6) Write Dale a note

7) Get the hell out of here before he gets home

I grabbed the bill box and scribbled checks for what was due in the next month. Luckily, thanks to Mrs. Keene's guidance, I had a checking account in just my name. After I paid the bills, I had about $150.00 left. It would have to work. I shoved everything in my purse. I'd get them to Dale at some point, but many of these bills were in my name, so I'd need to handle that first.

Then I shoved about half of Elizabeth's few toys, clothes, and all of mine into garbage bags. The last time my clothes were in garbage bags, I was leaving home. This time I was going home.

I wanted to take all of Elizabeth's things because I never wanted her in this trailer again. But Dale was her father, and optics matter. I hated leaving her crib, and I didn't know if I'd ever be able to get anything else out of here. But it was a risk I had to take.

The next thing I had to do was what this whole plan relied upon; calling my dad to ask if we could stay with him. Dad and Paula had just moved into a house this week that I hadn't even seen yet, and I didn't want to intrude on their new life. If staying with them wasn't an option, then we'd be sleeping in my car in a parking lot. I was never spending another night in this trailer.

I picked up the phone and dialed his number. "Hey, Dad."

"Hello there, Number One. How was the trip to your mom's? Levi and Amber settling in? I can't wait to get them back down here for a visit, especially now that I have more room.

"Good. Everyone's really good." I didn't have time to ease him into the conversation. The clock ticked. "I hate to ask you this, but I was wondering if Elizabeth and I could stay with you and Paula for a while? It turns out Dale and I aren't going to work." I crossed my fingers and held my breath.

He answered right away. "I've been hoping one day to get this call."

I bit my lip and held back the tears.

"You and Elizabeth come on. We'll discuss the details when you get here."

The tension in my neck released until I looked at the clock. My window of opportunity for getting out of here before Dale showed up was about to slam shut. He gave me the address and I scribbled it onto the back of my to-do list.

"Dad, thanks. Love you."

"Love you. Your room'll be ready when you get here."

My room. I was really going home.

I ripped my to-do list off the notepad and stuffed it in my back pocket. I had one more thing to write.

Dear Dale,

I have something important to tell you, and I hope you understand. Elizabeth and I are moving to my dad's. It's time. I don't think either one of us is really happy, and isn't that what life is all about, being happy? I want that for you, I want it for Elizabeth, and I want it for me, too. I don't know how this will work, but we'll figure it out. I paid the bills for the month and took the receipts so I can call and get what is in my name switched to yours. I'm going to spend the next few days just processing my emotions and letting you do the same. I'll call you later in the week. Maybe Elizabeth and I can come by next weekend so you can see her, and we can talk. We are both going to be okay.

Angela

I tried to be gentle. Not that he'd have a broken heart because I rarely saw signs he had one, but because he'd be angry. And once he told his family and friends that I left him, they would inflame his outrage. They'd say things like, "She always thought she was better than you," which I did, and "She's taking your kid away," which I was.

I used a fruit-shaped magnet and put it front and center on the fridge. The last thing I had left on a fridge for him was to get his attention, this time was to end it.

I lifted Elizabeth out of the swing and held her close. I scanned the trailer I'd lived in during my pregnancy and for all of Elizabeth's short life. She'd spent her first night home from the hospital here in bed with me. Along with her beautiful crib, I'd done my best with hand-me-downs and limited resources to make her a proper nursery.

She'd laid on a blanket many afternoons on the worn shag carpet while I did homework at the picnic kitchen table.

There were a lot of horrible memories in this place, but there were also some that I never wanted to forget. I rubbed the top of Elizabeth's soft head. Those memories, hers, were coming with me. The rest could die a slow, painful death.

CHAPTER SIXTY

GOING HOME

A LONG WINDING DIRT road led to Dad and Paula's new house. It sat in a neighborhood that used to be an old orange grove. A few remaining citrus trees that survived the freeze from years earlier, dotted the landscape—a refreshing reminder that life always finds a way.

I parked, popped Elizabeth's car seat out of its base, grabbed a bag, and walked toward the entrance to our new home. I wasn't sure if I'd sleep at all, but if I did, it would again be under my father's roof. And there was no place else I'd rather be.

Dad opened the door before I could knock and greeted me with, "There she is, Number One."

So far in my life, I hadn't done anything worthy of being called Number One, but that was about to change.

"Hey, Dad, Paula."

"Here, let me take her." Paula reached for Elizabeth.

I passed the heavy car seat over to her. "Thanks." It would be nice having someone's help with Elizabeth.

Dad took my bag. "Let's get your things unloaded."

The rest of the afternoon and early evening flew by. Paula looked after Elizabeth while Dad and I moved furniture around in their previous guest room. It was my room now. A small second room they'd used for storage housed Elizabeth's playpen. I had to figure out a way to get her crib. She deserved it.

After I bathed and fed Elizabeth, I laid her down. She fell right to sleep. This had to be hard on her. The last couple of days, she'd spent more time in her car seat than not. Hopefully, that was all over.

In the cozy living room, Paula curled up on a plush couch and under a fluffy quilt watching TV. She was much younger than my mother. I wondered if she and my dad would start their own family. She was about to get plenty of experience having a baby in the house.

When I entered, she used one of those fancy new remote controls to mute the TV. "Is Elizabeth asleep?"

"Yes. Out like a light."

"Good. Your dad's in the kitchen. I'll stay in here and give you two some privacy."

Dad sat at a round kitchen table in front of a cup of black coffee. I assumed he was gearing up for a long night of emotional testimony. But that wasn't the direction I planned this conversation to go. The things I'd told Harley, no dad needed to hear about their daughter. However, the night would still be long.

He held his mug in the air. "You want one?"

"Please."

"How do you like it?"

"A little coffee with my creamer."

He laughed. "Just like your mother."

"I need to get something out of the car. I'll be right back."

Outside, millions of stars flickered in the night sky. Funny how the darker the night, the brighter the stars. I'd lived through enough darkness. Now it was time for me to shine.

I opened the passenger door, reached into the glove box, and underneath my car's owner manual. There it was—the scholarship award letter from North Lake Community College.

When I got back inside, a steamy cup of coffee sat in front of an empty chair. I unfolded the letter and placed it on the table facing my father. He was the first person, other than me, to read it. I'd give anything to be in his head as he absorbed the words that would change his daughter's life forever.

He picked it up and put on his reading glasses.

I wrapped my hands around the warm mug. At one point, he choked up a little. Finally, I could make my father proud.

Before he had a chance to say anything, I spoke first. "I want to go to college for an education degree."

He pulled a pen from his front pocket and handed it to me. "Well, let's make it official."

As I was signing the acceptance letter, the phone rang. My hand trembled, and I botched my last name. Dad and I locked eyes. There'd only be one person calling this late.

"Want me to handle it?" he asked.

"No, I need to do this." I picked up the receiver and ducked between the kitchen and the entry.

I forced a cheery, "Hello."

"What's going on? You see your family, and the next thing I know, you're leaving. What kinda crap did they put in your head?"

"No one put anything into my head. I said everything I needed to say in the letter." Although my knees buckled, my voice was calm. It was a trick I'd mastered over the last year to diffuse him when he was angry. But I doubted it'd work this time.

"Well, I haven't said everything I need to say. You can't live with your daddy forever. You barely make minimum wage. And don't think you're getting a dime from me. This is Elizabeth's home."

"We won't have to live with my dad forever. I'm going to college to be a teacher. I'll be done by the time she starts school. We'll have the same schedule. It'll be great for her." I hoped Dale would consider what was best for his daughter. But if that also meant what was best for me, then I could forget it.

"You think you can just up and leave and go to college like some rich girl? You're nothing but trailer park trash. You think you're better than everybody else, but you're not. Elizabeth should be with me and my family. Mama's gonna help me look after her. You know Mama loves that baby."

The mention of Addis wanting my daughter boiled my blood. But I had to keep my cool. "I know she does. But this is between us. We need time to think and process. Then we can discuss what's best for Elizabeth later in the week."

"The next time you hear from me, it'll be through my attorney. Mama's already retained him, and he said since you ain't gotta house or a decent job, and some of the things you've done, I stand a better chance at getting custody of Elizabeth."

The room closed in around me at the mere mention of him trying to get custody of Elizabeth. "Please don't do that. Let's work this out between us."

"I'll do anything to prevent giving you one dime of child support. Anything." He screamed. Then, click, and a dial tone.

Even though I didn't think his threat held much merit, an irrational fear still flew through me. Because he was right about a few things. I didn't have my own place or a decent-paying job. I also couldn't afford to hire a lawyer to fight him. Attorney Graves was ruthless. He'd dig into my life until he found what he was looking for, then point it right back at me like a loaded gun.

But I did have one weapon to fight back with. And that weapon was the truth. I was not going to allow Dale Simmons to scare me anymore.

I walked back into the kitchen and hung up the phone.

"Anything you want to talk about?" Dad expected an answer, but he wasn't going to get it.

"No, sir."

It was time for me to call Officer Cresswell.

CHAPTER SIXTY-ONE

THE TRUTH

As expected, I'd laid awake much of the night before. Dale's threat of fighting for custody of Elizabeth crept into every thought I tried to think, every dream I tried to dream. My plan had to work. I couldn't bear the thought of her not with me and growing up in that trailer, or worse, in the Simmons' home.

Between her few bottles sprinkled throughout the night, Elizabeth slept like, well, a baby. Poor kid must have been so exhausted.

Fortunately, she, and everyone else, was still asleep when the sun broke, giving me some time to make a few private phone calls.

The first was to Alison. I couldn't work today. I told her I had a family emergency, which was partially true. She didn't ask questions, only said to take all the time I needed and that I was welcome to drop off Elizabeth. I thanked her and told her I'd be there soon.

Next, I pulled out Officer Cresswell's business card from my purse, picked the phone back up, and dialed the number. I didn't think Dale stood a chance at gaining custody of Elizabeth, but I needed to be certain. This was my only option.

"North Lake Police Department, how can I help you?"

If I crossed this line, I couldn't go back. But I had to do this—for Elizabeth. "Can I speak with Officer Cresswell?"

"Let me check if she's here. Hold on."

A growing fear made me worry I might be in trouble for lying in the first place. Before I had the chance to change my mind, she answered.

"This is Officer Creswell."

Time to do what must be done. "I don't know if you remember me, Angela Carter. About six months ago, you came to my school and asked me some questions about Dale Simmons." I hoped she remembered me.

"Yes, Miss Carter, I do. How can I help you?"

My shoulders relaxed. But then tensed again at what I was about to say. "You told me to call you if I remembered anything else about that night, the windshield. Well, I do." Line officially crossed.

She didn't hesitate. "Would you like to come to the station to amend your statement?"

And neither did I. "Yes, ma'am."

"Miss Carter, it's really hard for us to catch the bad guys if the good guys stand in the way. I'm glad your memory has offered up more details. I'll be here all morning."

"Thank you." After I hung up, I thought about what she said, and she was right. Dale was a bad guy, and I'd lied to cover for him. His attorney may have gotten him out of that DUI, but my secrets had kept him out of jail. As much as I didn't want to admit to what I'd seen, what I'd done, what had been done to me, it was time for me to tell the truth.

I left before Dad woke up. I didn't want him asking me questions because I didn't want to lie anymore. But I needed to do this alone and on my terms.

After I dropped Elizabeth off, I headed to the police station. I'd never been to one before. I hoped this would be my first and last time. "I'm here to see Officer Cresswell."

"Have a seat. She'll be right with you." The receptionist picked up the phone and told the officer I was there.

Before I even had time to sit down, she entered the room.

"Miss Carter, I'm glad to see you. Follow me." She led me to a small room with nothing but a table and a couple of chairs. But unlike the first time we spoke, I'd come to her this time. There'd be no interrogation because I was ready and willing to tell the truth.

"So, how this works"—She held out a notebook and a pen—"You're going to write down everything that happened that night. Feel free to include any other details that might help support your amended statement. When you're done, press the button by the door. I'll come back, make you a copy, and you're free to go."

It couldn't be that simple. "What happens after?"

"Since I conducted the preliminary investigation, one of our lead investigators and I will work to corroborate your new statement against the evidence and any witnesses. And just so you're aware, the statement will also go to Mr. Simmons' attorney. At that point, the attorney will most likely contact Mr. Simmons to discuss their next steps." Then she asked, "Are you still wanting to go through with this?"

I took the notepad and pen from her. "Absolutely."

"Good. Hopefully, what you write down on that notepad won't happen to anyone else."

After she shut the door, I closed my eyes. This was going to be one of the hardest things I'd ever done. To put the truth down in my own handwriting. Not only because I'd have to relive it, but also because the secrets I'd tried so hard to keep from everyone were about to become very public.

Then I thought about Dale behind bars, away from Elizabeth, away from me, unable to hurt anyone else. It was worth it. I opened my eyes, picked up the pen, and started to write.

CHAPTER SIXTY-TWO

A GREEN BACKPACK

I HAD ONE MORE stop before I picked up Elizabeth. I'd saved the best for last.

Even though I parked in the visitor lot, I pretended I was already a North Lake Community College student pulling up to go to class—that Julie and I had plans to meet in the cafeteria for coffee and to study for a test.

Thinking of Julie snapped me into the present. She and her family should be home Friday from their road trip. She'd been gone all summer and had no idea I'd left Dale, or we'd go to college together. Even though we'd each taken a different path, we still made it to the same destination.

I grabbed the manila folder Dad had put my scholarship acceptance letter in and entered the Admissions Office. "Hi, I'm here to see Mrs. Tibbals." I was really doing this.

The receptionist buzzed her. "She'll be right out."

"Thank you." The sign I'd seen months ago, "North Lake Community College Your Future Starts Here," was still on the wall. Back then, I hadn't believed my future would ever be here. Yet, the folder I held was proof that it would.

Mrs. Tibbals emerged from a hallway. "Hello. I'm sorry. Did we have an appointment? Nothing is on my calendar."

"No, ma'am. I just thought I'd try my luck. I met you a few months ago with my guidance counselor, Mr. Demalina. When I was in ETM at the Adult Education Center."

"Oh, that's right. I didn't recognize you without your cute little round belly. Angela, right?"

"Yes. I had the baby. A girl. Elizabeth. She's about three months old now."

"Congratulations. Come on back."

I followed her into her office. The last time I was here, I made excuses for why I couldn't go to college. This time I was here because I wanted to go.

I passed the folder to her. "I signed it. The scholarship acceptance letter."

"I'm so glad. This is a fantastic opportunity, and we are honored to have you join our student body. Let's get you formally admitted. Then I'll take you to meet with our academic advisor, and she'll register you for classes today. How does that sound?"

"Perfect." I couldn't believe I'd leave here today with a college class schedule in my hand when a year ago I'd considered dropping out of high school.

"Before we get started, we need to review the requirements for the scholarship. You must keep a three-point-zero GPA and complete thirty hours of community service per semester. Have you thought about what you might like to do?"

I knew exactly what I wanted to do. "Yes, ma'am. Last year, this teacher, Miss Jones, said I could visit her classroom anytime. She teaches fifth grade. I thought about asking her if I could be a volunteer since I want to be a teacher, too. Would that be okay?"

"That's more than okay. I think it's a great idea to get some real first-hand experience. Here's the timesheet we'll need her to sign each week."

I hadn't spoken with Miss Jones since Mrs. Elliott let me go, but I believed she'd love to have me.

Mrs. Tibbals finished my admissions paperwork, then brought me to the academic advisor. "This is Angela Carter. Please make sure she gets signed up for Study Skills. As an incoming freshman, I want to ensure she starts out on the right foot and keeps her scholarship." She placed my folder on the woman's desk.

"You got it."

Mrs. Tibbals held out her hand for a shake. "Welcome to North Lake Community College. See you next month and for the next four years."

"Yes, ma'am. Thank you." *The next four years.* I looked forward to every minute.

The academic advisor opened my folder. "Hello, Angela. I'm Mrs. Frazier. Congratulations on being this year's Adult Education Foundation Scholarship recipient."

I wasn't used to hearing accolades about my performance. "Thank you." I liked the new me already.

"Before we pick classes for this semester, we need to map out all the courses you'll take to get that degree in your hand. Then we will head to the campus bookstore to get your textbooks."

"Okay." I was grateful to have Mrs. Tibbals and Mrs. Frazier helping me. Apparently, you needed a college degree to figure out how to get a college degree.

She pulled out a sample of the Elementary Education course requirements. We moved a few things around, and within the hour, I had a plan of exactly what it would take to reach my end goal.

According to the document, in May of 1992, by my twenty-second birthday, I'd have a Bachelor of Arts in Elementary Education. Elizabeth would be four years old. I'd be a teacher, and she'd be a preschooler. So crazy to imagine. Crazy good.

"Oh, I almost forgot. Before we head to the bookstore, each scholarship recipient receives a backpack full of school supplies, a school t-shirt, and some other merch. Let me go get yours."

She returned carrying a green backpack with a suede bottom.

The day I visited here months ago, I had seen students with ones just like it over their shoulders. I never imagined I'd have one over mine.

"Thank you so very much." My life's path had gone from downhill fast to uphill even faster, and the speed of both made it hard to catch my breath.

"Of course. Now let's go fill that backpack with textbooks."

By the time we were done, it was heavy. Heavy with all the knowledge I'd learn over the next few months. I couldn't wait to get back to Dad's, back home, and start reading.

As I walked toward my car, I realized the next time I stepped foot on this campus would be my first day as a college student.

CHAPTER SIXTY-THREE

EARTH-TWO

Dale was radio silent all week. I assumed his attorney received my statement and advised him not to contact me. Eventually, I'd have to face him. And even though anxiety churned, I was confident I'd made the right decision. I shifted my focus from worrying about something I couldn't control to what I could—rebuilding a life without Dale.

I peeked in Elizabeth's playpen. She was fast asleep. Her dark eyelashes fluttered as if she was in the middle of a sweet dream. Finally, we were in a place where dreams were possible. I tiptoed out and headed to the kitchen.

"Good morning," I said as I walked into the sunny room. Freshly brewed coffee filled a carafe. Dad was dressed for work and reading the paper at the table. Paula, still in her terry cloth robe, stood at the stove frying eggs. This family scene was now my normal.

"Hey. You want some breakfast?" she asked.

I'd been so used to doing everything for myself that it was an adjustment to have someone do things for me. "Sure, thanks." But it was a welcome adjustment.

Dad peered over the paper, glanced at us both, and smiled.

"I'm gonna make a phone call first." I dialed the number to North Lake Elementary School and ducked around the corner for privacy. "Can I speak to Miss Jones?"

"Hold on. Let me see if she's in her classroom. Who's calling?"

"Tell her it's Angela Carter from the after-school program."

I couldn't believe this was happening. That last day with Miss Jones was one of the lowest points in my life. And now, here I'd come full circle.

"Angela, I'm so happy to hear from you. How are you? " I could hear her smiling.

"I'm good. I had a baby girl, Elizabeth. But that's not why I'm calling. I got a college scholarship. Does the offer still stand for me to volunteer in your classroom?" I crossed my fingers in hopes she'd say yes.

"Congratulations on your daughter. And absolutely, the offer still stands. I'm so proud of you. I can't wait to share the news with Mrs. Elliott this afternoon. The beginning of the year is a little hectic. Give me a couple of weeks, and then we'll work out a schedule. That'll also give you some time to adjust to being a college student."

"Perfect. I can't wait. And thank you for believing in me. I'll see you in a few weeks."

"Best of luck with a great start to your college career. You deserve it."

When I walked back into the kitchen to hang up the receiver, Dad asked, "So what put that huge grin on your face?"

"Everything, Dad. Everything." My heart was so full I expected it couldn't hold any more good news.

My next order of business was to drop Elizabeth off at Small Steps and talk to Alison. She and I agreed that when I started college, I'd switch to working with the after-school kids. Alison also said as long as I remained employed at Small Steps, even part-time, Elizabeth could continue free of charge.

That plan that everybody had kept asking me to make, I'd finally made it.

After I left the daycare, I drove to Julie's. I beamed when I saw an RV parked out front and her family unloading it. It hurt that I couldn't make those memories with her like we'd planned. But this summer had enabled me to get my life back on track. I'd miss nothing else.

As soon as I got out of my car, she ran over and threw her arms around my neck. "I missed you so much. Now, where's my favorite niece?"

"I missed you, too. She's at Small Steps. The daycare where I work now."

"Where you work? That's great news. I gotta help unload the RV. I wanna tell you all about our trip. But first, how was your summer?"

I couldn't wait for her reaction. "It was okay. I left Dale, moved in with my dad, and enrolled at North Lake Community College. Fairly uneventful."

"Wait, what? No offense, you aren't that funny, but is any of this a joke?"

I smiled. "No, it's all true."

"Ange, I didn't say anything because best friends don't judge, but I never understood why you stayed with him."

I'm sure everyone shared the same sentiment. "Jules, I wish I knew why." It was impossible to explain to my best friend what I'd gone through when I was just beginning to understand it myself—how feeling so low kept me trapped for so long.

"Well, the important thing is you aren't now. And school. You're going to North Lake with me. I can't believe it." She grabbed my hands, and we squealed and jumped up and down several times. When we finally stopped, she asked, "I just have one super important question, can we please get matching Hello Kitty lunchboxes?"

I couldn't ask for a better best friend. "Only if we can also get matching Trapper Keepers."

"Okay, you're a little bit funny. Not an option; after I finish up here, you and I are going out to celebrate tonight. Do you think your dad will babysit?"

"For sure. Oh, I have more news. Dad moved out of his apartment and into a house with his new awesome girlfriend, Paula."

"Seriously, I'm gone for a few weeks, and when I come back, I'm in an alternate universe on Earth-Two."

"I like Earth-Two a heck of a lot better than Earth-One." I scribbled Dad's new address down on the back of an old receipt and gave it to her.

Celebrating with my best friend was the perfect ending to the perfect day.

When I walked into the house, Dad was at the stove. The familiar scent of nutty roux filled the kitchen.

"Hey, Number One, it's your birthday next week. I thought we'd celebrate a little early with some 'All the Way' gumbo."

Before, when Dad left, I'd felt abandoned. But he believed he was doing everything possible to rebuild to provide a solid future for himself and us. Now, I appreciated it. "Thanks, Dad. Julie's back. Can you and Paula watch Elizabeth so she and I can go out tonight?"

"Absolutely," he answered without hesitation.

I almost wanted to pinch myself to prove this wasn't a dream. It didn't erase the last year of darkness, but if this was the light at the end of the tunnel, its brightness was blinding.

Julie showed up a little before dinner. "Hi, Mr. Carter. The gumbo smells delicious, and the house, I love it."

"Thanks. Plenty 'a room for the whole crew," he said as he held Elizabeth in one arm and stirred the gumbo with the other. He loved his hands-on grandad role. And I loved that he loved it.

After dinner, Julie and I got ready. She teased her hair and pulled the top half up in a scrunchie. Then she slipped into a denim mini skirt and white tank top and slid several bangle bracelets on her thin wrists. The best I had were fake leather pants and an old T-shirt. We looked like we were wearing Madonna and Joan Jett Halloween costumes.

"You still haven't told me where we're going."

"You'll love it. It's this under-twenty-one club called Weekends over in Mayflower. My friends and I used to go there senior year."

Her comment stung. "Oh, your friends." I'd lost my senior year—one of the many things Dale took from me. But Julie, she'd continued living her life, and done everything we should've done together with other people.

"Sorry, Ange, I never told you because I didn't want to hurt your feelings. You know you are and always have been my best friend."

She kept so much from me, but I understood why. "It's okay. It's not your fault. I was the one who screwed up. Withdrawing from everyone." How much misery I could have saved myself had I only spoken up. It was a tough pill to swallow.

"Well, that part of your life is over. And now, we can do things together again."

She was right. That part of my life was over. Even though it was like living inside a nightmare, one good—no great—thing had come out of it: Elizabeth.

I glossed my lips with a strawberry-flavored rollerball and smacked them together. "Okay, let's go. I can't wait to see what this Weekends place is like."

We skipped through the living room.

Paula said, "You girls look adorable. Lock your purses in the trunk so you don't have to keep up with them while dancing the night away."

"For sure, and thanks for looking after Elizabeth." I kissed my daughter on the top of her head while Paula fed her a bottle.

"Let's go," Julie said. "The parking lot gets full pretty fast."

As we walked out the front door, Dad added his two cents. "Stay safe and stay together."

But we weren't listening. We were too busy talking and laughing about the innocent things that occupied the brains of teen girls.

Chapter Sixty-Four

Weekends

One-way streets lined with unique gift shops, fancy restaurants, and cafes filled Mayflower. Weekends sat above a trendy bistro overlooking a park in the upscale town.

We shoved a few bucks and our IDs in our pockets and locked our purses in the trunk. As Paula said, we could dance the night away without having to keep up with them in the club.

A guy at the door checked our IDs, not to identify if we were old enough to get in, but to confirm we were young enough.

Inside the packed walls, a disco ball cast colorful light, and pop tunes blared. Some teenagers sat at tables munching nachos and sipping soft drinks. But most of them were on the dance floor—a last hoorah before saying goodbye to summer and hello to fall.

Julie's eyes lit up and she grabbed my hand. "Let's go."

We pushed through the crowd and inched into a small space on the elevated dance floor. We danced to Paula Abdul and the Go-Go's without a care in the world. The decibel of our laughter rivaled the music's volume.

Several girls from Julie's senior crew joined us. Like her, they all dressed as if part of an MTV music video. I needed to ask her to take me shopping. I wanted to look the part of my new, exciting life.

After about an hour of non-stop cardio, a Michael Jackson hit initiated a breakdance frenzy. Out of my limited wheelhouse of moves, this was the perfect time for a much-needed break. "Hey, Jules, I'm gonna slip outside for some fresh air. I'll be back in about ten or fifteen minutes."

She yelled over the music. "Okay, but hurry. I asked the DJ to play some special songs for you single ladies."

Single— I hadn't stopped long enough to register that. And even though Julie wasn't, I was happy my two best friends had found each other.

I yelled back. "Well, I definitely don't want to miss the Single Ladies Playlist."

"Right." She and her friends joined a group in a perfectly synchronized rendition of Thriller.

I fought my way through the maze of zombie-like dancing teens. Then stopped at the bar and ordered a soft drink. I wished I could have a Barq's Root Beer. But they weren't sold this far South. I'd have to wait for one the next time I visited the Panhandle, which I hoped was sooner than later. Instead, I ordered a Tab, my mother's soft drink of choice.

Outside, my throbbing eardrums took a few minutes to adjust to the quiet and my eyes to adjust to the dark. I walked down the steps and shuffled across the empty street into the park. A bench underneath the twinkling light-draped trees was the perfect spot to catch my breath and finish my Tab.

I had no idea when I lived with Dale, this was Julie's life. Just like I'd kept secrets from her, she kept some from me. I now knew all of hers. Soon she'd know all of mine. Eventually, everyone would because I'd written down every disgusting one of them in my own handwriting. I hoped once my friends and family knew those secrets, they'd still have faith I wasn't that person anymore.

A few twigs snapped in the bushes behind me. Probably an animal. Mysterious shadows lurked, and unidentifiable sounds now filled the initially inviting park. The flickering lights in the trees cast an eerie filter over skeletal-like branches. I remembered what my dad told Julie and me as we were leaving. I hadn't paid half a mind to it then, but now I wished I had. Because he'd said, "Stay safe and stay together."

I tossed the Tab into a trash can and readied myself to sprint back to the club. But someone grabbed my arms from behind, my previous gnawing anxiety embodied into flesh.

"We need to talk," Dale growled.

"Let me go. I don't have anything to say to you." I writhed and yanked as hard as I could to free my arm, but his grip was too tight. "Have you been following me?"

He pulled my arms tighter. "You think you can just write me off? It's not gonna be that easy. That statement you wrote, you're gonna visit your little friend at the police station and tell her it was all a lie. That the original story is the truth."

I refused to let him intimidate me any longer. "I'm not gonna do that. And if you don't wanna end up in jail tonight, you better let me go." I pulled again and failed to rip my arms free from his death-like grip.

"If you don't do what I say, my lawyer is prepared to fight for full custody of Elizabeth. Do you understand me?"

His sour breath yanked me back to the trailer. "I don't have to listen to you." My words narrowly burst through the wall of fear consuming me.

"Then you can say goodbye to that baby. Do you hear me?" he yelled.

His threat ignited a guttural instinct. "I'll never let you have custody of her. Never." I swung my head backward and smashed my skull into his face. Excruciating pain shot through me, and my vision blurred.

Dale screamed, and one of his hands involuntarily covered a bloody nose.

A shoulder popped and I broke free. Dizzy and disoriented, I ran toward the club. Footsteps closed in. *Faster, Angela. Faster.* A ringing in my ears muffled Dale's screams. Lights flickered. Flash after flash. Followed by blindness.

I pushed through unbearable pain, but I couldn't tell anymore where it was coming from. *Faster, Angela. Faster.* The flashes stopped, and darkness closed in. I tripped over a parking stop. My ankle snapped, and my leg buckled as gravity pulled me onto the pavement.

Dale pounced on top of me and pinned my wrists with one hand over my head.

"Please get off me, please," I begged in a low, muffled cry, Again, I was back in the trailer and Dale's helpless, pathetic victim.

He yanked up my head and screamed in my ear. "Say you'll do it." Eyes bulged on a bloodied face.

"Help me, help me," I weakly cried into the night. But no one was coming. I was nothing but unloved trailer trash lying on an asphalt deathbed.

"Say you'll do it. Say it now." Saliva sprayed and blood from his nose splattered on my face.

I collapsed under his weight. Lungs crushed—I stopped trying to breathe.

He grabbed my hair and pounded my head into the pavement. "Say you'll do it!"

I was in the car with him the night of the party. The screaming, the cursing, the accusing. But this time, I was the windshield. As the asphalt dug into my scalp, the all too familiar metallic taste of blood filled my mouth.

In a fading mental montage, I saw all the people who believed in me. All the people who tried to push me into the best version of myself. Even when I didn't know what that was, they did. And they knew it wasn't this. Their words of encouragement came at pivotal moments in my life and told me I was worth more.

They were right. I was worth more. I deserved to walk on a college campus. Elizabeth deserved a strong mother. I wasn't going to let Dale Simmons take anything else from me. And I didn't need anyone to save me. I could be my own hero.

As he readied to slam my head into the asphalt again, I shrieked through pain and broke one of my arms free.

Channeling every ounce of adrenaline left, I arched my back and struck him with my elbow square in his jaw. The crack of bone pierced the night. His body flew away from me like a rag doll and hit the pavement with a thud. He moaned as he melted into a puddle of useless flesh.

Dale Simmons would never hurt me again.

Shouting and hurried footsteps rushed in. A crowd formed. I sensed flashing lights and sirens off in the distance.

Julie burst through. "Oh my gosh. Are you okay? I'm so sorry. I should've never let you go outside alone." She cried and grabbed my hand as paramedics hoisted me onto a stretcher.

Because I was about to be rolled into an ambulance, I assumed my injuries must have been severe. But I felt no pain. The only thing I felt was pride. I cracked open swollen eyes. "Jules, it's not your fault. And it's okay. I won't have to worry about Dale ever again."

CHAPTER SIXTY-FIVE

THE STATEMENT

DAD AND JULIE WRAPPED their arms around my waist as we walked toward the building.

When we reached the entrance, Dad asked, "Are you sure you're up to this?"

I didn't want to put him through what he was about to experience, and justice had already been served, but this needed to happen for me to move on. I needed closure.

"Yes, sir. I am." With the arm not in a sling, I clutched the folder that held the painful words I'd soon read out loud. It was time to finally tell the truth.

Julie smiled. "You got this."

Even though she was my best friend, she didn't know what I'd been through. But going forward, I'd never keep secrets from her again. Because secrets, like the ones I'd kept, pierce your heart, and mine had nearly bled dry.

We sat at a table in the front of the small courtroom; Dad on one side, Julie on the other. Although my wounds were still visible, the healing on the inside had already started.

I should've been nervous. Saying out loud the things I was about to say, revealing my secrets to the world. But I wasn't. Because revealing mine meant revealing his, and it was time everyone knew the monster he was. It was time I had a voice.

Officer Cresswell came through a side door leading Dale, outfitted in an orange jumpsuit, hands cuffed behind his back. She nodded at me and offered a small, encouraging smile.

Addis, on the other hand, was in tears. She couldn't rescue her son this time.

For the last year, I'd felt like a prisoner, but now he was the one in jail. The tables had turned. Finally, the bad guy got what he deserved.

The judge broke the room's soundtrack of mumbling voices. "Miss Carter. The floor is yours."

I stood on my wobbly ankle, smoothed my pencil skirt with my non-slinged hand, and picked up the document off the table in front of me. "Thank you, Your Honor."

"My name is Angela Carter.

On the night of February 28, 1988, Dale Simmons and I went to a party at his cousin's house, Roger Olsen, at 337 County Road 88 in North Lake, Florida. I drove us there because Dale asked me to be his designated driver. And although I didn't want to go to the party, I did want him safe. After all, he was my unborn baby's father. When we got there, I ran into an old friend I hadn't seen in a while, Andrew Holmes. We spent the evening catching up. I didn't see Dale the rest of the night until he gripped the back of my arm and told me it was time to go. I could tell he had been drinking because he slurred as he spoke, and he was angry. He usually got angry when he drank. Andrew tried to talk to him, but Dale called him a punk and told him to stay away from me. He pushed me out of the trailer and flung open the passenger door of my car. Then threw me in. I said I should drive since he'd been drinking. That was the whole point for me coming. But he wouldn't let me and demanded I give him the keys. I was scared. All I wanted to do was get home safe. Once he started driving, he swerved all over the road. I tried to grab the wheel, but he shoved me into the passenger door. He was yelling and screaming at me and accusing me that the baby was Andrew's. But he knew that wasn't true because I'd never been with any guy other than him. He punched the windshield until it cracked. The car started to spin. I thought Dale was going to kill us that night. I didn't think I'd ever hold my baby. But finally, thankfully, the car stopped spinning and landed in a ditch off the side of the road. I got out. I couldn't believe I was okay. But then I got scared again. I ran to his parents' house and left him there. I'm sorry I lied the first time Officer Cresswell questioned me. Addis Simmons, Dale's mother, said I risked the baby being born without her father there if I told the truth. I was also afraid if I didn't do as she'd asked, Dale would be angry. When he was angry, I felt it in places you could see and places you couldn't. I have lived with Dale's physical, sexual, and emotional abuse for the last year and a half. And even though I have made some bad choices myself, I have never hurt anyone like he's hurt me—both that night and on many others. Someone told me you can't catch the bad guys if the good guys stand in the way. I am done standing in the way."

I tucked the document back into the folder. All eyes were on me, including Dale's. When I returned his gaze, he dropped his head. "Your Honor, I'm done."

"Thank you, Miss Carter." He pounded the gavel. "Everyone's adjourned."

The legs I stood firm on shook a little. And I finally breathed in deep. It was over.

Officer Cresswell led Dale back through the same door they'd entered. He couldn't hurt me or anyone else from the jail cell where he'd spend the next five years.

Tears streamed down Julie's face. "I had no idea. I'm a terrible friend. I should've known things were worse than you let on."

"Jules, you're a great friend. No one knew because I protected him."

Addis buried her face into John's chest. I pitied her a little. Knowing her son would be locked away had to be difficult. But now, at least, she knew he deserved it.

Dad put his arm around me. "Number One, I hate what you went through. And I'm sorry I didn't do more to protect you." He kissed the top of my head. "But today, I've never been prouder to be your father."

The weight of the truth now off me; I was his little girl again. "Daddy, take me home?"

As we headed toward the exit, Officer Creswell called, "Miss Carter, wait."

I turned to Dad and Julie, "I'll meet you guys at the car."

"Miss Carter, what you did in there, confronting your abuser; it's not an easy thing to do. I have the utmost respect for you. Your daughter, she's going to grow up with one heck of a role model."

"Thank you." Me as Elizabeth's role model, it was a role I was now ready to fill. "Officer Cresswell?"

"Yes?"

"Keep catching those bad guys."

"I plan on it. Enjoy the rest of your day." She offered me a salute, then walked away.

I beamed; I knew exactly what I would do with the rest of my day.

CHAPTER SIXTY-SIX

MOVING FORWARD

I STOOD ON MY tiptoes, brushed my hand across the top shelf of my closet and pulled down the cigar box my mother had given me for Christmas.

Sifting through its contents, I picked up the letter from her and brought it to my nose. Although faint, it was still there, Georgio. Thanksgiving break couldn't come soon enough.

I rubbed the smooth blue rubber keychain my father had given to me the day I told him I was pregnant. The logo "Clark's Cars, Your Number One Dealer," stirred a chuckle. My Dad had been my rock my entire life. He still was.

I held baby photos of me and Elizabeth side by side. We looked almost identical. The only exception—her olive skin. I hoped she'd one day be proud of the Simmons' Native American heritage.

Aha. Found it. The napkin. "904-555-0199. You got this. Harley."

I slowly dialed the number and tried to remember every detail of that night—his musky cologne, the song we danced to, my head on his chest. That night my life changed, and it was time to tell him.

My heart raced at his velvety hello.

"Hey, it's me, Angela."

"Good to hear from you. How are things?"

"They couldn't be better." But hearing his voice, maybe things could get better. "In case you didn't know, I live at my dad's now, and I'm going to school."

"I know. Levi's kept me up to date. I wanted to call. So many times. But I didn't want to get in your way."

"It's okay. That's why I didn't call either. I needed to get some things behind me." Now that I'd dealt with my past, I could focus on my future. "There's something I want you to know. That night I met you—it changed me. When I left that day, I wasn't the same person as when I arrived. I wanna thank you."

"I didn't do anything. You were ready. You just didn't know it yet. I'm glad I got to be a small part of your journey."

"You were more than a small part."

"Thanks. I've got some news of my own. I got accepted into that landscape design program in Jacksonville. Moving on campus in December. It sounds like we're both headed in the right direction."

It was only the right direction if our paths crossed again. "I'm so happy for you. And it's good you aren't leaving until December because Elizabeth and I are coming for Thanksgiving. If you wanna hang out?"

"Are you kidding? Of course. And this time, it won't be Ball Breakers."

We both laughed. When I first walked into that joint, my instinct had been to about-face and run. Now it'll forever be etched in my memory as the place where my life changed—for the better.

"A game of pool sounds pretty good to me right now." I didn't know where this thing with Harley would go. But the fact that there were possibilities was enough.

The alarm rang before the sun rose on my first official day as a college student. I slipped into the new Jordache jeans and Lacoste polo I'd bought with the money Dad had given me for school clothes. Then I put my already packed suede backpack by the front door and tiptoed into Elizabeth's room.

Coos drifted from her honey oak crib—the only thing I took from that trailer. "Good morning, Number One Baby Girl. It's a big day for your momma."

Paula popped her head in. "Hey, let me know when she's ready to go."

"Sure, thanks for dropping her off today. I really appreciate it." I couldn't do this without Dad and Paula's support, and they offered it in abundance.

"No problem. Busy day for you. I can't wait to hear all about it later at dinner."

All that time in the trailer, I had felt so alone. I kept waiting for someone to swoop in and rescue me. But that's not how it works. Just like Harley said, sometimes you have to be your own hero. I now knew that surrounding yourself with people you love and who love you back is how you build the strength to do it.

I fed and changed Elizabeth and Paula took her to daycare. Then I tossed my backpack in the front seat and drove to North Lake Community College.

When I arrived, I parked in the student parking lot, not the visitor's. This time I wasn't pretending. It was real. Sharpened pencils I was ready to dull and empty notebooks I was eager to fill stuffed my backpack.

My first class wasn't for another half hour. Julie and I were meeting in the courtyard and then going to the cafeteria for a quick cup of coffee before beginning our first day as college students.

I opened the car door and grabbed my backpack. I looked toward the campus where I'd spend the next four years, thankfully not having to worry about Dale in the background. The morning sun warmed my shoulders, shoulders that now didn't have the weight of the world piled on them.

I spotted Julie off in the distance running toward me. That girl. She wasn't the kind of friend who went into your dark hole with you. She was the kind who was optimistic you wouldn't stay there.

Getting here was not the result of a multi-year, carefully concocted plan. No, it was the culmination of many small and seemingly insignificant steps forward. It was the combination of the kindness and encouragement of others, often even strangers. Many of whom seamlessly drifted in and out of my life, but all sent the same message—you're worth more.

It was a mother's desire to provide for her child and to be a role model. Even when I lived in that dilapidated trailer, I knew there was more. I may not have known what it was, but I knew it was out there. I also knew the road to get there would be hard. Harder than anything I'd ever done in my life. But I also knew for me, for Elizabeth, the hard work would be worth it.

I shut my car door and took the first step toward my future.

EPILOGUE

MAY 2013

NINE O'CLOCK A.M. AND already ninety degrees. Thankfully, I'd worn a sleeveless dress—a new floral Lilly Pulitzer. Elizabeth's favorite designer. My poor husband was roasting in dark slacks and long sleeves, which he'd already rolled up. In weather like this, he ordinarily dressed in shorts and a t-shirt.

He placed a hand on the small of my back. "We'd better go grab our seats," he said as proud parents poured into the campus courtyard.

I hadn't seen Elizabeth since last night when we'd gone out to dinner with a few of her friends and their families. This morning, she and her friends had plans to sip mimosas while they got ready. Although I wanted to be there with her, this was their time. She'd made great friends here. Friends she'd have forever, like Julie and me.

Julie wanted to be here, too. But each graduate was only allotted two guests at the intimate ceremony. We were having a graduation party back at the house next week. The rest of the family would get the opportunity to congratulate Elizabeth then, and Julie was family.

I was kind of glad it was just the two of us, though. It meant I got to share this special day with just my husband. Even though Harley wasn't her biological father, you'd never know it. To Elizabeth, he was her dad, and to him, she was his daughter. It had been like that from day one.

The university president started the ceremony. Although I'm sure he said some wonderful and inspiring words, I couldn't hold on to them. I was too deep in thought. The Florida State Attorney General, a university professor, and a former student followed a few other speakers. But all of us were only here for one reason—to watch our loved ones walk across that stage.

Finally, the president reclaimed his position at the podium and readied to call names. The formerly distracted crowd, including me, now sat at full attention. One by one, the man handed the well-deserved students what they'd worked so hard for over the last several years.

"He's at the C's. Our girl will be up any minute." Harley squeezed my hand.

Tears welled.

Then the man said her name. "Elizabeth Carter-James."

She lifted the sides of the long deep purple robe and climbed the steps. Several honor cords draped her neck. Curled blonde hair fell from underneath a graduation cap and brushed her firm shoulders. My daughter then confidently walked across the stage at Stetson University College of Law and received her law degree.

The tears spilled.

Harley passed me the tissue I'd asked him to put in his pocket.

I thought about Elizabeth's humble beginnings. Her first home was in a trailer park. Her biological father—a prison inmate most of her life.

As a toddler, each month she stood in food stamp lines with me. Even with my father's help, being a single mother and college student wasn't always easy.

But we did it. She and I both achieved our dreams. From scared pregnant teen to now teaching alongside my mentor. This time it was me who shattered the glass—and now my daughter was bursting through it.

As I watched Elizabeth hold her law school degree in one hand and shake the president's hand with the other, I knew then, without a doubt, that everything—the hard things, the things that hurt, all of it. It had all been worth it.

Author's Note to the Teens in the Room

I see you. You have value. You have worth. You are not alone.

If, like Angela, you are in a challenging situation, please find a trusted adult to share what is happening in your life. Turn to a teacher, a guidance counselor, a friend's parent, or someone. Angela waited too long. You don't have to. Your life matters. YOU matter.

If, like Julie, you are fortunate enough to have a stable and loving family, first off, thank them. Secondly, be a friend like Julie. You never know what is happening in a friend's life behind closed doors. Never give up on them.

Author's Note to the Adults in the Room

Your note is going to be much longer. Because NO child should ever have to grow up too fast.

Teen pregnancy is a crisis. According to data collected by the CDC and Do Something.Org, of teens who give birth before graduating, only 50% have a high school diploma or GED by age 22, as opposed to 90% of students who aren't teen parents. Of those who do graduate, only around 2% earn a college degree by age 30. And an astonishing 25% have a second baby within 24 months. It should come as no surprise these teens are at much higher risk for poverty, dependence on governmental assistance, mental health challenges, substance abuse, and more.

The statistics for the children of teen parents aren't any better. They are at much higher risk for low birth weight, infant mortality, cognitive impairment, foster care placement, incarceration, poverty, and teen pregnancy themselves than children born to adult parents.

Additionally, if those statistics weren't staggering enough, the annual financial burden to our country as a result of teen pregnancies is in the billions.

My daughter and I, born when I was seventeen, are not part of those statistics. I clawed my way out of poverty, went to college, and enjoyed a twenty-year career as an educator. She was born healthy, excelled in school, and is now a Board-Certified Elder Law Attorney. I was also born to a teen mother, but the cycle stopped with me.

Why? Why did my story turn out differently than the majority of teens in the same situation?

I can tell you why. My school had supportive and encouraging teachers. My community had an educational program for teen mothers. My local community college provided scholarships for teen parents. My community provided me with support and opportunities many communities don't provide.

And this is a problem. It is a crisis every day that any child doesn't have access to what they need to be the best versions of themselves.

It is up to us, the adults in the room, to ensure accurate information and accessible resources are available to all children regardless of their needs. And, yes, teens are still children. We need to do better.

Their future is our future. And it's worth it.

ACKNOWLEDGEMENTS

Pardon me as I pick myself up from the puddle on the floor. Where to start? I have so many of you who have been the wind beneath my wings. I'm going to take a deep breath and start at the beginning.

Jenny, you were my Julie. You always will be. I'm going to leave it at that.

Danielle, I gave birth to you on March 28th, 1988. I was seventeen years old and had no idea what I was doing. Thank you for teaching me how to be your mom and inspiring me to write this story.

Brent, if you'd asked me a thousand times to read a revised version of the same sentence, I don't know how I would've reacted. But you listened—or cleverly pretended!

To all of my children, thank you for dealing with a little less of me during my writing and revising of this story. Oh, and you're welcome!

A15 Beta Readers, you told me this story was worth telling. I listened.

Dana, I'll never forget when at my lowest point you swooped in and said, "I got you." You took the reins and that's when the magic happened.

Shelby, you're the biggest cheerleader and I can never thank you enough for being mine.

Wild Ink Publishing, after more no's than I care to recount, thank you for giving me a yes!

To the whole of my family, this story is inspired by our lived experiences. But know that inspired by means I took many creative liberties. At the end of the day, I love you all, and throughout all our struggles, we all found our strengths.

That's the power of becoming your own hero!

About the Author

Amy Nielsen spent twenty years as a youth librarian sharing her love of books with young readers. Daily immersion in story took root and she penned her YA debut, WORTH IT, behind her circulation desk. Amy is the proud parent to four humans, one pup, and has more grand pups than she can count. When she's not reading or writing, Amy, her family, and at least two canine co-captains in mermaid life vests can be found boating the waters of Tampa Bay.

ALSO BY AMY NIELSEN

Goldilocks and the Three Bears:
Understanding Autism Spectrum Disorder

We all know the story of Goldilocks and the Three Bears.

But you may not know that this retelling of the familiar fairytale can also help us understand autism spectrum disorder.

As an added bonus, this one-of-a-kind story includes an ASD glossary of terms and discussion questions. It is perfect for libraries, classrooms, families of children with autism, or readers of all ages who want to learn more about ASD.

It Takes a Village: How to Build a Support System for Your
Exceptional Needs Family

With an authentic and conversational tone, *It Takes A Village* is an inspiring book that seeks to illuminate the challenges that parents of children with ADHD or Autism face, providing a wealth of practical strategies and advice for helping you navigate your role as a caregiver to neurodivergent kids.

Designed to help readers appreciate the value of a support system, this heartfelt book empowers parents of all backgrounds with the tools they need to surround themselves with positive, encouraging, and supportive people - from friends and family to professionals and non-profit groups. Plus, with a collection of exercises and prompts, you can keep track of your parenting journey and track your progress over time.